BEAST OF BURDEN

BEAST OF BURDEN
A Cal Innes Book

Ray Banks

First published in 2009 by Polygon,
an imprint of Birlinn Ltd

West Newington House
10 Newington Road
Edinburgh
EH9 1QS

9 8 7 6 5 4 3 2 1

www.birlinn.co.uk

ISBN 978 1 84697 098 6

British Library Cataloguing-in-Publication Data
A catalogue record for this book is available on request from the British Library.

Typeset by Hewer Text (UK) Ltd, Edinburgh
Printed in Great Britain by Clays Ltd, St Ives plc

To Anastasia,
I'll lose everything, but I won't let go of your hand.

And I keep my brother's blood. And I breathe my brother's love.
– 'My Brother's Man', Angels of Light

Revenge is a confession of pain.
– Latin proverb

PART ONE

Spasticus (Autisticus)

Declan was a suicide risk.

That's what the dumpy nurse told me, her specialist subject the totally fucking obvious. This rough voice on the phone, rattling out the rules, told me that if he wasn't awake when I arrived, I couldn't see him. No exceptions. And thanks to an overhead line fault at Dunbar, I didn't get to the hospital until well after visiting hours.

When I showed up in person, she softened a little. And when I opened my mouth to speak, that was it. She had no choice but to show me to my brother.

'We don't normally do this,' she said.

'Thanks.'

Declan was sparked out with the light on, which meant they'd dosed him. Usually, my brother needed it pitch black to sleep. A Louis L'Amour paperback sat on the bed, its cracked spine pointing up. One of my dad's – *The Strong Shall Live.* I remembered him trying to press it on us when we were younger. It was the kind of stuff he loved, inspirational reading for those with a Western bent, a bunch of short stories about plucky homesteaders triumphing over adversity. There was a heroic cowboy on the front cover, his rifle pointed to the ground, his gaze set on the vast Wyoming landscape.

Weird that my dad liked this stuff.

I picked up the book, dog-eared the page, and put it on the bedside table. Then I eased myself onto the chair by Declan's bed.

Uncle Kenny told me the suicide attempt was a cry for help. I didn't think so. I thought the cry for help came on an answering machine message Declan left me a week before he did it. I got Paulo to wipe it without listening, had enough of my own shite to deal with at the time, and I was under the impression his call was the usual monthly catch-up. In fact, the only reason I knew it was a cry for help was because Declan took the next logical step. He went out, hooked up with an old dealer, bought enough smack to fell a horse, and shot the lot.

He would've topped himself if it wasn't for his girlfriend. She was an ex-smackhead herself – they'd met through some Outreach group he kept going on about – so she didn't need any help to work out what had happened when she saw Declan turning blue in the bedroom.

Two or three years ago, I wouldn't have been surprised. That was the Declan who was too mashed to pick his brother up from outside the 'Ways on release day. It was that Declan who'd promised me then he was off the smack. Showed me his arms, the back of his knees, in between his toes, to prove it. But didn't hide the works, didn't hide the foil or the black smudges on his hands. So the same Declan got his arse handed to him by his younger brother because he was a lying junkie bastard. And afterwards, he'd sat there, his back to the wall with his knees up, snot, tears and blood on his face. One hand in his straggly hair, as he showed me his teeth but couldn't meet my gaze.

He dabbed at the blood on his top lip, fresh tears coming to his eyes.

He said he needed help.

He said it again, louder.

I put him on the next train to Waverley.

Then there was the Outreach, the girlfriend, the long road to recovery. The monthly phone calls that hammered the point home – he was doing okay, he was trying hard, he wasn't going to disappoint anyone who'd had faith in him, not this time. And every time he mentioned his life, it threw mine into stark relief. Like some born-again, he asked after my health. Like a full-blown addict, I lied through my teeth.

He was strong when he was clean. But only then.

I was glad he was asleep. I didn't want him to see me, not like this. A stroke victim with a walking stick, not even thirty and shuffling through the world like a fucking pensioner.

I sat with him for fifteen minutes. Watched him sleep. Then I left.

On the way out, I phoned my uncle. 'I saw him,' I said. 'He was asleep.'

'That's alright,' said Kenny. 'There's always tomorrow.'

Shook my head, even though Kenny couldn't see it. 'I've got to head off. Tell him I came though.'

Kenny made some noises, tried to persuade me to stay a wee while longer. I killed the call, caught a cab back to the station and just made the last train south.

A week out of the hospital, Dec had another shot at it. Locked the bathroom door, opened one arm from wrist to elbow, chased the pain with a thick shot to the thigh, then tried to open his other arm.

By the time paramedics got the door down, he was dead.

No longer a risk.

ONE

Innes

Mo Tiernan is dead.

And that's why I'm here right now. I'm not supposed to know, much less have something to do with it, so I play it dumb, which isn't too difficult. The past few months have given me time to get good at that particular game.

I'm sat in the lounge bar of the Wheatsheaf, the wall-hung wood-panelled jukebox playing Donovan, the music punctuated by the odd beep from the original Space Invaders machine in the corner.

Opposite me, Morris Tiernan. The Uncle himself. He appears to be staring out the window, but his eyes are too glazed to be looking anywhere but inwards.

'He's *missing*,' he says, turning to me finally.

I nod.

'Couple of months. At least.' He shakes his head. 'You heard?'

'No.'

'Really?'

'I just noticed,' I say.

'So he *is* missing.'

Tiernan doesn't need a reply to that. It's just something to say, a repeated lie told to divert his mind from the darker, more likely outcome. We both know that Mo couldn't disappear totally for one month, let alone two. The most you could hope for was a week out of circulation and even then he'd make his presence known when he returned. He'd be loud about being back in the game, scoring and selling, maybe glass some unfortunate bastard to cement his rep as a pin-pupil psycho. Silence is not an option for Mo Tiernan. Every time he makes some noise, it's a fuck-you to the father who kicked him out of the family.

But right now, it's too quiet.

'So,' I say.

Tiernan moves his head. Regards the pristine pint of Guinness on the table in front of him. He pushes his fingers across the tabletop. Normally he'd be smoking – ban be fucked – but there's no ashtray on the table, and now the music's stopped, I'm sure I can hear a ticking sound coming from the centre of Tiernan's chest. He breathes in slowly, then exhales as if he's taken a long drag from an imaginary cigarette. The tension leaves him along with the breath in his lungs.

'You find him for me.'

I shake my head.

'Yeah, you can.'

I look at him with a bland expression on my face. He can interpret it however he wants.

He wraps his hand around the bottom of the pint glass, but doesn't move it. 'The other thing,' he says. 'You handled that well enough.'

I cough. He takes it as sarcastic. Glances up at me.

'You got her back,' he says. 'That's all that matters.' One finger taps the side of the glass. There's something brown under a fingernail that could be dried blood. 'And you were discreet about it. I appreciated that.'

I look at the table. Don't say anything.

'Didn't use what you learned about our family against us. Someone else come across information like that, they'd think they had some dirt, something they could use to their advantage.' He bunches his lips, stares into his pint. 'You were bright enough to realise you didn't have nowt. Nowt you could think about using, anyway.'

'I know.'

'And that's why you're here.'

'Because I'm bright?'

'Because you're loyal.'

I stare at him. He's building up to something, but there's still that barrier. Maybe it's because he hasn't seen me in a while and now he has, there are doubts. Like maybe I can't be trusted to follow through on this, or maybe I'm not physically capable of doing the job.

Because he's heard what happened to me. But it's different seeing the results in the flesh.

His eyes twitch half-closed. He's obviously reached some sort of decision.

'Fuck it,' he says.

Fuck it?

That deep breath again, reminding me of the rumours flying about that Mo's disappearance has put Morris Senior on his guard, that maybe the Uncle's starting to fray around the edges, can't handle the pressure as well as he used to. Right enough, put me in a room and the place doesn't exactly feel very Zen, but Morris Tiernan's still not the kind to get jittery around the likes of me. Still, I'd credited him with a strong enough gut to look me in the face, and that hasn't happened yet.

So maybe I'm wrong. Maybe I do make him uncomfortable.

Good.

He waves his free hand. 'This . . . Whatever this is . . .'

I wait for him.

'If this is what we think it might be, then it's possible it could be personal.'

'Personal,' I say, as if I know exactly what he's talking about.

'With Mo.'

And now I *do* know exactly what he's talking about.

Never occurred to me that this would be the reason Morris Tiernan called me in. He reckons that if his son's got himself so fucked up that he's missing or worse, it's got something to do with him. That someone's using Mo to get to him in some way, because that person didn't get the circular telling everyone that Mo wasn't an official Tiernan anymore. Even if that's *not* the case, I get the idea that Tiernan thinks this thing with Mo is going to bite him on the arse the minute his back is turned. And for the first time since I met him, it looks like the Uncle's actually worried.

But it's not about Mo. Can't be. He made his feelings about his son pretty clear a while ago.

'Nobody's been in touch,' he says, running a hand over his chin. 'Could be something, could be nothing. I don't know who's playing the game these days, never mind who's winning it. Don't need to know. Could be Mo's playing funny buggers somewhere, could be he's jumped on a Dutch deal. It's happened before, but Mo's never had the ambition to piss off anyone serious.' He pauses, pitches a sigh. 'Either way, it wouldn't do me any good to be seen asking questions.'

No, it wouldn't. Man like Morris Tiernan, he asks after his son, it'll look like a U-turn on the exile. If Mo's out, Mo's out. Supposed to be as good as dead, end of story, and Tiernan can't be seen as a man who changes his mind at the first sniff of shit. He made his rep on being a mulish bastard, devoid of sentimentality and violent enough to make might equal right.

'Which is where you come in,' says Tiernan. 'You know his mates.'

I don't say anything. Don't move my head either. Watch him look at that pint. He's waiting for me to agree, but I'm not saying one fucking word until he looks up at me. I want him to know who he's seeing, who he's been talking to, because I get this sinking feeling that he reckons he's talking to the Callum Michael Innes who just got out of prison, the one scared of the family name and hungry for paying work. That very same bloke who was asked to track down ten grand and a runaway daughter last year, ended up the six-foot pile of shite that I am now.

So Tiernan needs to see my lopsided face, the sink of my right-hand side. He needs to see me move with my walking stick. He needs to listen closely when I speak, see my spastic lips and tongue try to form words my brain knows but my mouth has forgotten. He needs to drink all this in, and then he needs to understand that it was him and his fucked up family that did this to me.

But he doesn't. When he raises his head to look at me, there's a flicker of disgust, but not much more.

Certainly no guilt.

'You know what I heard?' he says.

I can guess, but I shake my head.

'That you're a full-on mong now.'

I shrug.

'That you're all . . . brain-damaged.'

If he's trying to get a rise out of me, he'll be disappointed. None of this 'mong' shite is anything I haven't already heard from kids on the street.

Tiernan shifts his gaze back to his pint. 'You even working now?'

I nod. I have an office, letterhead, small business client list with occasional private work, the whole shebang. Even got a stack of professionally printed business cards, 400gsm, thick as you like. He knows all this. I wouldn't be here without an up-to-date background check.

After a minute's silence, he says, 'Well?'

Finally, he's looking at me right in the eyes and holding it. I stare back. He doesn't waver for a second. If he's desperate enough to look at me full on, we're off to a good start.

I give him my own special brand of half-smile, really milking the difference between the good and bad sides of my face. He blinks, but keeps whatever discomfort he's feeling under wraps.

'Just tell me how much,' he says.

I smile wider on the left side of my face. Then I give him the standard look-see price. I could skin the bloke, but I choose not to. After all, he's paying me to ask a couple of questions to the right people. That's all.

And besides, the price Tiernan's going to pay has fuck all to do with money.

TWO

Innes

I'm already out of the Wheatsheaf, hobbling across the car park to my Micra, when my mobile rings. It's Frank, calling to see where I am.

'Still in Starbucks.' I pull open the car door, and hope that he doesn't pick up that I'm obviously outdoors.

'Still?'

I get in the car, toss my stick onto the passenger seat and pull the driver's door almost closed to kill some of the ambient sound. 'There's a queue. Out the door.'

Frank sighs down the phone. He's got a proper pet lip on by the sounds of it. 'Right, okay.'

'I'll be back soon,' I say.

'Paulo's being a pain.'

'He's had a lot of practice.'

'He wants his coffee.'

'Then he knows . . . where the *kettle* is.'

'Cal—'

I hang up on him, slam the car door closed, and start the engine.

There's a reason I'm stalling, other than the meeting with Tiernan. One of the major drawbacks of working for a gay bloke is his coffee order. With Paulo it's a Caramel Macchiato, extra sugar, soy milk and a skinny lemon and poppyseed muffin. It's an embarrassment, ordering that. And to make matters worse, he thinks that by sending me to get his order, he's doing me a favour. Getting me out into the world, forcing me to interact with other people, making me better.

Because even though he hasn't said as much, he knows I'm not doing the speech therapy or the physio. He doesn't need to ask me, so I don't need to lie. But I'm still glad I told Frank that I was going for coffees. Frank's easier to lie to; he's still daft enough to believe the best of people.

But then fate always did have a bastard streak: when I get to Starbucks, wouldn't you know it, the place is fucking packed.

Late morning, midweek, it shouldn't be like this. But then I'd forgotten what any calendar or charity shop could've told me: the students are back in town. Loud voices with non-Manc accents compete with the screech of the steamer. Too much youth in this place, the smell of what I presume is popular aftershave (more like perfume to me) mixed with the smell of burned coffee, the blokes with the kind of haircut a kid fashions in the bath with shampoo suds, the girls rich and cold enough to bundle themselves up in what look like their grandmother's clothes. Experience makes me watch my step round here. I haven't had the best of times in student company, and it pays to be wary.

I catch sight of a guy in one of the back nooks, got the big black Buddy Holly glasses and the look of a serial mouthbreather. When we accidentally lock stares, he pushes his glasses and drops his gaze to the silver laptop in front of him.

A brief shuffle, and the queue moves forward enough for me to reach a bottle of orange and mango juice for Frank. He's not one for hot drinks, our Francis. More often than not, he feeds the vending machine, but all that Coke's given him chronic wind, clear teeth, and the beginnings of a stomach ulcer, so for all our sakes, we've been trying to get him to switch to juice.

I don't mind. If this trip was all about buying a fucking smoothie, I wouldn't be sweating cobs right now.

Talking is a problem. Words don't stay. One minute I'll have a sentence all ready to go, almost *feel* it sitting there on my tongue, and the next it's gone, or else mangled into gibberish. And even when I manage to get the words right, the voice that struggles out of the working side of my mouth isn't mine anymore. I hear myself talking, it's like there's a mental case in the room, and I'm stuck with him twenty-four hours a day.

On the plus side, I can say just about anything I want to people and they can't take offence, because their automatic response is that I'm just a mong. But it takes me so long to say anything, most of the time an insult isn't worth the effort. So I'd rather not say anything these days, especially to strangers, unless I absolutely have to.

Which means dealing with a minimum-wager isn't exactly an experience I relish.

'Next, please.'

I don't look at the girl behind the counter. I already know what she looks like – blonde hair pulled back, weak chin, large blue eyes and a badly hidden spot just under one nostril. But even though it's been a good couple of months since the stroke, it's still difficult for me to deal with that initial reaction. So I stare up at the false chalk menu, thinking about the words, running them through my head.

'Americano. Large with a shot. Of ex-press . . . *Espresso.*' I breathe out. Hear it in my head, then repeat slowly. Sound out the syllables. 'Caramel . . . Macc-hiato. With soy milk. Please.'

The girl's staring at me, I can feel it. I wipe my mouth – force of habit – and find my hand comes away wet with drool. Trying not to show my discomfort, so I show her the juice instead, point at the skinny lemon and poppyseed.

'Okay,' she says. 'You . . . sitting in?'

Those strangled pauses are infectious.

I shake my head, concentrate. 'No. There's a sign. In the window?'

I have to look at her now. After a few moments, she realises that I'm waiting on an answer to go with my change. As she drops coins into my left hand, she glances across at the front windows. When she realises what I'm talking about, she swallows. Half-expect her to start tugging at her collar.

'The part-time barista job?' she says.

I nod.

'You want an application form?'

I blink. 'Yes.'

'Okay. ' She starts nodding, as if she's waiting for me to realise what an insane request it is, just marking time until I change my mind. That, or she's mesmerised by my face. It's happened before.

'Yes, *please*?'

She glances over my shoulder at the queue. 'Right, yeah, I'll see if we've got any.'

Then she calls for one of the other baristas to take over as she pulls herself away from the counter with a smile. I move out of the way, shuffle off to wait for the coffees and application form.

I didn't ask for the form to make her uncomfortable; this is a genuine career option for me.

Thing is, on the most basic practical level, I can't really work as a PI – I can't speak properly enough to ask questions, and walking more than six feet in one go is a real endurance test. But this barista job – what would I do in here? Shuffle from one end of the counter to the other, which is what I'd be doing in physio anyway, and learn a few stock phrases to perfection, which is what I'd be doing in speech therapy. I'd be rehabilitating myself, and getting paid for it. I know Paulo and Frank don't think the same way – they're entirely convinced that if I just went to the hospital every now and then, I'd be back working private cases in no time, but neither of those blokes is exactly known for their realistic worldview.

So I've been collecting application forms, filled out a couple, ruined more than that. My right hand used to be dominant, but since the stroke I've tried and failed to get anything but basic movement out of it. I've been trying to teach myself to write with my left hand, but I'm still at the barely legible scrawl stage. Which doesn't matter so much with application forms – most of them are happy with everything in block capitals – but there's the added problem of an unreliable arm. Every now and then, especially when I'm channelling all my energy into controlling my left hand, something will spike up my arm, spasm a streak of ink across the paper. And then all I can do is pour another drink to steady my nerves, dump the application, and try to forget about it until I see another McJob that I think I could do.

'Okay,' says the girl, a booklet in her hand, though it might as well be Bible-sized. She leans over the counter to hand it to me. 'If you just want to fill this out and post it back to the head office, they'll take it from there.'

I look at the application pack. 'Post?'

She keeps smiling at me. I don't try to return it, wouldn't want to upset her.

'Or you could bring it back in here. That's not a problem. But, y'know, I don't actually think we *hire* from here? So we'd have to forward it on for you, but that's okay, we can do that.'

'Right.' Nodding. 'Thanks.'

I move back up the counter to wait for the coffees. Scan through the application pack. Turns out that Starbucks are more than happy to employ someone like me – or at least they make a point of saying it on the application – but they're also keen to know every detail about my incarceration.

Fuck it.

I let out another breath, look up from the form to catch Buddy Holly staring at me again. Lower the form, try to straighten up as best I can.

'Problem?' I say, nice and loud.

Buddy doesn't say anything. Pulls on his glasses, wets his bottom lip. He doesn't need to say a word – that look on his face is all too fucking familiar. He's giving me the rubberneck double-take in all its limited glory.

The first look catches an image of me that isn't quite whole, but enough to jar.

That first thought: *Something's the matter with that bloke.*

Another look, and in a flash they connect the walking stick with the apparent slackness in my right cheek. If I happen to be moving or talking, it's clear as day.

Then the second thought: *Oh Jesus, he's had a fucking stroke or something.*

And then there's a choice that needs to be made. *What do we go for here, disgust or pity?*

Sometimes it's an either-or, but most people tend to combine.

Yeah, and thank the Cree-ay-tor they're not in the state I'm in.

I make a move towards Buddy. The look on his face just switched from disgust into one I haven't seen before, not in this context.

Fear.

Good. 'I said, *problem*?'

'No, what?' He holds up one chair, shifting back on the pleather chair. 'There's no problem here, mate.'

'Fuck . . . you . . . looking at, then?'

'Sorry?'

I take another awkward step towards him, make sure to bang the bottom of the stick against the wooden floor. Wanker wants to have a staring match, he can do it with someone else. Because he's still not looked away from me. Like it's impossible for him. He's frozen to the spot, and I'm a fucking Intercity, coming right at him.

'You get a good look. You get a good . . . *fuckin'* look, eh?'

'Wait a second, mate. I didn't mean anything . . .'

'The fuck you . . . didn't. Cunt.'

Another step. Buddy gets out of his seat, showing his hands at the same time. This just got a little bit more interesting to everyone else in the shop. I already knew I was drawing stares, but even the ones who were desperately trying to look away are openly interested now. The noise of voices in here is now almost non-existent. They all want to know how far I'm going to go.

I point at Buddy. 'You're fuckin'—'

'Sir?'

It's the girl who gave me the application form. I don't say anything. Keep staring at Buddy.

'Look, mate,' he says quietly, 'I didn't mean anything by it, alright?'

'Uh-huh.'

He takes off his glasses, a move that's supposed to make him more vulnerable, but which makes me think that he'd rather see me out of focus. 'Didn't mean to stare at you. I'm sorry if I did.'

Silence.

'Uh, sir?' I can hear the girl move her feet, as if she doesn't know what to do with the homicidal special case in front of her. Like I'm her responsibility because she talked to me, and her manager's going to take it out on her if she doesn't calm me down and get me the fuck out.

I blink at Buddy.

'I really am sorry, man,' he says. And he sounds it.

'Fuckin'—'

'Sir, if you could—'

'Fuck's sake, *what*?'

I turn around, ready to kick off with her, too. In front of her are an Americano and a Caramel Macchiato with soy milk. The cups sit in a cardboard tray. Means I can carry the lot in one hand.

The whole place is silent apart from the relentless bubble of the machines, everyone watching me. Lapping it up. I lower my head, grab the coffees and head for the exit, a path opening up as I hobble across the shop floor. I don't hear any conversation until the door's almost closed, and even then it's quieter than it was. I leg it up the street, but stop before I get to my car to fling the application pack at the nearest bin. It bounces off the rim, hits the pavement.

I make a move towards it, then realise I'd never be able to pick up the forms without doing myself damage and, worse than that, spilling Paulo's coffee.

So I leave it, push on to where I parked the Micra. Someone's parked their big black Hummer in front of my car. As I get closer, I see someone's taken a key to it, scraped the same word three times down the paintwork on the driver's door.

WRONG.

WRONG.

WRONG.

I get into the Micra, secure the coffees, muffin and juice. Sit and look at the Hummer as I start the engine. Catch a glimpse of my face in the rear-view mirror.

Wrong.

Yeah, that about sums it up.

THREE

Donkin

Innes. There was a good chance he was at the poof's place. But the problem with going round the poof's place was the poof himself.

His name was Paulo Gray, and I knew him to look at, talked to him a couple times, but I wouldn't go so far as to call us bosom buddies or owt like that. In fact, if anyone was going to refuse their membership to the Detective Sergeant Donkin Fan Club (early days yet, only one member, but he was dedicated), it was him. His problem was that he was an uppity fucker, quick to protect his boyfriend Innes. Quick to deny he was his boyfriend, too, but the way I saw it, I didn't live in a world where an older poof took in a younger man and helped him out unless someone was getting his oil changed.

Anyway, it didn't matter when I got to the club, because Paulo was nowhere to be seen. I made a point of pushing the doors hard so they bounced against the wall on either side. I was a sheriff pushing into a dusty saloon, even threw a little swagger into my walk so there wasn't any confusion. Got a few of the lads staring my way, but I didn't stare them back. Headed straight for the office at the back of the place, the one with the daft little sign by the door, like it was a proper business instead of a fuck-around tax dodge.

In the office was the big bastard that worked with Innes. He got me itching, this lad, because I was positive I'd seen him before I caught him working here, supposedly legit. Definitely had the look about him that he'd done bird at some point in his life and he didn't like it one bit. Strangeways sharpened a couple of edges on Innes, but sometimes it worked the opposite way. Like with this bloke, looked as if the time he'd done had drained something fundamental out of him, left him all squidgy and terrified.

I pushed open the office door, parked myself in the doorway. He turned around, saw us there and looked like he soiled himself.

'Y'alright?' I said, all nice and friendly, like.

He kept schtum.

'You seen your mate about?'

He blinked.

'Callum Innes,' I said, just to remind him. 'You know him. You work with him.'

'No,' he said, and his voice cracked. 'Haven't seen him.'

'Where is he?'

'He's out. Can I take a message for you or something?'

I narrowed my eyes, positive I'd seen this bloke somewhere before. 'What's your name again?'

There was a pause before he said, 'Frank.'

'Both of them.'

Shook his head a little bit, like he wasn't sure.

'I ask where's Frank, people are going to say Frank who?'

'Oh, right.' He attempted a smile, but it didn't stay long enough on his face for it to register properly. 'Collier. Frank Collier.'

'Right.' Name didn't mean anything to us. 'I know you around, do I?'

'You asked us that the last time you came round, Detective.'

'So you remember who I am.'

'Yeah.'

'And what did you say when I asked you?'

'I said . . .' He trailed off, thinking about it. Wanting to get it right for us because I was a copper. Common enough reaction for a recidivist. 'I said I didn't know.'

'And you still don't know?'

Frank Collier rubbed his nose. 'I don't . . . Sorry, you're going to have to excuse us, but what did you want?'

'Innes,' I said.

Frank frowned. Frank Collier. That name flicking at something in my head, but not enough to flip the switch. Not yet. Give it time, though. I'd get him in the end.

'I told you,' he said. 'He's not here.'

I pulled out my rollie tin. Dipped fingers for a paper and some baccy. 'You done bird, Frank Collier?'

When I looked at him, he was bricking it. I rolled a cigarette and put it in my mouth. When I replaced my tin, started patting around for my lighter, I swear to God I thought the bloke was going to have a heart attack or something.

'Sorry, no,' he said. 'No, you can't.'

'What's that?'

'You can't smoke in here.'

'Like fuck I can't.'

'It's a workplace. You can't smoke. It's against the law.'

'I *am* the law, Frank Collier.' But I took the ciggie out of my mouth and used it to point at him. 'You know something, you remind us of someone. You sure our paths haven't crossed at some point, eh?'

'I'm sure,' he said. And he crossed his arms, which bumped up his biceps, made him look like a right bruiser.

'You ever work the doors, Frank?' I said. 'Maybe down Moss Side, the Buccaneer, somewhere like that?'

'No.'

'You've knocked a few heads in your time, though, haven't you, eh? I'm right in thinking that.'

His face got tight. 'I told you already that Mr Innes isn't here—'

'Mr Innes, is it, son?'

'—and if you don't have any other questions—'

'He's your gaffer now, is he?'

'—I've got work to be getting on with.'

'But I've got other questions, Frank, mate. I want to know about you.'

Frank pushed back out of his chair with a sharp sigh. He got to his feet and I nudged myself off the doorway.

'Going somewhere, are you?' I said. 'Don't think I gave you permission.'

'There a problem here, Frank?'

A different voice, the poof finally making an appearance. Brought out of hiding by the possibility of his loose cannon mate here kicking off with the CID. I turned around and looked at him, this expression on his face like someone'd farted and he was pretty sure it was me.

'I'm looking for Innes,' I said.

'I know you are.' He was nodding. 'Every time you come around here, you're looking for him.'

'Because he's never here, is he?' I smiled, tried to keep it light. I heard about this bastard, used to be a bit of a fighter back in his day, and while I was curious about Collier, this one I *knew* had bird under his belt. Hard times an' all. Not that I was scared of him, mind – we were just two old hands playing an even older game.

'You want to step into my office?' he said.

'Nah.'

He gave us a look, then he glanced at Frank. 'Okay. You want to give us a second here, Frank?'

I didn't see Frank nod, but I guessed he did, because he was out of there sharpish. Paulo backed us into the office and closed the door behind him. Soon as that door clicked shut, I have to say, I got a bit uneasy. I didn't like being in this close with a homosexual. Not that I had owt against them or anything, nothing fucking *homophobic* about it; I just didn't want my arse felt.

So I put the ciggie in my mouth and sniffed at him like I didn't give a fuck.

'You can't smoke in here, Detective,' he said.

'You got a problem with it an' all, do you?'

'You should know the law.'

'Right.' I put the ciggie back in the tin. 'So what is it you wanted to say to us? Hopefully you're going to tell us where Innes is—'

'Why do you need him?'

'I don't have to tell you that.'

'He done something?'

I shrugged.

'The reason I ask,' he said, 'is because this is a place of business. You know what we do here?'

I sat on the edge of the desk, folded my arms. I had a million cracks to dish out to him, but this wasn't the right time, so I said: 'Boxing.'

'Boxing,' said Paulo. 'Yeah, you're close.'

'It's a fuckin' gym, mate. I'm not blind.'

'It's a special gym, Detective. We deal with lads who've been in trouble with the law. They've already served their time and they need a place to deal with whatever impulses put them into care in the first place.'

'I know. I recognise some of them.'

'And they know you.'

'That right? My reputation precedes us, eh?'

'Yeah,' he said, stretching it out. 'You could say that.'

'Marvellous.'

'Something else you could say – they know you, they know what you're fuckin' like, and the ones that don't think you're a fuckin' joke reckon you're bent as a nine-bob note.'

'Pot, kettle.'

'You know what I mean.'

I took that in, let it settle, gazed out at the gym. There was a couple lads out there watching us. Joke or bent as fuck. I didn't know which one I preferred. Nah, scrub that, of course I did. I preferred bent. Because bent meant dangerous, bent meant I could fuck you up and I had the nous to get away with it.

'Which ones said I was a joke?' I said, nice and quiet.

'Don't get me wrong, Detective. I don't mean to insult you, I'm just spelling out the situation.'

'Nice of you.'

'I don't want you to think that every time you kick open those doors that you're scaring the shit out of us, because that's not the case. You might think that you have an audience here while you wait for Callum to turn up, but what you don't know is most of that audience is laughing at you.'

'Really,' I said. 'That's interesting.'

'Plus, if you take him to the floor in here, you'll have to bring reinforcements.'

I pulled myself up straighter on the desk. 'And what's that, then? You threatening me, Mr Gray?'

'No,' he said. 'I'm just giving you a likely scenario if you get nasty here. I've got the future of this place to think about, so I wouldn't want you pounded any more than you need to be. But I'm warning you, if you keep coming in here thinking you're invincible, spouting off and throwing your sizeable fuckin' weight around, one day someone's going to call you on it.'

'You?'

The poof moved closer to us. I didn't move, wasn't about to let someone like him call the shots, so I straightened up full height to make my point. It'd been a good while since I'd gone the rounds with someone bigger and stronger. And, I'll admit, recent circumstances had put us sufficiently on edge that a good fight might've been just what I needed.

'Calm it,' he said.

'Back,' I said.

'What I'm saying—'

'You're saying you want to be arrested for assaulting a police officer, you don't back the fuck up, big lad.'

He stepped off. 'Be an adult about this, Detective. All I'm saying is you want to talk to Callum Innes, be a copper about it and find out where he actually is. I'm saying use what they taught you your first day about adapting to situations in order to avoid conflict. And I'm also saying that if you continue to show your face round here, causing trouble for people like Frank – who's done his time, completely rehabilitated himself, and is now a productive member of that society you've promised to protect – then I'll have no option but to file a formal complaint with your superiors.'

I thought about what he said for a good long while, took on his arguments, digested them.

Then I gave him my answer: 'Get fucked.'

'I could complain about you now, anyway. And I will if you don't haul your arse out of my club in the next ten seconds.'

I pointed at him. 'I won't be threatened.'

'You're not being threatened.'

'Nah, I'm not going to be threatened by some poof fuckin' jailbird—'

'You're being *promised*, Detective. Cal's a good lad, but if he's hit, he'll hit back, sometimes a little too hard for his own good. And I don't need you provoking him on my premises. You want to get your jollies harassing ex-cons, do it somewhere else.'

A pause, let the tension bubble for a minute, then I smiled at him, nodded my head like everything was matey. 'Right. Okay, I get you.'

'Yeah?'

'Yeah,' I said. 'No problems here.'

He moved out of my way, waved at the door. 'Glad we understand each other.'

I went out into the gym, saw the lads who'd been watching go back to punch bags and sparring. I opened my baccy tin, pulled out the ciggie I rolled before and put it in my mouth. Halfway across the gym, I sparked it up. Made sure I'd smoked it down by the time I got to the front doors, then I dropped and stamped, turned round to see the poof glaring at us from the doorway to the office.

Let him file his fucking complaints. We both knew I'd be back, and that I'd *keep* coming back until I got a hold of Callum Innes.

FOUR

Donkin

I was fucked if I went back to the station, and my hackles were still well and truly up, so instead of calling it a morning, I decided to cruise round the old estates, looking for a familiar face.

Pissed us off that Innes wasn't at the poof's club, but it pissed us off even more that I didn't have an official reason for going round there. I'd heard that he was a mong or whatever, reckoned I had a spare morning, I might as well go round there and take the piss out of him for a bit. But then the poof had to stick his fucking nose in, take the fun out of the situation.

So I had an itch that needed to be scratched. And I didn't think I was going to get any relief until I saw Paddy Reece.

The first thing about Paddy Reece, he wasn't Irish, but every March he'd be on the streets and in most of the pubs, making out he was blarney as fuck in order to get a free pint. Second thing, Paddy was a nine-carat smackhead. Not only that, but he was the kind of bastard you wouldn't want round to babysit, not with his priors. Two girls, they were fourteen and he was eighteen. Didn't matter that both girls were early drinkers, or that both looked like they were forty years old with the experience to match. Whatever it said on their birth certificate was what the court prosecuted, and smackhead Reece, for poking the pair of them in a drunken haze, found himself down for a two-stretch as an adult kiddie-fiddler. After he got out, he kept himself to himself, except for when he needed to score or when I managed to get my hands on him.

I drew my car up alongside Paddy as he walked. When I honked the horn, two short bursts, he near shit himself.

'Y'alright, Paddy? I didn't know you were out.'

He saw us, pulled a face. 'Aw, fuck.'

'That's not much of a hello, is it?' I cranked the wheel, jumped the pavement. This lad wanted to pump his feet, I could keep driving, run the bastard down. I flung open the car door and he backed up a couple of steps. I got out of the car, pulled out my baccy tin, started to roll a ciggie. 'Were you going to run there, Pads?'

'Nah,' he said, wiping his feet like he had an itch on the soles. 'I wouldn't run, Sergeant.'

'*Detective.*'

'Right. Detective. Not daft enough to run, am I?'

'Used to be a fuckin' rabbit, as I recall.' I looked around the street, but the place was dead apart from a slow rain that'd started as soon as I left the poof's club. Right enough, most people who lived out here, they'd still be in their kip, sleeping it off. 'Didn't know you lived round here.'

'I don't,' said Paddy.

Stuck the cigarette in my mouth, lit it. 'Thought you did.'

'No, I never lived round here.'

'Then what you doing?'

'I was just walking, like.'

He couldn't get his eyes on me. I blew the first lungful of smoke his way and got a bit closer. 'Where from?'

'Just walking, Detective. No law—'

'You must've come from somewhere, though. Y'know, if you don't live round here. So where was it? You still getting your piss test at the clinic up the road, are you?'

'Nah.'

'You don't do 'em anymore, is that it?'

'I do 'em.'

'But not today, right?'

He pulled a De Niro. Just for a second.

'Whoa, the fuck was that, Paddy?'

'Nowt.'

'That face you just pulled at us.'

'Nowt,' he said. 'I dunno what you mean.'

I got right in there, stared at him. Caught a sniff of some nasty Superdrug aftershave he was wearing. 'Oof, Jesus, what you wearing that for?'

He shook his head.

'Fuckin' hummin', that. You got a fuckin' gash round here or what?'

He looked around him, didn't say anything. Probably searching for an escape route.

'I asked you a question. Last thing I knew, you were a bloke with a fuckin' tongue in his head, could answer questions when someone asked them at you, am I right?'

'Yeah,' he said.

'Fuckin' hell, it speaks. So you got a lady friend round here? Hope for your sake she's done her GCSEs.'

'A mate,' he said, his lips dead thin. Looking at us now, almost had this defiant glint in his eyes. And a glint of *any* kind in Paddy's eyes was a weird sight. 'Up the road.'

'This mate a bloke?'

'Yeah.'

'And you went to see him with aftershave on?'

'Yeah.'

'You turn poof in the nick, Pads?'

'Nah.'

'You did something,' I said, pointing at him. Gave him a wink. 'I know you did something.'

His voice got big. 'I was just seeing a mate, wasn't I?'

Paddy was lying to us. He was the same as all the rest, got shouty when they knew they were caught, played indignant to get out of the cuffs. And I would've let it go, except Paddy got mouthier than usual, moved his face back into mine.

'You can't stop us like this,' he said. 'It's not legal. You want to watch I don't put in a complaint about you.'

'For what?' I said.

'For fuckin' harassment, that's what.'

'Right y'are.' I stared at the bastard for a good long time. He knew the moment he made a move to run, I'd be on him, and it'd be the worst kicking he ever got. So he shifted his weight, one leg to the other, and he tried to keep his gaze anywhere but at me. When he finally found a spot on the wall next to him to look at, I spoke. Kept my voice low as I said, 'How's about you and me, we go up that alley over there? I think we need to have a quiet word.'

I pointed up behind him. An alley, long and narrow, boxed in high on both sides, led to the other estate. Looked like the kind of corridor Paddy used to squat down when he was committed fully to the smack and fuck knows what else. He obviously didn't like the idea, pulled another De Niro face.

'You still on the gear?' I said.

'No.'

'Right then.' I pointed the way. 'Up you go.'

'The fuck?'

I put a hand on him, pushed him in his hollow chest towards the alley. He was a streak of piss, nearly buckled under my shove, and when I pushed him again, he flinched like he was set to come back at us.

'What?' I said. 'You want something, Paddy?'

Yeah, he wanted to get fucking bolshy, push us back. But he knew, he put a finger on us, I'd have him back in a piss-soaked cell, the kind with that thick stink that got right in your clothes. See how he fancied going back to his 'mate' with that smell on him.

Paddy trudged into the alley. I checked behind us, made sure there was nobody with a nose on them, or about to do one with my car. Then I followed him, rubbing my hands to get them warm. I saw the puke and broken glass on the ground, reckoned this'd be perfect. It was even slightly sheltered against the rain.

'Up against the wall,' I said.

'Eh?'

'Don't waste my fuckin' time, Paddy. Get your back scraping that wall, son.'

He did what I told him, but he still had a face on.

'You testing?' I said.

'Yeah.'

'Showing clean?'

'Wouldn't be here if I wasn't, would I?' Big grin on his face now, of the fuck-you variety. He rolled up the sleeves of his jumper and slapped his arms to show them unmarked. 'Kind of daft fuckin' question's that?'

I scratched my cheek. 'Alright, it's time to listen to us now, Paddy. This is important an' all so do us a favour and pay very close attention. You can slap your arms all you fuckin' want, son, but that doesn't mean you're not a smackhead, so don't treat us like your fuckin' PO. You're sharp as a baby's fingernails, Paddy, I'll give you that, but you're not as sharp as me. Not even close.'

Paddy didn't say anything.

'So I'll ask you again, and this time you'll stow the attitude. Are you clean?'

'Yeah,' he said.

'You're clean.' I could taste blood coming from somewhere in my mouth. I looked at Paddy's feet. Pumas, box-white. Someone was getting paid these days.

'So is that it?' he said.

'You're definitely clean?'

'I told you.'

'Okay.'

'Right.' He made a move off the wall.

I put a hand on his chest, pushed him back. 'So if I got you to turn out your pockets, I'm not going to find anything?'

Paddy's face pinched up. 'You're not—'

'I'm not going to find smack, anything like that? You haven't shifted onto coke or nowt?'

'Fuck off, you can't—'

I slapped him, open hand. Once. Hard. Paddy didn't see it, didn't roll, caught it all. His face flared where I hit him, and he clamped a hand over the mark, his mouth open.

'Don't interrupt us, Paddy. From now on you speak when you're fuckin' well spoken to. Now, is there anything on your person that you think I should know about, given our current situation?'

'I don't—'

'I know, none of the gear. I know it, I'm aware. But you wouldn't happen to have any pills, resin, owt like that? Doesn't have to be intent to sell. Even if it's a smidge, I need to know.'

'Fuckin' *shite*.' His eyes were red and shiny.

I pulled the cigarette from my mouth and chucked it down the alley. Looked around to make sure we were still alone. 'Turn 'em out, son.'

Paddy sucked his teeth.

'Here or down the nick, whichever way you want to play it. If it's down the nick, mind, you know I'll have to charge you.' I sniffed. 'So chop-chop, eh?'

Paddy paused, then dug his hands into his pockets, started to turn them out, and what a stash it was, more than enough to warrant the stop and search. Got what looked like about an eighth of resin in foil, scraped down from what was probably a quarter at one point. Meant he was selling, because there wasn't a testing smackhead in the world would risk pissing dirty because he'd been smoking resin. Other stuff: Clipper lighter, flint rod sticking out, Zig Zags pack with the front flap all ripped up. Ten pack of Bensons. Flipped that open, found four and a half cigarettes left. I took one of the full ciggies, lit it and blinked against the smoke.

'Other one,' I said.

The other pocket wasn't half as exciting, but I still scored a wrap of speed in amongst the fluff and change. When I looked up at Paddy, he was pale as fuck. Sweating despite the chill. I stuffed the haul into my leather jacket, craned to see the lip of the alley. My car was still up there. Untouched, as far as I could see, but I didn't want to push my luck much more.

'Well?' he said.

I sniffed, then blew smoke. 'Shoes.'

'You what?'

'I'm not joking, and I don't have all day. Take 'em off.'

'Why?'

'Need to make sure you're not a terrorist. What the fuck difference does it make? I tell you to do something, you fuckin' well do it.'

Paddy leaned back against the wall, scooched down a bit and grabbed his left trainer. Undid the laces, handed me the shoe with his sock foot against the wall. I looked inside the trainer. Nothing. I didn't think there would be, like, but I thought I'd pretend to be interested anyway.

'And the other one.'

He pulled a face at us, but I didn't bite this time. Then he rocked on his heels, leaned on the ball of his sock foot and yanked the other trainer off.

'Jesus, the stink doesn't really hit you until you've got the pair, does it?'

That must've hit a nerve, because Paddy turned on the charm. 'The fuck is this about, Donkey?'

And as soon as the word spilled out of his mouth, he knew he'd fucked up big-style.

Not that I didn't know that people called us Donkey. It was a nickname that'd stuck to me like shit to a quilt. It was just that most people had the common decency not to call us it to my face. And Paddy Reece was the kind of bloke who was never above getting a solid beating at the best of times, so I didn't know where the fuck he got the idea he could up the ante by calling me that.

'What's that, Pads?'

'Nothing.'

'Didn't quite catch it. Say it again.'

He mumbled something, shook his head, already the colour back in his face.

I held up one shoe, squinted down the alley. Then I pulled back and flung his Puma as far as I could. It flew for a good distance, then bounced off a bin and landed hole-down in a puddle. Paddy groaned loud.

'What'd you do that for?' he said.

'There was nothing in it.'

He made a move to get up. I kicked him in the middle of his chest. Paddy hit the wall, scuffed down a bit further, his face twisted and the breath torn from his lungs. I leaned over, held the other trainer up so he could see it.

'You want to fuck about your whole life, that's fine by me. But if you choose to fuck about with the men in charge, they're liable to make that life seriously fuckin' uncomfortable.'

I hefted the weight of his other trainer in my hand, then started back to my car.

'Wait a minute,' he said.

I looked back at him. He stared up the alley at the thrown trainer, then back at me. Struggled upright, put one of his feet on the ground and withdrew it sharply.

'Mind yourself walking,' I said. 'Think some dirty fuckin' smackhead's been using it as a shooting gallery.'

'Detective Donkin, come on—'

'I just taught you an important lesson, Patrick, and I didn't have to kick shite out of you to do it. You should be grateful.'

I turned to the street, spotted a variety of targets, and finally picked a cat that was stretching on a wheelie bin across the road. I chucked Paddy's trainer as hard as I could. It bounced off the side of the wheelie bin, scared the shit out of the cat. Behind us, Paddy let out this long sigh.

'You got off light, son,' I told him, getting into the car. 'Next time you see fit to mess us around, I'll put you in the fuckin' hospital. Think on.'

FIVE

Innes

The sign outside the Lads' Club reads IC INVESTIGATIONS.

The I stands for Innes, the C for Collier. It was a long, draining and argumentative night when we finally agreed on a name. Look at it now, and it still seems a little naff, but it's too late to change and besides, the eyeball logo doesn't look too bad. One of the lads who used to come to the club was on his art foundation course, and he needed a stuffed portfolio more than cash. Managed to get some mileage out of that eye – not only does it grace the sign outside, but it's a metallic fixture of our fancy new business cards. The silvery finish was Paulo's idea, and to hell with the cost, we'll make the money back. But while he's optimistic about this little venture, I still think the idea of Frank and me as trustworthy professional private investigators seems, well, *sarcastic.*

I nudge open the doors with my stick and push into the Lads' Club. Slowly, my fingers white around the cardboard tray, I manage to slip through into the gym. In the large championship ring at the back of the place, two of Paulo's top lads are slapping gloves. The blond kid who's about to batter hell out of the other lad is Jason Kelly. He's this year's Liam Wooley, without so many priors. Jason's not the aggro type, but it was drug trouble that put him in the institution. Now he works as a plasterer's apprentice, but he's obviously better with his fists than he is with a trowel and paddle, because Paulo's taken a keen interest.

Other than that, I don't know much about him. As soon as Paulo registered a stake in the lad's career, I backed off, barely spoke to him. I might be superstitious about it, but after the Los Angeles thing, I've found it's best to separate myself from most of what happens in the club. And the continued success of Paulo's boxers leaves me feeling that I was definitely the jinx that fucked Liam Wooley's career.

The two lads are still circling. Paulo watches them from the ropes. He has a foul look on his face. When the doors scream closed behind me, he glances over, but doesn't acknowledge me. I'm halfway across the gym when I see Frank emerge from the back office. And my stomach turns. The way he's coming at me, his face all creased, it looks as if he's had a full-blown panic attack and I'm the cause.

He stops in front of me, and the expression doesn't change. 'Where've you been?'

I hold up the coffees.

'All this time?' Looking at his watch as if he can't believe it, it would be comical if it weren't so annoying. 'Really?'

'What is it?'

He looks over at Paulo, who leans forward to clang the bell. The two lads break and head to their respective corners. Paulo swings under the rope, starts telling them both what they were doing wrong in a loud voice that seems aimed at me. Frank grabs my arm, jostling the coffees. 'Jesus, Frank.'

'Can't talk about it out here,' he says, ushering me towards the office.

'Alright, just . . . don't be handy.'

He leads the way into the office. He closes the door as I put the coffees down on his desk. The furniture's arranged in an L shape around the room, my desk facing the door, Frank's backing onto a window that has a fine view of the bins but very little else. Frank watches Paulo through the partition window. When he finally turns my way, I hand him his juice.

'Frank, tell me.'

'You had someone round asking for you.'

'Who?'

'A policeman. Big guy, looked like he wanted to beat the snot out of you, actually . . .'

'Uniform?'

'No.' He uncaps his juice. 'Said his name was Detective Sergeant Donkin.'

I move over to my desk, pull out my chair and ease down onto it. Reach for my coffee and take a sip. It's still hot enough to sit for a while, and when I look up, Frank's standing there looking at me, looks like he's waiting for an answer to a question I didn't hear.

'You know him.'

I nod. 'What'd he say?'

'He wanted to talk to you.'

'Why?'

'He didn't say.'

'He come to . . . arrest me?'

'Just wanted to talk, he said. Came in specially to see you, though.'

'About what?'

'Wouldn't tell us.'

'Then it's nowt.'

Frank squints at me. 'You think?'

'Trust me. He just wanted . . . to fuck with me. Wind me up.'

'Because I'll tell you, Cal, I was worried.'

I keep nodding like I understand, it's nothing, don't worry about it, not worth your time. Frank's not used to coppers like Donkey, doesn't know how to handle them.

'If he's after you for something—'

'He's not.'

'—we should probably talk about it.'

'It's *nothing*.' I stare at him. 'Okay?'

Frank leans against his desk, watches me, his arms folded. He cricks his neck, doesn't look at me when he says, 'You sure? Because if this is going to have a knock-on effect on our business here, Callum, you should tell us what's going on. I mean, you saw Paulo.'

I look out the window at the gym. 'He was here?'

'Yeah, took him to one side.'

'Who did?'

'Paulo did, took the copper to one side.'

I pick up my coffee again, thumb off the lid and blow on the contents. 'He . . . pissed off?'

'He's something. Not been right since he had a word with the policeman.'

'That's usual. He's angry.'

'Why?'

I think about what I'm going to say. Breathe slowly. 'Because he doesn't like . . . having *coppers* around. Does he? It's nothing. How many . . . *times* do I have to. Tell you?'

'Okay, okay.' He gulps down half his juice, sucks on his bottom lip. 'I'm just making sure. I don't want anything coming out of the woodwork to bite us on the you-know-what.'

Jesus, a grown man with a criminal record and he doesn't swear. This is what I have to work with.

'I know.'

He holds up the juice bottle, pushing himself off the desk at the same time. 'Thanks for this.'

'Don't mention it.'

Points at the door. 'I'm just going—'

'Yeah.'

To the toilet, I know. It's pretty regular halfway down a juice, but he still feels the need to tell me. And because the man has the bladder of an infant, I hear it about nine times a day if I'm stuck in the office. I'm actually beginning to think there might be something wrong with his prostate, but I don't want to say anything. Fuck it, I'm not sure I *can* say anything.

I watch him go, the door easing closed behind him. Take another sip of my coffee.

Donkey's got some fucking timing, I'll give him that. If he's sniffing around, it means one thing – he's bored and he wants to sweat someone. Which is stupid, considering I'm clean as soap and he knows it. Unless he's heard about the stroke and wants to rub it in. Wouldn't put it past him.

Of course, he might've heard that I'm working for Tiernan.

No. Not possible. I just got in from seeing him. Word doesn't travel that fast, but I'm still checking off the people who might've seen Tiernan and me together. Only one I can come up with is Brian, the landlord of the Wheatsheaf, and he's not stupid or unlucky enough to be one of Donkey's grasses.

Still, it's only a matter of time. I get to my feet as Frank emerges from the toilets, the sound of a flush following him out. He opens the office door as I approach it.

'Going somewhere?' he says.

I nod. Frank shifts out of the way, holds the door open for me. 'Where?'

Trying to think of an answer, gazing out across the gym. I watch one of the lads head towards the double doors, a bag in his hand. He puts one hand on the door, grey light leaking in for a second.

'I need to—'

There's a muffled crack and the lad ducks back into the club. 'Fuckin' hell!'

I nod towards the front door. Frank follows my gaze.

Paulo's out in the middle of the gym, half-jogging to the lad who shouted. The bag's on the floor now and I think I can see blood on the lad's trackie bottoms. Paulo looks back to us, and Frank runs across. I follow as quickly as I can.

'. . . fuckin' *mentalist*,' says the lad as I get within earshot. He's staring at the double doors. Definitely blood on the back of his leg, but it's not a gusher. 'Fuckin' *shot* us.'

A loud crack, and we all flinch. Paulo crouches as the doors fly open and a couple more lads burst into the gym. He waves them through. Someone screams outside. It's a shrill sound, could be a woman. And another shot makes Paulo whip his head away from the open door. A crowd develops around the wounded lad.

'Get him away from the door,' Paulo says.

Frank grabs the wounded lad and drags him across the wooden floor, the lad moaning.

'What's up?' I say.

It's Jason who speaks. 'Aaron says there's a fuckin' mental case out there.'

'See what it was?'

The lad called Aaron stops screaming long enough to shout, 'She was fuckin' *shooting* at us.'

Another series of loud, dry bangs, a triple bill. Paulo doesn't flinch this time. 'It's okay. It's just an air rifle.'

'Get out here!'

I push to the doors, peek out. Right enough, there's a woman out on the street in front of the club, looks to be in her early fifties and has the air of a senior librarian gone Michael Ryan with an air rifle. Her face looks like a used tissue, screwed up and wet with tears.

She's shouting, 'Get out here, get out here this *instant*. I'm not going anywhere. I can stand here all day until you come out, so you get *out* here.'

Over and over again, the same pitch and volume, like a screaming mantra.

'What d'you think?' says Frank.

Paulo sniffs, reaches into his jeans for his mobile. 'Call the police.'

'No,' I say.

Paulo glares at me. 'What?'

'You serious? You want the police round here?'

He works his mouth, keeps quiet. I straighten up as best I can. The woman's still screaming for someone to come outside, that she knows they're in there somewhere and she won't leave until she sees them.

'Let me handle it,' I say.

Frank shakes his head, his eyes wide. 'You can't go out there.'

'Course I can.'

'She's mental.'

'She won't shoot *me*.'

'Why not?'

'Look at me,' I say, as I put my hand on the door. 'Too . . . *pathetic* to shoot.'

At least I hope that's the case.

SIX

Innes

Call me a hero if you like, but there's something to be said for looking vulnerable. As soon as the woman sees me, the rifle is up and pointed at me, but the barrel shakes and there's doubt on her face. I think it's doubt, anyway. Could well be grim determination at this distance.

I stop in front of the Lads' Club, raise one hand. Feels like I should be waving a white hankie or something: *We surrender.* She glances at my other hand, which is gripping my walking stick.

'Don't shoot,' I say, with no irony whatsoever.

She keeps the rifle pointed my way, moves her head slightly to one side as if she's spotted something behind me. 'Where are they?'

'Who?'

Back to me now, and her eyes are narrowed, but there's the tremble in the gun that means she's scared. She wasn't expecting someone like me. 'You work in there?'

I gesture to the sign by the door. 'I'm the I.'

She squints at the sign. Looks like someone forgot their glasses, which means she probably couldn't hit a barn door right now. She still hit that lad, but I get the feeling it was a lucky shot. I'd make a move for the gun if it wouldn't take me half a fucking hour.

'I can't . . . what is it?' she says.

'IC Investigations.'

'Then it's not you. I don't want you. I want the boys.'

'What boys?'

'I'll know them when I see them.'

'You sure?' I say, thinking about those missing glasses.

She tightens her grip on the gun. 'Yes.'

'Why?'

'They're criminals.'

'Okay,' I say. 'But not anymore.'

'They're vandals.'

'Some of them. *Were.*'

'No, they're vandals *now*,' she says. 'I know it's them.'

I wave my hand at her. 'You want to . . . put the gun *down*.'

'No.' Shaking her head, but her eyes are fixed on me. 'You bring them out here.'

'We can talk.'

'We *are* talking. You bring them out.'

'I don't know who . . . you mean.'

'You *do*.'

There's a desperation in her voice that I don't like. She's breathing too hard, looks like she might hyperventilate and keel over.

'Please. Put it down.' I take a couple of steps towards her.

She looks at me, obviously thinking about it. But wondering why I'm talking to her as if she's dangerous. Then she glances behind me, I hear some movement, and her arm straightens. I don't need to turn to know that Paulo just stepped out of the gym. If he thinks this is something to do with his lads, he'll be out to defend them, whatever the cost.

'Which lads?' he says.

'I can pick them out.'

'Pick 'em *off*, more like.'

'I don't know their names.'

'But you know what they look like.'

Confusion clouds her face, and she blinks. 'There's . . . too many of them.'

I hear Paulo breathe out. 'Look, I'm trying to help you here, love, but you're not exactly making it easy for us, are you? You reckon you've got something to tell us about the lads in there, it'll be better for you if you get specific, know what I mean? Otherwise you're going to look like a fuckin' basket case.'

'I'm not a . . .' She pinches her mouth closed, swallows the phrase. 'Don't use language like that in front of me, please.'

'He's sorry,' I say.

'It's raining. He doesn't like . . . the *rain*.'

She looks back to me. I extend my hand, start hobbling towards her. Nice and slow, deliberate movements, don't want to spook her. Make it obvious that I'm not going to break into a run or make a sudden grab for the rifle. Instead, I'm going to ask nicely.

'C'mon,' I say. 'Give me the gun.'

She backs up, takes aim. Rainwater drips off her nose. She sniffs some of it up one nostril.

'We really want to help you, love,' says Paulo, and it sounds like a warning. 'But if you're going to act like a Care in the Community, we can just let the police sort it out.'

'Call the police,' she says. 'I don't care.'

'Alright.' I hear the door to the club opening.

'Don't, Paulo.'

I turn and look at him.

Shaking my head: 'Don't.'

Don't make this worse, mate. You bring the police into this, you up the ante, and things'll only go to shit after that. She'll probably start shooting again, and guess who's the nearest fucking target?

My hand stays up, palm out. 'Don't shoot.'

She shakes her head. Tears mixing with the rain.

'Come on,' I say.

Want to say, don't be a fucking idiot, hand me the gun before this all blows up in your face. You seem like a nice enough biddy, but you give it a couple more minutes of this stand-off, and Paulo's going to pull out his mobile and call the police.

That's if Frank hasn't already done it. It'd be just like him.

'Missus,' I say. 'Please. Don't do this. It's not worth it.'

She works her mouth. Looks as if the rifle weighs a ton. Doesn't seem to know what she's doing with the weapon now, as if she's fallen back into her old librarian life. And when she lands, it's obviously painful. Her eyes are red-rimmed, her hand shaking.

'It's okay. Just . . . you know.'

She offers me the rifle. I take it by the barrel, carefully. Tears streaming down her face, her mouth turning in on itself, her entire body shaking with sobs.

I hand the rifle to Paulo.

'Thanks.'

And somewhere behind me I can hear Paulo saying, 'Frank, while you're doing fuck all, mate, how's about you make us a brew, eh? Soaked to the skin out here.'

The woman's name is Elizabeth Sadler, she's a history teacher at Buile Hill, which isn't that far from here, but still makes me wonder what connections she's made. Now she's sat in the back office clutching a mug of tea in both hands, she's noticeably more relaxed, even slightly embarrassed at all the fuss she's caused. The rifle's propped up behind my desk, out of reach.

You never know.

Frank asks all the questions, slightly louder than usual because of the rain that buckshots the windows. Since we got in, it's been coming down in sheets, and I wouldn't be surprised if the rain had actually turned to hail, from the sound of it. Paulo doesn't say anything, standing by the door to the office, watching the lads on the couch outside.

Our chief suspects. Three of them. Mrs Sadler pointed them out as soon as she managed to calm down. One kid, Justin Scott, is a proper vandal, done youth time for it. Keen on burning stuff at one point, from what I hear. The other two are brothers, Aaron and Karl Hills, ginger twins who were a double pain in the arse, one of whom *has* a pain in the arse thanks to Mrs Sadler. But they're nothing special, tagged a couple of buildings in their time, never struck me as more than a couple of delinquent Weasleys.

Still, when Karl makes a move from the couch, Paulo's on him.

'The fuck d'you think you're going?'

'Bog.'

'Sit down.'

'I'm fuckin' *bursting*.'

'You'll park your arse or I'll put a clout on you, son.'

'He's going to piss on the couch, then,' says Aaron.

'You piss on the couch, you're cleaning it up after.'

'I can't hold it in.'

'You're a grown fuckin' lad, you *can* hold it in. Get your brother to tie a knot in it if you want, but I see you shift from that seat, I'll do you.'

'It wasn't us,' says Justin.

'We'll see.'

'Here,' says Aaron. 'Whatever happened to innocent until proven guilty?'

'Whatever happened to children being seen and not fuckin' heard?'

Justin blinks at that one. Paulo points a warning finger at the three of them, then closes the office door. It's a few seconds before he realises that everyone's looking at him.

'You finished?' says Frank.

Paulo's eyes narrow for a second, until he realises that he interrupted one of Frank's questions. Then he folds his arms and pulls a face that reminds me of the dad on *The Wonder Years*. He nods at Frank. 'Sorry. You carry on.'

Frank rubs the corner of his mouth. While he's been talking to Mrs Sadler, he's been rolling a Chupa Chup around his gob, which hardly makes him the most intimidating interrogator in the world. Now he points at the floor with the lolly, gesturing for Mrs Sadler to continue.

'I'm sorry,' she says, 'I don't remember what the question was.'

'That's okay. I just asked you what you were alleging against those boys out there.'

Alleging. Paulo and I glance at each other, both wondering who bought Frank the Word-A-Day calendar. Mrs Sadler looks into her tea, then up at Frank, who's put the lolly back in his mouth.

'They slashed my car tyres,' she says. 'Put bricks through my window. They left . . . *dog mess* on my doorstep, scrawled things on the back door of my house. I can forgive general mischief, Mr Collier, but this isn't just youthful exuberance.'

'Nobody said it was,' says Frank in a low voice.

'You're sure it's them lads out there that did it?' says Paulo.

Mrs Sadler opens her mouth to speak, then stops herself. She sips her tea, heavily sugared by Frank to help with the stress of the situation. The action reminds us we all have our own drinks going cold, and when I knock back the dregs of the Americano, they twist my gut into a knot.

'Well?'

Frank shoots Paulo a glance – don't be so aggressive with her – which Paulo sees and promptly ignores, moving closer to Mrs Sadler. Because he won't believe that those lads outside the office had anything to do with this. He still reckons she's a mental case, but he has to hear her out because she's committed to punishing his lads. And nobody's going to punish Paulo's lads except Paulo.

So he nods when Mrs Sadler finally says, 'No.'

'No, you're not sure?' says Frank.

Paulo's already pushed himself off the desk and stalked to the door.

'You three,' he mouths. 'Fuck off.'

Karl leaps from the couch and sprints to the toilets. The other two stand there looking stupid, not entirely sure that they're allowed to go. Paulo takes a step towards them and they move off, backwards.

'Go on,' he says.

Justin and Aaron head across the gym, talking to each other with occasional glances back at the office. Aaron puts on a heavy limp as he walks.

'I'm sorry,' says Mrs Sadler when Paulo returns to the office.

'It's fine,' he says. 'Just needed to be sure.'

She sniffs, and tears aren't far behind. 'It's just, I don't know what to do. I was *positive* it was them. I'm sorry, it's really . . .'

'Here.' Frank holds out a tissue. 'It's okay. No harm done.'

Paulo glances at me, his eyebrows raised.

'I thought I clipped one of your boys,' says Mrs Sadler.

'You did,' says Paulo. 'But he walked out of here, so he should be alright. Any problems with the guardians, I might have to come back to you, mind.'

'I'm sure that won't be an issue,' says Frank.

'I'm so sorry, it's just too much for me at the moment.' She makes a rattling sound as she blows her nose. 'You try to help these kids, and some of them, I'm sure they think it's just a *lark*, you know?'

'When was the last time something happened?'

'This morning. My car. All four tyres. I'm supposed to be at work right now, but I just can't face it.'

Frank looks at me. Only a quick glance, so Mrs Sadler doesn't pick it up, her face buried in the tissue as she goes in for another blow. I shake my head at him. Irritation flickers on his face, then he turns back to her.

Doesn't matter that I think it's a waste of time, Frank's heart-strings have been tugged, and there's nothing I can do about it.

'Look,' he says, 'maybe there's something we can do.'

'Sorry?' She sniffs. 'I don't understand.'

'We can find out who's doing this to you.'

She looks across at Paulo, then at me. Weighing us up. 'No, I'm sorry. I really don't have that kind of money.'

I want to tell Frank to shut up right now, but the words don't hit my mouth quick enough to interrupt.

'We could consider this *pro bono*,' he says.

That fucking calendar, swear to God . . .

'Free? Really?'

A favour case, fine, but it's *his* fucking favour. I chuck my empty coffee cup into the bin.

'I don't see why not,' says Frank. Then, to me, as I push past him: 'And where're you going?'

'Out. *Paying* work.'

Truth is, I can't hang around here much longer even if I wanted to. If Donkey's been round once, he'll be back soon enough. Besides, I've got to chase up a few leads on Mo. And by my watch, it's time for early doors at the Harvester.

SEVEN

Donkin

Course, the first thing I heard when I got back to the station was that bastard Bowie song.

Nothing against the man personally, but I couldn't say that being screamed at by a dodgy trannie with two different-coloured eyes and fucked teeth was something I wanted to suffer on a regular basis. And it didn't help his case that he wrote that fucking song, which I hated even more now that it came out of the mouth of a proper arsehole.

Detective Inspector Colin Kennedy – call him by the initials DICK – a Scouse twat who obviously couldn't hack it on the Mersey beat, and Greater Manchester was starving for DIs, so they chucked him out here for us to deal with. Came to us last year, breezed in through the doors like he owned the place, and he took a fancy to me in particular, been riding us ever since. He was a right fucking comedian, more gags than Monkhouse, and ninety per cent of them at my expense.

Including that fucking Bowie song, 'Life on Mars'.

Hilarious. Especially that stuff about the law man beating up the wrong guy, because that was what stuck in my head. Not just mine. It was a catchy song alright – I might not have had much time for Bowie, but I could admit that much – and it wasn't just me it caught. It got so Kennedy didn't even need to sing it anymore. It was like that Russian bloke's dog, the rest of the bastards in the office would sing it soon as they saw us walking in the door. Wouldn't have minded so much, but the fucking programme it was off wasn't even on the telly anymore.

It was time to knock it on the head, so when I came in the office, and Kennedy started humming away, I had to say something.

'Y'alright?'

Kennedy stopped humming, nodded. 'Yeah, Iain. How're you?'

I looked at him hard. He gave nothing away, the twat. Probably prided himself on that, if I knew him right. A calm sea, not a ripple showing, but the other bastards in the office looked like their heads were going to explode from keeping in their laughter. I chucked my bacon and sausage barm onto my desk, turned to Kennedy. 'You got something to say?'

'You what?'

'With the humming.'

'I don't get you,' he said, smiling. 'I'm just humming.'

'That tune.'

'What tune?'

I didn't answer him. Kept staring. This close to putting his head through his fucking desk.

'Look, it's a catchy tune,' he said.

'Too fuckin' right it is.'

I went to my desk, a plywood piece of shit covered in paperwork, some of it mine, most of it other people's because they liked to use my workspace as a dumping ground for anything they couldn't be arsed filing. But when I got there, it wasn't the papers I was bothered about.

'Alright,' I said, nice and loud so everyone could hear. 'Who's had it?'

A sea of blank faces, those that were brave enough to make eye contact with us. Then I looked at Kennedy. The fucker had this oily smirk on his face.

'Well?' I said.

He shook his head, playing innocent again. 'Sorry?'

'You had a stroke or something? What's with your face?'

'I'm not doing anything with my face, Iain.'

'You know something or not?'

'What's up?'

I showed him the empty space where my chair used to be.

'Nothing there,' he said.

'I know there's not.'

Shook his head again, pulled a face like he didn't understand what I was driving at.

'Where's my chair?'

'Oh, right, yeah,' he said. 'I get you now. You've lost your chair somewhere.'

'Uh-huh. That's right. And I'm guessing you're just the bastard that knows something about it.'

That pulled him up. Didn't like being called a bastard, did Kennedy. Touched a nerve. Probably his mam called him it once, it was that psychologically raw for him. 'What'd you just say?'

That was when I saw DS Adams move for the door. He was a milksop twat, reed-skinny in a cheap suit and what they used to call Cuban heels, but what I wanted to call platforms every time I saw him. He was proper lairy about his skin, pretty much ducked his head any time someone looked at him straight. Didn't help he was so blonde as to be almost albino, and when you got him in a corner, he blushed so hard, you could toast bread on his cratered cheeks. The bloke was a mess, but he was trustworthy. So I watched him slink around the edge of the room, waited until he got to the door, then grabbed his arm. Kennedy laughed at us, but I didn't care.

'Derek, you seen my chair?'

He pulled away from us, shaking his head, but I followed him until he hit the filing cabinets. Looked like he was trying to retract his head into his collar, which meant he knew exactly what was going on.

'I've not seen it, no,' he said. 'Look, Iain, I'm really busy.'

'You sure?'

'Yeah, I'm positive. Can I just squeeze past you there?'

'Where you going?'

He nodded towards the door. 'It's just an interview.'

'Let him go, Iain.' Kennedy, and the smirk was gone. 'You heard him. He doesn't know anything about your chair, he's got someone in interview, and you're holding him up. Bloke's got a job to do, you might want to do the same.'

'Did I ask you, son? I'm talking to Derek, didn't call out for a fuckin' three-way, did I?' Back to Adams. 'And who the fuck have you got in interview that's more important than my chair?'

He cleared his throat. 'I'm not saying he's more important—'

'Who is it?'

'Bloke's name is Brian Conroy.'

Adams moved away from us. I dogged him.

'Conroy? What you got him on?'

One hand on the door, Adams looked confused, like he didn't understand how I knew the name. 'Uh, fenced goods. Nothing major.'

'He's a fuckin' smackhead.'

'He's a smackhead with a stash of twenty boxed and hooky IPhones.'

'Where the fuck did he get them?'

'Well, that's what I'm going to ask him, Iain.'

'No, you can't do that,' I said.

'Sorry?'

I lowered my voice. 'He's one of mine.'

Adams looked me right in the eye. 'I don't follow.'

'He's one of mine.' I nodded at the door. 'Brian Conroy's one of my' – paused it here, knowing fine well that Kennedy was having a beak, so I had to whisper – '*confidential informants.*'

Somewhere behind us, Kennedy let out a single, barked laugh. I let it go. Didn't want to deal with him just yet. More important things.

'Well,' said Adams. 'That is a problem.'

'He's your collar, is he?'

He looked up at us. 'Yeah, he's definitely caught.'

'He given up his source? Guarantee you he never had the opportunity to nick that many. He picked 'em up from someone.'

'He wouldn't do that, he's not daft. And he's used to how it works in here, obviously.'

'So what're you going to do?' I said. 'You have owt to offer?'

'Offer? No.'

'That's what he's waiting on.'

Adams frowned. 'No, we're going to *charge* him, Iain. If he wants to give up his source, that's fine, but it's a clean collar. I'm not going to *offer* him anything.'

'Tell you what, let me talk to him.'

He shook his head. 'I can't do that.'

'No, it's okay. I'll go in there, have a little word with the lad, get you something a bit juicier to hang a charge on than a bunch of hooky fuckin' phones.'

'I don't think so, Iain.'

I got in between him and the door, pushed it for him. Held up my hands, gave him the smile. 'Ten minutes, mate. Tell you, won't be a single second longer.'

'Iain, really, I can't—'

'Donkey, leave the lad alone.'

Kennedy again. This time with the fucking nickname.

'What you doing, Colin, sticking your oar in, when I already told you this is between me and Derek here?'

Kennedy gestured at Adams. 'Bloke won't tell you to leave it, someone has to.'

'Here, can you not just mind your own business, alright?'

'It's not your interview. He already told you he doesn't want you in there, messing with his collar.'

'Iain,' said Adams, but I wasn't bothered about him anymore.

I turned around, rolled my shoulders. 'It's got nowt to do with you, Colin.'

He put down the folder he was looking at, cocked his head at us. 'I work in this office, I have to hear it all the bloody time. You're a bully, and right now, you're trying to barge your way in on someone else's collar because you can't make the numbers.'

'Yeah?'

'I notice you don't try that shit on me, Iain.'

'I'm not interested in your suspects, Colin, because you're not clever enough to pick up my CIs.'

'Come on, Conroy's a smackhead who could use a spell in the nick, clean him up.' Kennedy sucked his teeth at us. 'You tell him he's a *confidential informant,* or whatever you call a grass these days, he's going to get ideas. And when a bloke like that gets ideas, he starts thinking the law doesn't apply to him.'

I moved towards Kennedy. He straightened his neck when he saw us coming.

'Problem, Colin?'

'Told you, didn't I?'

'I come in, you're humming that fuckin' song—'

'Iain, get a grip on yourself, will you? Jesus, you look like you're about to have a heart attack, mate.'

'You're humming that fuckin' song, you nick my fuckin' chair, you call us Donkey and now you're telling us to back off what's probably going to be a sticky situation if Adams charges one of my valued informants.'

He grinned, folded his arms. 'It bothers you that much, does it?'

'What?'

'The name,' he said. '*Donkey.*'

'Nah,' I said.

'You're sure? Doesn't hurt your feelings or anything?'

'Nah.'

'Got this little kid thing going, so I wondered about it.'

I got right up to him. 'You keep talking like an arse, I'll slap you like one.'

'Go on, then.'

He didn't back down. He was supposed to. Everyone else did when I got this close, this aggro. I didn't say anything to him.

So he said, 'Go on. Show us what you're made of, big lad.'

Stared at him.

'You want something from me, you come ahead.'

And I did want to step up, put that fucker to the floor, start kicking shit out of him, but there was this alarm ringing in the back of my head. He might've been a bastard, but he was a Detective Inspector, too. Rank counted. And that meant he was the bloke in the right if I kicked off. One thing you could always rely on – the brass would cover for the superior officer.

'Forget it,' I said.

'Right.'

'Forget. It.'

'Yeah,' he said with this big grin, his lips wet. 'Forget *it*. Hardarse, eh?'

I turned around, looked around at the rest of the office. Everyone was watching us. Fucking mouths were open, me and Kennedy were like *Lost* to this shower of shite. Probably waiting to see who would come out on top if we went at it, who'd land the first good punch.

No, hang on a sec. That wasn't it.

They were waiting on Kennedy to fuck us up. Which, thinking about it, was the most likely scenario if it came to a one-on-one and I didn't have the jump on him. Kennedy was a serious gym rat, and he was lean enough for me to forget about it, especially when I had my blood up.

I looked at him; he looked back. That smirk was back in evidence.

Yeah, he knew he could take us, which was one of the reasons he was acting the twat. My problem was I got too close too fucking quick. I'd have to watch that in future.

I pulled at my jacket, tried to cover some of my gut, like it was no big deal. Adams was still there by the door, watching us, both his eyebrows pointing up.

'Forget about it,' I said. 'You do what you want, Derek. Just tell Conroy I said hello.'

I pushed past him out of the office, walked quickly to the stairs. This was why I didn't come round the station if I could help it.

I was walking out when I realised I'd left my bacon and sausage barm on my desk. *Fuck.* Still, Kennedy could have it. I hoped it'd choke him, no more than the wanker deserved.

EIGHT

Innes

'Been a while, Innes. I heard you went all fuckin' special on us. Heard you were in a fuckin' wheelchair an' that, couldn't walk or nowt.'

'Nope.'

Baz raises his head, his eyes half-closed. He's either knackered or piss-drunk. I wouldn't be surprised if it was the latter, considering the place is heaving now, the early liquid lunch brigade out for the afternoon. I find him at the same table he used to occupy with Mo and Rossie. Back to the wall, good view of the rest of the pub, it was a position that mirrored Morris Tiernan's seat in the Wheatsheaf. But now that Baz is the only one here, and the drinkers on either side are seeping into the spaces that Mo and Rossie used to occupy, he's become a bloated ghost. Off to one side, as if he's still waiting for Mo to come back, shoulders bunched up at his ears, one hand protective of his pint. Last time I saw him, the hands were bandaged. Now when he shows his palms, I can see the scar tissue shine like plastic.

'You got a stick,' he says in a low slur. 'What happened to you anyway? I heard something like fuckin' *popped* in your brain.'

I don't answer, don't react. Make it obvious to him that he's not going to wind me up. Instead, I clear my throat and say, 'I asked you a question, Barry.'

He tightens his fingers around his pint, takes a large swallow that spills out, leaving his lips wet and shining. After he puts the glass down, he looks at me straight, his eyelids still heavy. 'Last time I saw Mo, you threatened to kill him.'

'Really,' I say.

'Remember that?' He's genuinely interested.

'Yeah. I remember.'

Mo was slumped on the carpet right where I'm standing now, his hands up over his face, a large blood bubble oozing from the wad of chewed meat that used to be his nose and top lip. And I stood over him with broken, red hands.

'*I see you anywhere near Paulo, near the lads that go to his place, near the club, near me, I'm going to kill you on sight.*'

I look at Baz's scarred hands, see fire blackened walls and the sick grin on Mo's face that meant him and his two mates were behind it all. But he's still lying, having a pop at me because he's pissed up and amused at the state I'm in. Reckons I'm a far cry from the bloke who dragged Mo Tiernan over a table and beat him until his knuckles broke.

'You haven't . . . *seen* him. Since then?'

'Who?' he says, squinting at me.

Still playing games.

'Mo.'

'Ah, Mo.' He shifts in his seat, taps the side of his pint glass. 'Aye, you're right.'

'So, when?'

'I need a slash,' he says.

Baz knocks his pint into a wobble as he tries to pull himself from behind the table. A guy in a tweedy jacket with the smell of years-old whisky sweat on him shifts towards me as Baz lurches past. I make the mistake of putting a hand on the guy's arm, and my fingers come away damp. With what, I don't want to know.

'Baz,' I say, as he moves towards the toilets.

He doesn't answer, pulls a face as if he's thinking about knocking me down, and as he does his skin creases, showing wrinkles that weren't there the last time I saw him. Now I see him moving, I notice the weight on him, too, and I wonder how long it's been.

Can't be any more than five months, but there's been some damage done in that time.

When I look up, Baz has already gone, headed for the gents'. I get up, head to the short corridor that leads to both sets of toilets, and I lean on the old cigarette machine. I'm not about to follow him in. Bad memories associated with that particular pisser, and I like the idea of being out in the open just in case the drink makes Baz handier than usual. That way, at least I've got plenty of witnesses.

Just like when I beat the shit out of Mo. Some of them are in this afternoon, and they remember me. Something about that incident managed to stick well into their otherwise booze-blasted memory. Looking around the Harvester, I realise that Baz wasn't the only one around here to get older and fatter. They never were a pretty bunch, but now it's definitely a pub you walk into drunk for fear of seeing who you're drinking with. The bloke in the tweed glances at me over the rim of his lager. One eye is haemorrhaged and swollen, a dispute ended with a single blow; his nose is a burst strawberry well past its sell-by. When he catches me looking at him, he attempts a Paddington stare. Then he puts down his lager and shouts something at me. I don't make out the words. Sounds like he's barking.

'What'd you say to piss Hamish off?' says Baz.

I put a hand on his chest, nudge him back into the corridor. There's a fizz behind his eyes that tells me he didn't just have a slash.

'When did . . . you see him?'

'Fuckin' hell, you know what you sound like?' He tilts his head to one side. 'You sound like a right fuckin' joey.'

'I know.'

Baz was never like this before. Out of the pair of Mo's lads, it was Rossie who acted the hardarse; he was the one more likely to go aggro on you. But with Rossie absent, Baz seems to have bristled right up, bent himself all out of shape to project an image he needs a wrap of speed to maintain.

And I know why: Baz was the butt of the trio. Used to be, because Mo was the one in charge, he'd put Baz under his boot more often than he'd give him a voice. Now Mo's gone, Baz has had to build himself up like he doesn't need the bloke anymore.

But it's a cowboy job – Baz's problem is he thought he had something to say only while he was forbidden to say it. Now he realises, he's just as fucking useless as Mo told him he was.

'You dealing?' I say.

'Eh? What'd you say, Mong?'

'Speed. You dealing?'

'You got cash on you, maybe I am.'

Shake my head. 'You take over, Baz?'

Baz sticks his tongue under his bottom lip, breathing through his nose. 'Take over what?'

I grip the handle of my walking stick, lean into him. Smell the booze on his breath. 'You and Mo, Baz. Did it not . . . work out?'

He flinches back, the speed prickling at him. 'You what?'

'You know. Mo's gone. You're selling. What happened?'

Baz backs up further, looking at me with wide eyes. There's a smile that keeps trying to sneak its way onto his face, but he won't let it pitch tent because his brain is too busy sifting through possible answers and because Baz is such a thick bastard, it could take a while, even with the speed kicking in. He starts working his mouth, chewing invisible gum. I watch him, blocking his exit back to the main bar, the only close sound the intermittent flush of the urinals.

'What you saying?'

I stare at him. He knows only too well what I'm saying. Wants me to repeat it so he has an excuse to kick off.

'What, that I had summat to do with Mo, is that it?'

'He dead?'

His eyes shock wider for a second. 'I didn't say that.'

'Don't fuck about.'

He breathes through his teeth. I can almost hear his heart thumping in his chest. That wrap was a tough one, ripped the water out of him, as he smacks his lips. The only thing he wants right now is a pint, and I'm hardly in a position to get in his way for long. He knows that, too.

'Fuck off.'

Baz steps forward and my first instinct kicks in, which is to stand firm. He slams me into the wall, the impact knocking the wind from me. As I peel myself from the wallpaper, I can't do anything but watch him march out into the main bar.

I take my time, stare at the swirls on the carpet until I catch my breath. Once I'm mobile, I swing out after him, arrive at the bar just as Baz gets his pint. He picks up the glass, raising it to his mouth as I double-grip my walking stick and swing at him.

The rubber end of the stick catches the edge of his glass, whips it out of his hands and into the bottles lined along the back bar. There's a terrific crash, shit lager spraying the bar, Baz and anyone within a four-foot radius. The landlord, a fucking bull of a man with more tattoos than skin, shouts: 'The fuck d'you think you're playing at?'

I'm staring at Baz. Fucking fearless. Bring it on.

He turns to me, sucking beer from his thumb, looks like some giant psychotic baby. Thoughts churning, he's trying to work out what to do, whether to give in to the simple chemical urge to break me down quick and nasty.

'Talking to *you*, you fuckin' cunt.' The landlord again, getting closer. 'The fuck you think you are, you spastic fuck, come in here—'

'Morris Tiernan,' I say.

I don't need to see the landlord to know he's stopped in his tracks. Don't need to hear him to know he's wondering what the hell Morris Tiernan has to do with his wrecked back bar. But he's not about to ask any questions. I might as well have said Candyman five times into his cracked bar mirror.

'He wants to know.' I take a breath. 'Where his son is.'

The landlord doesn't say anything. Neither does Baz, but he's gone grey and he's stopped staring at me, started staring *through* me. And with the speed well in his system by now, those thoughts have jumped the rails, become full-tilt paranoia.

'We need to talk,' I tell him. 'Like fuckin' *adults.*'

He looks around him as if he's just sobered up after a fortnight drunk, wondering where the fuck he's ended up. I dig around in my jacket pocket, find my cigarettes and hold the pack out to Baz.

'You want a smoke?' I say.

Baz looks at the Embassys, pitches a sigh, and reaches for the pack.

'Outside, lads,' says the landlord.

'I know.'

Baz reaches for a cigarette, and I nod towards the doors. He trudges out into the street, and I'm not far behind.

NINE

Innes

'So where's Rossie?'

The rain has eased off to a shower, but it's still cold enough to prompt a shiver from Baz as he sucks on a filter round the Harvester's 'beer garden', which is basically a trestle table and an ashtray. He rubs his nose as he contemplates his answer. We seem to be the only things moving out here. The houses across the way look abandoned, but someone has to call this place their local.

'You never talked to him, then,' he says.

'Don't know . . . where he is.'

'He's out of it.'

'Left town?'

'Left the game,' says Baz. 'Been looking for an excuse to fuck off since he started knocking off that skank up Cheetham Hill.'

'You keep in touch?'

'Last I heard, he was working full-time in fuckin' *Currys*.'

'Delivering them?'

'The shop. In the Trafford.'

Never expected Rossie to go straight, and I certainly never expected him to go into a job-type job. Which makes me think it wasn't just the skank who made him leave. 'What about Mo?'

Baz breathes smoke down through his nostrils as he plucks the cigarette from his mouth. 'I don't know. He was bad.'

'What's that mean?'

'Since his dad chucked him out, y'know, he was just doing *bad*. Wasn't right in the head most of the time, that thing with his dad just like fuckin' turned it up. I've known him since first school, right, but I swear to God I never seen him so bad as after his dad cut him loose. That was like the final fuckin' straw. You know, Rossie told us Mo didn't even know who his mam was? I mean, Mo always reckoned it was this one bird, but she was already long gone by the time he could ask any questions.'

'Gone?'

'Dead or left.' Baz pulls a face. 'Doesn't matter which, does it? But my fuckin' point is, you forgive him a lot of the shit he did 'cause, y'know, what else was he supposed to fuckin' turn out like, you get me? Tapped at the source. So it's no wonder he did what he did.'

'Like his sister.'

'*Half*-sister. But yeah, that.' The orange glow on the end of his cigarette bobs as he moves his head. He blows some more smoke. 'I never said it was legal or nowt like that. I'm just trying to give you some background on it, 'cause I know you didn't look at that whole thing the same fuckin' way we did.'

'How'd you see it?'

'Just that Mo loved her.'

'Fuck off.'

'Nah, see, different fuckin' ways of seeing it. And you never saw him when it was going on. It was true love to him. Didn't matter that they was fuckin' related.'

'Yeah, I know this. True love. Okay.'

'And when she went and fucked off with that bloke, you got to understand, he's already got this shite with his dad, not thinking he's up to snuff, now his fuckin' *bird*'s pulling the same. Y'know, *plus* he's never been right in the head in the first fuckin' place . . . it was never going to end well.'

I glare at him. 'You think?'

'All I'm saying, you want to blame anyone for what's happened, don't fuckin' put it all on Mo. And if owt's happened to him, then it's probably not deserved that much.'

'What *has* . . . happened to him?'

'I don't know.'

'Last time you saw him?'

Baz takes a long drag on the cigarette, then another, until there's the smell of burning filter in the air. He pulls the butt from his mouth, flicks it into a puddle. He points to the pub. 'In there.'

'When?'

'Couple month back.'

That's about right. 'Was Rossie there?'

'Just me and Mo.'

'And?'

'And, what else do you do in a fuckin' pub?' He spits at the pavement. 'We were drinking, and he was in a fuckin' state, wasn't he? He was talking about his dad, which he usually did when he'd had a few.'

'How?'

'Like the usual.' Baz moved his shoulders. 'Like he was going to show his dad that he wasn't a fuck-up, and did I know that Uncle Morris treated him like shit his entire life, never gave him a chance to stand up, work on a bigger scale. Course I fuckin' did, it was all he ever talked about when he had a couple pints in him. And then he started talking about Rossie, and wondering where he was, so I told him he was working in Currys. He said we should go and fuck him up, him and his missus. And I said I wasn't going to fuckin' do that. Rossie was a mate, wasn't he? Then he got all fuckin' lairy with us, started on that I was a fat, useless cunt.' Baz sniffs, his eyes wide and glazed. He looks up at me, shrugs again. 'Usual shite.'

It was. Any time I'd spent around the three of them, it was always Baz that got the shitty end of the stick. And I can only think Mo was well and truly hacked off to be left with Baz as company.

'So I told him to fuck off,' says Baz. 'I wasn't taking his shite anymore, I couldn't be fuckin' arsed with it. And then he was like, he didn't need us anyway, I was a fuckin' baby, slowing him down.'

'He had plans?' I say.

'Mo always had plans. You know that. This time, he was going on about a *proper* job, something that would bring in the cash. Then he wouldn't have to spend his time in a shithole pub with a fuckin' brain dead sidekick. That's what he said, anyway.'

'What d'you mean . . . *proper*?'

Baz shuffles closer into the smokers' alcove, peers at the dark grey sky. 'I don't know, do I? Fuckin' Mo was always going on about Amsterdam, wasn't he? Reckoned he knew this bloke over there was going to hook him up a fuckin' distribution deal over here. Nobody in their right fuckin' mind would risk that much for three quid fuckin' pills, know what I mean? You're gonna bring in the Class As, you might as well bring in smack, get a better mark-up and the same fuckin' time if you're nabbed.'

'You setting up?'

'Me?' Shakes his head, wipes his nose. 'Like fuck. You got another ciggie?'

I hand him the pack. He pulls out an Embassy, grunts his thanks, then sparks it with a disposable lighter.

'You not in . . . business, then?' I say.

He glares at me through a cloud of smoke. 'Not like that, nah. Not like a proper fuckin' big-time job. I punt on if I get it, the usual. You know. Nowt fuckin' changes with me, mate. I'm the last proper gangster in Manchester.' He laughs, and as he winds down, I hear the wheeze tacked on the end of it. 'I'm in with Tiernan, but way fuckin' down the totem, know what I mean? Out of sight, out of mind. One thing I learned being with Mo.'

'That's it?'

He nods, blows smoke out the side of his mouth. 'He tried calling us once after that. I didn't talk to him.'

'And you haven't . . . seen him? Anywhere?'

'Not since, no. I told you.'

'Where's he living?'

Baz scratches at the corner of his mouth, picks at some dry skin there. 'I know where he *was* living.'

'That'll do.'

'Might not be there now, like.'

'Last known's good.'

'Out at Miles Platting. He had this squat in Sutpen Court, used to kip down there sometimes.'

'Write it down.' I hand him a bookie pen and a bus ticket. 'Thought he had a flat.'

'Yeah, he *did*,' he says as he scrawls on the ticket. 'But he sold it. Y'know, after what happened with his old man—'

'*He* sold it?'

He hands me the address. 'Said he didn't want to live where his dad could get to him. Just because he wanted to kill his fuckin' dad, reckoned it was the other way around an' all. And the way he told it, he needed the money.'

'For what?'

'Didn't ask. Just thought he needed it for this proper job he was talking about. Like fuckin' seed money or summat.'

'And?'

'And, I don't fuckin' know, do I? Either he did it and he's fucked off, or summat happened to him and he didn't.'

'You try to find him?'

He doesn't answer, turns his face away. When he breathes out, smoke spills out of his mouth, seems to go on forever. Then he closes his mouth, and the muscles in his jaw twitch like insects under his skin.

'Baz,' I say.

'Nah.'

'Why not?'

He thinks about it, takes another drag on the cigarette. Sucks his teeth and turns back to me.

Then he says, 'Because I realised that I was better off without that cunt in my life.'

TEN

Donkin

So yeah, I was hungry by the time I got out the station, kind of miserable into the bargain. On top of that, it was pissing down, so I had to stay in the entrance to light my cigarette. Glad I did, mind, because I got to see the jam sandwich rolling in up front, and who happened to be in the back seat but Paddy Reece, his face all knotted up.

As I stepped out into the rain, moving quick to my car, I called out to the bobby who'd brought him in. When he turned round, I waved at him to come over, then I got in my car, wound the window down.

'Detective,' he said, all professional, like.

'Your man in there, what you got him on?'

'Why d'you ask?' He was smiling with his mouth only, all professionalism gone out the window when he started to think I was after his collar. I didn't know what the fuck was the matter with people at this station, they were scared out of their minds about losing their arrests.

I looked at him through the smoke. 'Answer a question with a question, why don't you?'

He didn't catch that, though, so there was this long, uncomfortable pause, me just staring at the daft twat, waiting for him to carry on. In the end, I gave a little Queen wave to get him rolling.

'Well?' I said.

'Shoplifting.'

I craned around in time to see Paddy disappearing into the station. Right enough, he was still in his socked feet. 'Let me guess, fuckin' Foot Locker, was it?'

'TK Maxx.'

I laughed. 'Fuckin' right y'are. Jesus Christ . . .'

'Pair of trainers on special.'

'Better get him banged up, then.' I started the engine, revved it good and hard. 'Christ, you can't have a dangerous bloke like that walking the fuckin' streets, eh? Specially not in his stocking feet.'

I backed the car out of the space, turned towards the exit. Couldn't help myself laughing, thinking about poor old Paddy hopscotching his way into town, looking for the nearest shoe shop. Made us wonder why he never bothered going back to see his mate, get a pair of shoes off him. And I made a mental note to have a word with Paddy as soon as he got out. The bugger was definitely keeping something from us, and I wouldn't let it go until I found out what it was.

I started towards Salford, thinking I'd catch Innes at home and wind him up. He wasn't in, so I hung around outside for a while.

When I caught myself dozing off, I reckoned I'd best have a drive around, see if I couldn't wake up a bit.

As I was driving down into Castlefield, my mobile went off. I wouldn't normally have answered it, but the display showed ANNIE, so I had to.

'Yeah?' I said.

'You driving?'

'Yeah, aye.'

'Okay, then can you call me back when you've stopped?'

'No, it's alright. I can drive and—'

'Iain, you can't. It's illegal.'

'You're on the fuckin' hands-free, woman,' I said.

'There's an echo on the hands-free. So I know when I'm on, and I'm not on now. Pull over and call me back, okay?'

'For fuck's—'

She hung up. I wanted to pitch my mobile through the fucking windscreen, but I kept it subdued, worked through it like I was supposed to. Turned my lips in, gnawed on the bottom one as I looked for places to turn in. Up ahead, a Gala Bingo, so I swung into the car park, found a nice quiet space and killed the engine.

Annie was always on at us about the fucking mobile, but it was always her that called us on it. She wouldn't call the home number, knew that I never answered it and wouldn't check for messages like she always used to do. So she called us on the mobile, but wouldn't talk to us unless I was stationary.

And me being the soft twat I was, I did what she told us to do. Because if I did that, then there was a bigger chance of her talking to us in person the next time.

'I'm parked up. Happy now?'

'Yes,' she said. 'I needed to talk to you, it's kind of important. To do with Shannon.'

'What's she into?'

'Nothing.'

'You sure? You can tell us, you know that. I'll sort it out, no muss, no fuckin' fuss. Drugs or lads, either one. It's easily taken care of, I just need names.'

'She's fine, Iain. Don't worry about that.'

'Then what is it?'

'Christmas.'

'What about it?'

'We need to sort out who she's spending it with this year.'

I looked out the side window, watching the cars go by on the main road. 'I don't know. She lives with you.'

'And she hasn't seen you in ages.'

I sniffed. 'I don't think she wants to, does she?'

'Iain—'

'Nah, it's fine. I don't mind. She lives with you, seems only right she spends Christmas with you. Y'know, you got that home all sorted out, I got my place – *our* place.'

'Your place.'

'My place, it's . . .' I breathed out, then laughed once. 'Looks like you just left, actually, like. Haven't had a chance to get it sorted.'

'Okay.'

'I mean, I could come round, bring presents an' that.'

'I don't think so.'

'It's no trouble, and I won't stay long. Just drop 'em off, like.'

'You know why that can't happen, Iain.'

'It's five minutes.'

'It doesn't matter.'

I wanted to scream at her. Wanted to ask her again why the fuck she thought making it legal was a good idea, even though I knew the answer. But I was a changed bloke, took a good long look at myself and did what I needed to do. I didn't need a fucking court-ordered injunction to keep us in line, punch or no punch.

'Fine,' I said. 'You do what you fuckin' want, Annie. I'll dump the presents by the side of the road, you can come pick 'em up whenever, like a fuckin' ransom drop. Y'know, just in case we accidentally fuckin' see each other in person.'

'See, this is why I don't like doing this.'

'Fuckin' easy answer to that, then, isn't there?'

I cut off the call, turned off my mobile and slung it onto the dashboard. Soon as my mind stopped raging, I regretted it. But I didn't turn it back on. There was nothing to say to her. As I started the engine again, I realised that she hadn't been ringing to ask us about Christmas; she was *telling* us that Shannon would be spending it with her.

Fine. It was fine. They deserved each other. Christ, the last thing I wanted was a fourteen-year-old in the bastard house over Christmas, when I was trying to get nicely bladdered. Even thinking about it gave us a thirst, so I headed round the offie, picked up a crate for the fridge, then went down to Wilmslow Road. Popped out of the car at The Balti King, but I kept an eye on the car while I was in there.

Nobody turned up, and by the time I got back to the car, it was already getting dark. I shoved my lamb jalfrezi, pilau and nan (so greasy you could see through the paper bag) into the passenger seat, and headed home, the smell killing us with hunger every minute I was driving.

By the time I got in, I was feeling it. And by the time I got the curry down us, plus five cans, I was seriously knackered. I tore off some bog roll and mopped up some sauce from the settee. It wouldn't come out all the way, so I thought fuck it.

Everything was fucking work these days. Since Annie did her bunk, I was stuck with a place that didn't want to stay clean. I mean, I wasn't the kind of bloke to plastic-wrap his furniture, but the fact was that the chintzy shit she left us with attracted dirt. And it wasn't like I could get rid of it, either, not when I reckoned that it was only a matter of time before she came to her fucking senses. So the place was getting manky, and I was in no mood to clean it up. Especially not after I'd drunk those cans. A couple more, and I was getting thirsty for the Grouse in the kitchen cupboard.

I didn't need to check my watch to know it was getting late. If I turned on the telly right now, there'd be that saucy brunette on ITV Play telling all those sad, hopeful bastards out there in the dark that if they just got the *right* word in tonight's Wordfind, they'd win ten grand. And then I got to thinking that her and the bog roll would go together like ham and pease pudding, might wake us up a bit.

Instead, I sat looking at myself in the dead screen. Kennedy had already popped in my head, and that was enough to kill any urges I might've had. A bloke in my head when I was handling myself, that was the first step on a dark path. Especially one like Kennedy, a put-on merchant, right down to his fucking accent. You got the bloke talking to a scally, he was all phlegm in the throat, a hundred per cent Scouser right from the streets, but as soon as the DCI wanted a word, that accent went out the fucking window. He was clipped, he was professional, and most of all he was full of shite.

And yet, *I* was the joke of the office. It was like a conspiracy against us these days.

I felt around for my baccy tin. Found it wedged down the back of the settee. Rolled myself a thick one, hands going numb with the drink, and pulled my lighter. There was baccy falling out the ends, but I reckoned it would smoke good enough. I lit it and took a big enough draw to bring an itch to my lungs. When I finished coughing, I thought about that last bit again.

Right enough, I hadn't been doing that well recently. Couple of bad collars that came back to bite us in the arse because I may've used a little too much force when cuffing them, and a shoplifter who swore blind I put my hand up her crack when I didn't. But a few bad arrests didn't make a whole lot of difference outside the station, and that attitude on Paddy Reece had been bothering us. It was like he'd heard something along the line that I'd lost whatever respect I once had, that I wasn't hard enough anymore. I took another drag on my ciggie, leaned forward on the settee. Wondered how that could've happened.

It was someone who'd decided to mess around with us. Putting about that I'd gone soft or something. And me a peaceful bloke, didn't want to knock heads unless I absolutely had to in order to get the job done. If someone gave us lip, I'd fatten it, but I didn't go out of my way to get into fights. Someone was spreading shit about us.

So who was it? Kennedy?

Kennedy was a Scouse twat, but he hadn't been at the nick long enough to get any informants of his own, so there was no way he could put any kind of word out. And everyone else in the nick knew better than to fuck us off.

I heard the crackle of the paper going up, felt the heat near my fingers. Dropped the ciggie into the large glass ashtray on the coffee table, breathed smoke.

'That fucking cunt,' I said to the floor.

Because I knew who it was right then.

Callum bastard Innes.

ELEVEN

Donkin

The more I thought about it, the more it made sense.

Innes knew how I worked. I had a carefully constructed network of gobs and grasses stretched across Greater Manchester like an invisible spider web. If someone nicked a load of Motorolas in Crumpsall, I'd know the bastard within the hour, thanks to a dippy slut called Mandy Corr. Down Prestwich, if you were to tell us that one of those nice Victorian terraces got broke into, that'd be a quick call and a boot up the ring of former daytime burglar Gerald Moss. And say a granny got lamped and robbed down Eccles New Road, that was a case for the gob who called himself Just Dom.

One thing tied all these people together, and that was the gear. Every time I heard that crime problem was a drug problem, I knew that the drugs were also part of the solution, because there was nowt as gabby and unscrupulous as a needy smackhead. Nobody outside of your tight-arsed and tanned white-collar criminal is more scared of a prison term, either, because it meant they'd have to clean up. And as much as they all said they wanted to clean up, fact remained that they were smackheads, and if there was one thing smackheads loved, it was smack.

My favourite grass was long gone, though. And I still reckoned that was an issue with me and Innes.

His brother, Declan. A piece of work, and a dream come true to a copper like me. The lad was well in with the Tiernans and he had a fierce hunger for pretty much any downer he could lay his hands on. Didn't take much to get him trained up. He took to the rules pretty quickly. It wasn't long before if I wanted anything connected to the Tiernans, I'd pull Declan Innes. And the brass would let us do it, no questions asked.

Get him sat in an interview room for a couple of hours, just enough time for the blood to leech from his face and for his skin to prickle. Then I'd leave him another hour, just to be on the safe side. By the time I pushed open the door, he'd be ready to talk. Most of the time he'd give us solid information, and because the Tiernans knew he wasn't giving us anything directly related to them, they let him keep walking around.

Then along came his fucking brother to muddy up the waters.

I thought it'd be great, a brother in the mix, more emotional. Didn't exactly turn out like that, though.

I remember after that security guard got his napper stoved in, I brought Declan down the nick, and made sure to sweat him hard before I came back. When I did, he looked like he was about to puke on the fucking floor.

'How you hanging, old son?' I said.

He didn't say, too busy hugging himself. He wagged his head, his eyes bugging at the floor.

'Jesus, Declan, what *are* you doing with your life, eh?'

Nothing again.

'I'll tell you what you're doing with it, you're watching it go down the fuckin' plughole, and we all know whose fault that is.' I walked behind the table, stopped and watched him suffer. 'You know that cunt Mo's going to drag you right down into the shit with him, don't you?'

Declan hugged harder. Drew a long, wet breath up through his nose.

'You want to end up in the fuckin' 'Ways, son?'

He shook his head.

'Because I'll tell you, Declan, I like you.' He pulled a face at us, but I smiled. 'No, I do. And I'll tell you straight, no word of a lie, I reckon you're a good lad. You've done us some good turns over the years, and I really don't want to see you banged up.'

He stuck his bottom teeth out, then he smacked his lips and swallowed. Looked to me like he was trying not to cry.

'You're not a strong lad,' I said.

'I'm fine.'

'You're fine.' I laughed at him. 'I leave you in here much longer without a fuckin' fix, you'll be climbing the bastard walls.'

Shaking his head, breathing through his nose so there was this weird whistling sound in the room. I wanted to slap him so he'd breathe through his mouth like a normal human being, but instead, I leaned on the table, fixed him with a stare.

'You're a fuckin' smackhead,' I said. 'You're fuckin' fragile. And you're not going to get any better unless you face up to that fact. So when I ask you questions next time, I want to make sure you tell me what I need to know.'

Then I straightened up, and left him in there for another hour and a half.

It was good stewing time, and it gave him time to hit that core of self-loathing that I knew he carried around with him. What I heard, his old man was a bit of an arsehole, but obviously knew that a backhander to the mug was worth a thousand angry words. Having a smackhead as a son, I had no doubt that Innes Senior would've done what any father worth his balls would do, and that was to make his eldest feel like shit. I wanted to bring all those feelings right back, break him down to the point where it didn't matter if the Tiernans *killed* him – the only thing he'd want was to get out of that interview room.

When I went back in, he'd near melted into a puddle of his own sweat.

'So, you going to tell us about that robbery, then, Declan?'

His face crumpled up. That was the last thing he wanted to talk about.

'I heard about it,' I said. 'Heard your kid, whassisname – *Callum*, is it? – got picked up. On his own. Or near enough. There was this almost dead security guard with him. Looked like your little brother smacked him over the head with something, except here's the thing – whatever he smacked the guard over the head with, it wasn't around anymore. But he was. Funny that, innit?'

Declan shook his head.

'Did I get something wrong?' I said.

'I don't know—'

'Fuck off, you don't know.'

'I'm telling you—'

'Here, I've got a good sense of humour, Declan. You know that, we've had a few laughs over the years, me and you. So I'm willing to let that first one slide, know what I mean? But the thing about jokes is you can't really tell them to the same person twice because then they stop being funny.'

I pointed at him, and he jerked so hard I thought for a second I'd hit him with a lightning bolt.

'I'm sorry,' he said. 'I can't tell you anything.'

'You want to continue this discussion tomorrow morning?'

He looked at us, and his eyes were fucked. Like he was knackered, but he wouldn't be able to sleep for ages.

'What do you want?' he said.

'I know you were there. Your kid wouldn't do nowt without his big brother's say-so, am I right? Especially when he's new in town.'

Declan kept quiet.

'So you must've been there. And I know that you wouldn't dare try to pull a warehouse, just you and your brother, so I'm guessing that you had a couple mates along for the ride.' I smiled at him. '*And*, knowing you the way I *do* fuckin' know you, reckon it'd be safe to assume that those mates were Mo Tiernan and his boys. Am I warm?'

He set his jaw, kept his gob shut. And inside, I bet he was eating himself alive.

'So what're you going to tell us here, Dec? What you got?'

He moved his head, looked at the floor. I got in a bit closer. Leaned forward and grabbed his face. He reacted like my hand was red hot, made a hissing noise through his teeth.

'Yes or no, those lads were there.'

He screwed his eyes shut. Made a choking noise like he was going to either puke or start crying. I let go of his face, pushed off the table.

'You want to play this formal, we can.' I pointed at the door. 'I can take you out there, chuck you in a cell and watch you tear your fuckin' hair out. But after that, I'll bring you out here again and I'll ask you the same questions. You don't tell us what I want to know, I'll put you back. I can do that, Declan, because I have every reason to suspect that you were on the scene.'

Hugged himself so hard, I thought he was going to snap his own spine.

'Wasn't your brother put the guard down. Wasn't you, neither.'

He took a deep, ragged breath in.

'You hear a guard coming, you'd fucking leg it, wouldn't you? He catches you, you want to put up a fight, see if you can get away, but it's not like you go *looking* for trouble, is it?' I pointed at him again; he doesn't see it to flinch. '*You* don't lamp a cunt just because he's there.'

He let out the breath with a small noise like a sob.

'So tell us.'

'I don't know what you're talking about.'

I was on him before he could react. Grabbed his hair tight in one fist and pulled him out of the chair. The chair hit the floor, and he kicked at it, yelping. I dragged the fucker to the corner of the room, threw him into the wall, one hand against the back of his neck as I jabbed him hard and low in the kidney. He cried out again, and I stepped back to watch the pain shudder through him.

He leaned into the corner of the room, his mouth open but no sound coming out.

There was a knock at the interview room door. A voice outside, asking if everything was okay. I told them to fuck off.

They fucked off. Back then I still commanded enough respect to make that happen. Back then, I could even be in here with a suspect on my own. Didn't need a uniform watching over us every step of the way.

Declan started to curl as he went to the floor.

'We got your brother,' I said. 'You know that.'

He nodded, hearing us through the pain. His lips disappeared – he looked like a fucking muppet.

'You go on tape, tell us what happened, I can do things for you. Do things for your little brother an' all. Bring in Mo, keep him here.'

Declan sobbed, then he said, 'No.'

'No?'

He shook his head. Pitched a painful sigh.

'No,' I said. 'Even though if we get Mo, he'll be gone for a while. We get Mo and your brother's given a slap sentence, a six-month trip, out in three.'

'I can't—'

'We *don't* get Mo, your brother's looking at a maximum of five. You fuckin' *know* it.'

He shut up. Put a fist to his mouth and coughed hard. His head was lowered, his shoulders up. I caught a glimpse of his face – it was all over the place, past the point of tears and anticipating a punch that I wasn't going to throw.

'You're the one sending him to prison,' I said. 'You fuckin' well remember that.'

There was another knock at the door, but I didn't tell this one to fuck off. Instead, I left the room and told the constable on the other side of the door to clean up the mess.

That was the only time he never spilled. And I took it upon myself to punish the bastard while his brother was in prison. I felt justified.

I always reckoned that Callum Innes would come out of the 'Ways a rangy cunt, and I wasn't far off the mark. You do a couple of years in that place, you're liable to pick up a thing or two. Mostly hepatitis if you let them get you on your belly, but you're also liable to change deep inside. That definitely happened with Innes, now I came to think of it. Wasn't just the edges sharpened. Something snapped in that lad, something that would probably make him an easy collar one of these days, but he'd been slippery so far.

Which made us positive it was him behind the rumours. I wouldn't put it past him to spread shit about us, not only for turning his brother into a grass, but because I was determined to get him working for us, too. There was no one else I knew with the connections or the motive.

That was why I was headed out to his place now. Smoking another shitty roll-up, because I needed to clear my head. Didn't want to be dopey when I got round there. If I was lucky, it being late, I'd catch him in his kip. Drag him out, just like the old days. I had no doubt he was up to his neck in shit; he always was. The only question was, could I use it to my advantage?

And the answer would be: absolutely I fucking could.

TWELVE

Innes

Baz might as well have talked about Mo in the past tense, for all he cares. As far as he's concerned, Mo's dead to him and good fucking riddance. Haven't talked to Rossie yet, but I can guess that his reaction's going to be similar. The only person who actually seems to care about Mo's fate is his dad, the very same guy Mo would've been happy to watch bleed out. Makes you wonder who's actually going to miss you when you're gone.

Your estranged father.

Your sister.

As far as I can see, Alison Tiernan hasn't changed much since she did a runner to Newcastle with ten grand in stolen cash and a boyfriend old enough to be her dad. She was a dirty version of an old song, sixteen going on seventeen, but she wasn't timid, shy or scared about it. Hardly jailbait in the popular sense, being plain as a brick, but there's blokes out there who'd happily fuck a piranha if it was young enough.

One of those blokes is leaving her house right now. He's tall, greyish hair, obviously older than Alison, which makes him a dead ringer for Rob Stokes, so probably her new boyfriend. I watch him walk across the rain-drenched street to his car. Looks like a Mazda, which means this guy's a prize prick. Alison stands in the lit doorway of the brand new semi-detached. No prizes for guessing who put the money down for the place, especially considering it's out here in Oldham, away from danger and any temptations that might lead to it.

The boyfriend starts his engine. I watch Alison wave at him, then the Mazda peels away from the kerb. I don't take my eyes off the house as the car passes by my Micra. As soon as I see the brake lights disappear, I push open the driver's door.

'Alison.'

She's about to close the door when she looks my way. It takes her a moment to recognise me. I'd like to think it's the gloom that made her hesitant, but I know different.

'Shit,' she says.

I was hoping for a hello, but her reaction is closer to what I actually expected, and it'll have to do. 'Alison.'

'What d'you want?' She looks up and down the street, checking to see if anyone's watching. Then she leans against the door jamb, jerks her chin at me. I'm not a threat to her, at least.

'Your brother.'

'What're you talking about? Mo's not here.'

'Where is he?'

She blinks at me, totally incredulous. 'How the fuck am I supposed to know?'

I nod at the hall and she pulls the door closed so I can't see into the house.

'No way,' she says. 'You're not coming in.'

'I need to talk.'

'About what? Mo? No. I'm not going to talk about him.' She does another quick recce of the street. 'Not here. Not now.'

'Your dad sent me.'

'I don't give a *fuck*.' She sighs, catches her temper, and her voice drops when she says, 'You know what he did to us, right?'

'Yes.'

'So why would I want to see him?'

'Might not be . . . about *want*.'

'If he's gone, fuckin' great. My dad knows that. He wouldn't send you round here. He could ask us right out if he's interested, and I'd tell him the same thing.'

'Which is?'

'Which is, I haven't fuckin' seen him, I wouldn't want to fuckin' see him, and if I ever did fuckin' see him, I'd slam the door on his face. You get me?'

'Okay,' I say.

Silence. I stare at her, unmoving. Her hair's tied back, and that combined with the attitude makes her look almost like an adult. There's a long strand of hair on her top. I reach forward; she flinches back as I pluck the hair from her shoulder, hold it up to the light. She reacts badly, as if I've intruded on her personal space. My presence makes her uncomfortable.

Good.

I step back onto the path, smile with half my face so she gets the full effect. 'I should've thought. About your past.' I shake my head, try to look vaguely remorseful. 'Daft of me to come. Thought you could help.'

'Well, I don't know where he is,' she says. 'I haven't seen him.'

'I know. You told me.'

She steps back a little into the hall, opening the door wider. For a second, I think I'm about to be invited in, but her hand's still on the door, and that door looks as if it's going to be closing soon enough. As she starts to push, my mobile rings.

'There's nothing else, is there?' she says.

I want to tell her that I've plenty more, but nothing springs to mind. Before I know it, the door's half-closed and I pick my mobile out of my pocket, still trying to think of something to stop Alison from shutting me out.

A soft click, and she's gone. I connect the call in the dark.

'Callum, it's Frank.'

I watch the front door. Had my chance, blew it. I start back to my car. 'What's up?'

'You still got that digital camera at your place?'

I turn as I catch movement behind the curtains in the ground-floor window. She's watching me leave. 'Yeah.'

'Don't suppose you could bring it over to us, could you?'

'What, now?'

'Yeah.'

'Seriously? Tonight? You can't wait?'

His voice takes on a pompous tone I don't like much. 'I'm in the middle of the Sadler case here, Callum.'

'Where?'

He gives me an address. It's not that far from where I live.

'Her house?' I say.

'Yeah.'

I take one last look at the light in the window of Alison's house, then trudge back to the Micra. 'Fuckin' freebies.'

'It's a favour, Cal. Helping someone out. You're not against a bit of charity, are you?'

'I've done favours before.'

Frank's set up shop in a light blue Ford Fiesta, barely visible in the darkness opposite Mrs Sadler's house. I park behind him, limp over to the side of the car and pass him the camera through the open window. I had to go by my flat to pick it up, which was a pain in the arse, but I'd promised, and if there was one thing you didn't do to Frank, it was break a promise. You'd hear about it for days.

'There you go.'

'Is it charged?'

'Aw, fuck, no. I forgot. Probably doesn't work.'

There's a momentary look of panic on Frank's face as he contemplates all the problems he's going to have if this camera doesn't work. Then he turns it on, sees the full battery bar and breathes out.

'Funny,' he says.

'You watching out . . . for bad guys?'

He shoots me a look. 'Thanks for the camera.'

'You're welcome.'

'Sorry to get you out of bed.'

'I wasn't in bed.'

'Out of the pub, then.'

I turn to look at him. He's sulky about something. Busy staring out of the windscreen at the house opposite, not a light in the whole place. From what I can make out, it's a nice enough Victorian semi with two of the panes in the living room bay put out and replaced with cardboard from a Walkers box. I check my watch – it's already way past my bedtime now, but I've got one more thing to do before I call it a night.

'You need anything else?' I say.

'You got somewhere to be?'

'As it happens.'

He nods, chewing his lip. Then he moves his face into the shadow. 'Okay.'

'You alright, Frank?'

I get the feeling he's looking at me, but I can't see him. 'Yeah, I'm fine.'

'Good.'

'Thought you might want to help out,' he says.

'Right. I can't.'

'You don't want to, that's fine. I know you think this is a waste of time.'

'It's not that. I just can't.'

'Okay,' he says. 'See you later, then.'

I knock him on the shoulder. 'Try not to doze off, eh?'

'I won't.'

I head back to the Micra, look over my shoulder at Frank, but he's winding up the window, apparently still intent on the house across the road. I should hang about, offer to take a shift off him so he can get some sleep if he needs it, but this is a bullshit freebie job he's taken on against my wishes, so let him stick it out all by himself. Might teach the bugger a lesson. Also, I don't fancy being cooped up in a Fiesta with him for too long. I remember long nights, just him and me in the Micra, waiting to evict people. I could live the rest of my life quite happily never doing that again.

But I've got other things to do. Number one is check out the address that Baz gave me. After all, some thing are more important than a terrorised teacher.

I get back in the Micra, slip behind the wheel. By rights, I shouldn't be driving, not when I'm prone to sudden spasms or seizures that could freeze up my right-hand side. It's not as if I haven't already had a few shots across the bough. There was an incident last week; I couldn't move, thought I was going to go off the road and became suddenly thankful for the paralysis because it would mean less pain on impact. But then the feeling came back, and I wrestled the car back into a straight line.

I haven't mentioned it to anyone. Knowing Paulo, he'd take my car keys.

But the way I see it, as I turn the key in the ignition, so what if every drive might be my last? At least I'll be killed on my own fucking terms. Which is the least anyone can ask for.

THIRTEEN

Innes

I know Miles Platting reasonably well, been out here more times than I'd care to mention. It's mostly cheap rentals round here, except the only landlord is Manchester City Council, and the houses are stacked one on top of the other. Like all the grimy areas of Manchester, they're trying to tart it up and sell it on to the professional classes. Up the road, a large sign proclaims that Lovell are down to build *one thousand* new homes and luxury apartments *right here.*

It won't matter. They can put in as much Warmsafe as they want, it'll be like smearing lipstick on a pig.

And as pigs go, there's none more ugly or angry than Sutpen Court.

I leave the Micra in a spot I hope proves safe enough. Head across chipped concrete, past broken glass and takeaway papers which shift along the ground like urban tumbleweed. Look up: Sutpen Court looms overhead, a crumbling monolith. When they finally pull the plug on this place, I'm guessing this block'll be one of the first to fall.

The communal entrance doors are propped open with an overturned Kwik Save trolley. The smell of bleach and cheap wine catches my nose as I step into the hallway. I don't bother with the lift, even if there wasn't a sign taped to the doors saying it was 'FUCKED'. Another look at the address Baz gave me, and it looks like I'm going to have to drag myself up to the sixth floor, which turns out to be a long, slow business. By the time I hit the right landing, my lungs feel as though they've pressed themselves tight to the inside of my chest. There's a spin in my head, and I grip the railing tighter to stop from hitting the deck.

They're not all squats up here, judging from the sounds coming from behind some of the doors. The number Baz gave me looks to be at the end of the hall to my right. As I get closer, I can see the metal brace across the door, a large Yale padlock hanging open. There's a notice of eviction in a plastic sheet taped to the door.

I nudge open the door with my stick and as the air inside circulates, a rotten smell kicks me in the throat. I put my arm to my nose and mouth, try to swallow the nausea. The light from the hallway shows an edge of a mattress way inside the flat. I can't see anything else, but I've suddenly got a fair idea of what I can expect.

I don't want to go any further. But if I'm going to do this, I need to go all the way.

Normally these places creak with slow and slight movement. Not much; just enough to get from mattress to pipe, from chair to works.

But there's nothing here. No sound. No presence. I fumble about in my pocket for keys, fiddle with the tiny torch keyring I got out of a cracker.

People have been here, but I'd be lying if I said it was recent. Pizza boxes, polystyrene cartons and newspapers litter the floor. I can see that the carpet's been scorched in a couple of places, or else stained dark. I flick the thin beam around, but I know I'm just killing time, working up the nerve to turn the torch on the mattress in the corner of the room.

Because that's where the smell's coming from.

Mo.

Or what *used* to be Mo. A reasonable, but rotting, facsimile.

He's laid out on the mattress, one leg cocked at the knee, one sleeve rolled up to expose tracks: some are old, some more recent and already festering. No needle in sight, but I could just be missing it. His favourite Berghaus is on the floor next to the mattress, splattered with blood. As I shift round, I can also see a stain behind his head and a larger one around his crotch and arse from his final evacuation, his trackie bottoms stuck tight to the body. Break the seal on that and there'd be complaints from up the hall.

I stare at him until the shock wears off. Lean on my stick, my nose and mouth still buried in the crook of my elbow. Should've guessed it would turn out like this. Mo never could take no for an answer, never could see beyond himself and what he wanted. Just like my brother, got himself into a pattern of behaviour that he couldn't escape in the end.

And what's that they say about hell? Something about making the same mistakes over and over again.

I prod open Mo's jacket with the end of my walking stick. As I lean over to reach into his inside pocket, I catch movement in the torch beam. I shake a long hair from my hand, watch it drift for a moment before I realise where it's from.

Alison's hair finally settles across one of Mo's open palms.

There's a part of me that feels kind of sorry for him, especially considering what's happened. Kicked out of his family, unequipped to do anything but deal, and even that at a low level. Throw in the speed, amphetamine and heroin cocktails he'd obviously been taking, and you've got a brain corroded until one crystal thought remained – the reminder that he was Morris Tiernan's son, and he was a failure at that.

Course, that sympathy only lasts as long as I don't think about everything the cunt did to me and my brother.

I straighten up, feel the weight of the cane in both hands and shift my feet so I'm balanced.

Take a breath, relish that filthy smell, let it out, and bring the handle of my stick down across the bridge of Mo's nose. Fucker went and died, doesn't mean I can't beat the shit out of him. The rap across the nose felt good. So I do it again. And again.

That's for Declan.

That's for my prison time.

No.

That's for the first month I spent inside. That's for the second. The third . . .

And one more each for the sister who had me beaten, the blokes she got to do it, and the father that sent me on a wild goose chase, the first fatal mistake that kick-started me down this fucking road.

And as I lose the strength to continue, as my chest aches with the exertion and my arms start to feel like steel pins have been shot through them, I find myself slowing to a stop. Finally lower the stick, the handle slick with blood. I lean on it, look at the floor.

Check the evidence trail. Cover my arse.

I got the address from Baz. So he knew where Mo was living, and I'm sure there's motive to kill him. That many years with Mo calling him all the bastards in the book, I'm sure that'd be enough to make anyone snap.

Alison's hair, now in Mo's hand. A strange place to be if she maintains that she hasn't seen him since Newcastle.

And again, plenty of motive.

I look at Mo. Only the eyes and nose are recognisable as facial features, the rest is guesswork. When the police arrive, they'll have some digging to do. And with a little luck, they'll have an Orient Express on their hands.

I step back from Mo, scuff my cane marks away from the dirt on the floor, then reach into his Berghaus and take the wallet in his inside pocket. Nothing much in there apart from the usual shite and a photograph, folded in half, that has the colours of an eighties Kodak moment. A woman, big hair, skinny otherwise, sitting in a brown fabric chair with tassels along the bottom. Her legs crossed, her skirt hitched up and tight to the thigh, with an unseen man's hand on her knee. She has a wide, white smile and her large blue eyes are a little too close together. A vague resemblance to Mo, and I guess that it's his mother.

I take a photo ID out of the wallet, toss it onto the floor. That should speed things up. Then I tuck the wallet into my jacket pocket.

Head out of the room, making sure not to touch anything on the way. I draw the door closed with the end of my walking stick, bringing a fresh wave of stink out into the corridor. Then I wipe my hands on my T-shirt, the handle of the walking stick, too. Hope I'm clean enough that people don't scream when they see me, then zip my jacket up. Further up the corridor, the door to the occupied flat is still closed, and the television is still on. I try to walk as evenly as I can – the last thing I need is someone telling the police they heard someone limping around outside their door.

I need a story for Tiernan, and I think I have one: I got a note of Mo's old address from one of his mates, and I was all set to check it out in the morning, but when I got there, the place was swarming with busies. Which they will be once I drop a twenty on the whereabouts of Mo's corpse. That's it. Son found, give me my fucking money and I'll be on my way.

I know it won't end like that. But I need Tiernan to be the one to instigate it.

The last landing, and a final flight of stairs. There's a pain in my leg, which is unusual, and a tightness in my chest which isn't. Above all that, though, there's this nagging sense that everything just went to shit, that I'd missed something, maybe left some incriminating evidence up there that would make the police come straight to me.

Think about it. I took his wallet, but that'll come in handy later. Other than that, I didn't touch anything, and fingerprints are hardly that important. The hair's not mine, and it's unlikely that I've left any of my own, considering how short I keep it. It's possible that I could've moved some dust or something – it was dark enough so that I wouldn't see – but I don't think so.

Doesn't matter. Everything's fine. Even if I have left some evidence up there, the police will naturally think it's from whoever rang in the body. Which, if they come to me, is what I'll say. Anything else, it's me worrying about fuck all. I just need to get it over with.

I head down the rest of the stairs, pull my mobile out of my pocket as I walk through the lobby and barge through the exit. It's cold out here, feels like it's getting colder all the time.

But I'll soon be home. Still a little blood on my walking stick, plenty more on my T-shirt, and there's an image of Mo that I'll need to kill with a couple of swift drinks and some sleeping pills.

I'm about to dial 999 when I see the car.

A big, old car. Someone behind the wheel with a cigarette in their mouth. The engine's running, which is enough to make the temperature around me drop even further. I stop, clear the number from my phone display.

Then the headlights come up full glare. I shield my eyes, blinking at the sudden light.

The engine keeps running. The sound feels industrial, ominous. Whoever this is, he likes his fucking drama.

'Y'alright, Innes?'

Fuck. Should've guessed.

I push the mobile back into my pocket and wave my hand at the lights. They dip to a normal level, and I manage to blink away the afterburn in time to see Donkey getting out of the car. More blinking, and I can see the grin on his face.

That grin says he knows everything, that he's caught me red-handed.

FOURTEEN

Donkin

I wished I had a camera because, seriously, his face was fucking priceless.

Switched on the headlights and he was caught like a rabbit, big wide eyes. I had to watch myself, because when I saw the dopey look on his face, I almost burst out laughing. And that certainly wasn't the plan – I had to be serious about this. Mind you, I made a mental note to use the headlight trick in the future. If it shat anyone else up like it did the cripple, it was a technique worth remembering.

'Y'alright, Innes?' Nice and loud so he knew it was me.

He didn't say anything. Screwed up half his face.

'Asked you a question, like.'

I was trying to keep it friendly, but reckoned if this bastard didn't feel like talking, I could always knock his stick out, see how he liked that.

Instead, I saw him nod. 'I know.'

'And?'

'Not bad.'

'Fuckin' terrific night for it, isn't it?' I walked over to him – proper strolled like I was enjoying the night air, always come round here to do it – and I said, 'I love it this time of year.'

'Yeah?'

'Yeah, smells like Christmas.'

He stood in the middle of the car park, didn't move. Probably reckoned that if he moved, I'd be on him, which was pretty clever of him. Because he knew if he did a runner, that'd just be worse later on when I *did* catch up with him. Anyone who knew us was quick to learn that.

'You know what I mean when I say that, don't you?' I said. 'Like it's all *crisp* an' that. Course, not so much now. *Now* it's just brass fuckin' monkeys and reeks like a fuckin' canal, and I don't want to be out here longer than I have to. Which is a pain in the arse, because I've been sat in my car waiting for you to finish whatever the fuck it is you were doing in there. You *are* finished, aren't you?'

He rubbed one eye and sniffed. Didn't say anything.

'So,' I said, 'what's the score?'

'Score?'

'You heard.'

'Looking to . . . move here.'

'That right?'

'No.'

'Never mind. Least you're talking, eh? So what're you doing out here?'

'Nowt.'

He gave us a smile, but it only worked on half his face, just like when he scrunched it up before.

'Don't play funny buggers,' I said. 'You know what I can do to you.'

He shook his head, still had that twisted smile on his face. 'Not on licence. Not anymore.' He pointed at us. 'You can't . . . do *nowt*. Donkey.'

And I nodded. Because there was the dilemma. There were plenty of people I knew who didn't reckon that I gave much thought to my actions. There'd been reports I'd seen with the words 'IMPULSE CONTROL ISSUES' written all in capitals, like that was the key to my personality. But I *did* think about my actions, right then especially. I stood there, my arms folded against the cold. In any normal situation, I'd be well within my rights to grab the cunt and slam his head in his car door. But the problem was, it was obvious to us that Innes was a special needs. And not just any special needs, either. It honestly looked like something'd just mangled fuck out of him, inside and out.

So there it was: I wanted to kick shite out of him, but he was a cripple. And there was no kudos in kicking shite out of a cripple. Even if the cripple was an arsehole. -

'I heard something bad happened to you,' I said.

He squinted at us.

I waggled a finger at him, then folded my arms again. 'So what was it?'

He shook his head and made a move for his car. I watched him hobble over to the Micra, then followed him over. Waited for him to put his hand on the door. When he pulled it open, I kicked it hard, slammed it shut. Hey, fuck him if he got hurt by accident, right? Hardly my fault if that happened. And he shuffled back quickly, like I almost clipped. him. Then he stood, one hand gripping the handle of his walking stick tight, looking like he wanted to plant one on us. There was something smeared on his hand and the stick.

'You got something you want to say, son?' I looked him in the eyes. 'Because you feel like you want to take a swing at us, you be my fuckin' guest. Reckon I never had too much trouble putting the fuckin' pain on you when you were whole, I don't think you're going to pose any particular problems now that you're the walking fuckin' wounded, what do you think? And then it won't matter if you're on licence or not, will it?'

He cleared his throat, spat something at the ground. Then he started talking to us again, and there was something about the way he spoke, like he was saying everything all over-clear, like *I* was the fucking mong. 'What do you want?'

'I wanted to talk to you, didn't I?'

'About what?'

'Been looking all over the place for you, but you're an elusive bastard, I'll give you that. Fuckin' slippery.' I smiled. 'Got so's your poof mate doesn't want to see us round the club no more. Apparently I'm scaring the kids, like.'

Didn't get a reaction, but then that was usual. This fucker was internal all the way and, at the moment, he seemed calm with it. Like he was just waiting for us to stop talking so's he could go home. Back in the day, he would've kicked off with us. Course, back in the day, he was a bloke with a bit of fight in him. Now, he looked like someone'd nicked his balls.

Or maybe he just needed a bit more of a prod.

'How's your brother?' I said.

'Dead.'

'Yeah? How?'

I saw his neck move. 'Overdose.'

'Once a smackhead, eh?'

'Yeah.'

'Don't get us wrong, like. Feeling your pain an' that, but I'm guessing you saw it coming.'

'Not really.'

'Well, you should have. I mean, I don't know much about smackheads other than, y'know, what I have to deal with every day, but the one thing I do know? Once they're on, they're never off. Even when they think they are, know what I mean?' I went into my pocket for my tin, held it out to Innes.

He wasn't having any of it. Fair enough.

I put the roll-up in my mouth and lit it. Took in the smoke, then let it go as I said, 'So you ask *me*, it was just a matter of time before something sparked him off and he went and scored from the wrong bloke. I mean, let's face it, if there's one thing that smackheads can't deal with, it's stress, eh?'

Watched him, tried to wait him out for a reply, but he still wasn't playing. I moved a bit closer to him.

'I'm right, aren't I?' I said. 'I mean, I liked your brother an' that – he was a great fuckin' grass – but he was a smackhead. Which is probably why he didn't save your skin when he could've. But then you know all about that.'

Innes tried to keep his face straight, but I could see something fizz.

'He did top himself, didn't he?' I said. 'You wouldn't have had anything to do with it?'

'No.'

'That's a shame,' I said, blowing more smoke at him. 'So what were you doing in that block of flats, then?'

Blindsided the bastard; he never expected that.

'Following up,' he said.

'On what?'

'A lead.'

'What fuckin' lead?'

He looked back at the flats, and I watched that half-smile tug at his cheek. 'You wouldn't . . . be interested.'

'Try us.'

He turned back to me. 'It's a case. I'm working on.'

'A case? You still up to your neck in that, eh?'

'Yeah.'

'Who for?'

He paused, looked like he was thinking about it. Then he said, 'Morris Tiernan.'

My turn to pause. I wanted to tell him he was full of shite, but there was a look in his eyes that meant he wasn't. Still, I had to ask. 'Serious?'

He nodded. I looked over at the flats. After everything I heard about Innes, the last person I expected he'd take a job off was Morris Tiernan. If this was back in the day, then fine, okay, I could expect it – this twat wasn't too picky about working the dodgy jobs back then. But since he got out? No. It was what made him resistant to being a proper grass. If he wasn't up to anything untoward, I couldn't threaten him with prison, could I?

'What you doing for him?'

Again, he said, 'Confidential.'

'C'mon, son, you know there's nowt confidential with me. I out-rank you. I mean, you want us to haul you up the nick, I can do that. But you're going to have to let us know if you're on any meds, just in case we accidentally forget to let you have them when you're supposed to.'

'You don't have to . . . do that.'

'No, I don't, you're right. But I can.'

He cleared his throat again, second time since he saw me, there must've been something wrong with his lungs. I could see him running his options, maybe even rehearsing a couple of lies in his head, just to see how they sounded. Normally I would've cut those thoughts right off, nip it in the bud, save us all some time, but I knew Innes wasn't daft. He already knew I was a one-man lie detector, so it wasn't worth him working his bastard ticket.

'Mo,' he said.

'What about him?'

'He's missing. I'm working on . . . finding him.'

'Right.'

He jerked a thumb at the flats. 'This here is . . . his *last* known.'

'You find him?'

He didn't say anything for a few seconds. Then he nodded. 'I think so.'

'Where?'

'In there.'

'So that's you finished, then, isn't it? Job's a fuckin' good 'un.'

'Yup.' The smile returned. 'Course, he's dead.'

I looked at him. The smile almost gone to a grin, like he was having fun with us. And for no good reason other than that, I was ready to belt fuck out of him. But I kept it down, dropped my ciggie onto the ground, and said, nice and low, 'He's dead.'

'Up there, yeah.' Innes rubbed his cheek. 'You should . . . *investigate*. Make your career.'

'What you being a smartarse for?'

'I'm not.'

'Sound like a cheeky cunt.'

'Telling you . . . the truth. *Detective*.'

Acting the twat, alright, and why? What, because he was working for Tiernan he thought he could get away with it? I smiled, he half-smiled back, and I turned away from him for a second. Took a deep breath in through my nose, held it, then turned back and smacked Innes in the face. Snapped the cunt's neck round and bust his mouth at the same time. He let out this grunt, bounced off the side of his car. Planted his stick on the ground so he wouldn't fall.

I thought about kicking it away, but I didn't fancy helping him back up. And my conscience would make us do that.

He half-stood there, leaning against the stick, rubbing his face. Looking at the ground like, *what the fuck was that for?*

I got in close again, smelled blood on him. 'You're a cheeky cunt, Innes.' Slapped him soft to get his attention, made him look us in the eyes. Rammed a finger against the side of his head. 'You should know better an' all. You can fuckin' limp all you want, but you don't get a mong pass out of me, son, d'you understand?'

He nodded, kept dabbing at his lip with the sleeve of his jacket.

I shoved him against his car. 'Now fuck off out of it.'

He watched us.

'I mean it, fuck off. Out of my fuckin' sight.'

Innes pulled open his car door, then suddenly let go of it like it was hot. I wondered why, then realised he probably reckoned I was going to kick it again. Meant he was back scared of us again.

I stopped halfway to the Granada, turned back to him. 'One more thing.'

He was already in his car, looking at us through the windscreen.

'I hear you been spreading shite about us again, I'll ram that walking stick up your arse, alright?'

He looked confused.

'I'm watching you,' I said.

Innes nodded, started the engine. I didn't get into the Granada until I was sure he was gone. Then I looked up at the block of flats. Place looked like it stank from foundation to roof. Nah, there was no way I was going in there, not even on the slim chance that Innes was telling us the truth. He was just fucking us about. So I got into my car, turned the key.

I had cans at home, but they didn't seem too appetising. Took too long to get pissed on them, anyway. So I decided I'd go round the Bell on Hope Street. That place was always having lock-ins. Maybe I'd have a word with the landlord, scare up one of them big bottles of Grouse. This job had to have some perks.

Either way, I needed some booze in my system. I blamed Innes. That bastard had a way of killing a buzz.

FIFTEEN

Innes

Five minutes by my watch, and then Donkey's Granada pulls out from the car park in front of Sutpen Court. The car kangaroo-jumps once as he accidentally stalls it, then heads out towards the main road. I wind down the driver's window, lean out to see the brake lights kick in as Donkey approaches a junction.

Then he's gone.

My face hurts. Honestly didn't expect Donkey to punch me like that. I'd get a slap, maybe. A stern word, certainly. I was angling for both, but the jab in the mouth was still a surprise. But then it was my own fucking fault, should've seen from the moment Donkey made his presence known that he was pissed up and spoiling for a fight.

He was following me, though. Must've been. And I didn't see him until he wanted me to. Which makes my gut twitch and the rest of me paranoid.

Of course, that's what he wanted me to think. First I saw of him, I thought that was it, the game was up. But then as soon as he let that punch fly, I realised he didn't know a thing. He was just pissed off that I'd been out of his orbit for so long.

So I should be relaxed about the situation, but I'm still coming down, mopping the last of the blood from my split lip and watching a dead road.

It was a stupid move to tell him what I was doing there. Even dafter to tell him that I'd found Mo dead. But the thing is about

Donkey, he's never believed I was much of a PI, so it stands to reason that he doesn't think I'm clever enough to find a body without the police finding it first. I can understand that. But then Donkey wouldn't have found Mo's body with a fucking map, X marking the spot, not without having it verified first by his network of grasses.

And that's the point. Donkey's always puffing himself up about how he can sniff out a liar, and the truth is he's just playing the odds. If most of the people you come into contact with lie to you, then you're not going to believe the truth if you hear it right off the bat. Besides, there's no way Donkey'd climb six flights on a tip from me. But if I'd lied about it, that'd be me in a cell right now. And once that bastard gets you in custody, that's you charged with whatever he can get, no matter how ridiculous. Longer he keeps you in there, the more likely it is he'll find out what you're really feeling guilty about. It's an old tactic.

I pull out my mobile, look at the display, then stare into the middle distance.

Donkey can place me at the scene. And he'll remember what I told him, especially when it proves to be true. When he gets an official whiff of a corpse, he's going to come at me like a fucking bull.

I could walk away right now. It's what I should do.

But I can't. Because if I do, I don't want to think about what'll happen.

I put my mobile back in my jacket pocket. I can't do it on my mobile anyway. They'll keep a log of the numbers, and I wouldn't put it past Donkey to do some extra-curricular investigation as soon as he's convinced that I'm involved.

Start the engine, put the car into gear and pull out. Thinking it through at the same time. Weighing up my options.

He knows I got the last known address from someone. So if he finds out about Mo, chances are he'll come round to twist a name out of me, along with any other information he thinks is necessary. Then it's a question of whether I give him Baz or Rossie. Donkey's always carried a half-on for making me his grass. Might be time to give the bastard what he wants.

But first things first.

I pass a phone box. Carry on up the road and turn off at the first corner, kill the engine. Sit for a moment, psyching myself up, then get out of the car. I look around the street – dead this time of night. Not a light in any of the windows. No witnesses, though there's always a chance that someone around will find me suspicious. After all, you use a phone box these days, you're probably up to something. Otherwise you'd use your mobile.

And if you don't have a mobile?

Well then, there's *definitely* something the matter with you.

I stop in the middle of the street, light a cigarette. Like everything else, I'm not supposed to be smoking, and like everything else I'm not supposed to be doing, I couldn't give a fuck. What doesn't kill me makes me stronger.

Yeah, says the bloke with the fucking walking stick.

I stroll to the phone box as nonchalantly as I can, get the cold night air in my gills. Then I finish off the rest of the cigarette, flick it out into the middle of the street, and pull open the door to the booth.

Stand in the dark, practising what I have to say. Repeat it in my head, then whispering it to myself. Over and over, until it's less a collection of words than it is a string of connected sounds, like a song with nonsense lyrics. Someone in prison once told me that the secret to forging a signature was to turn it upside down and draw it. Once the words have no meaning, they're easier to deal with. Same principle as when I have to say a glut of words in one go.

I pick up the receiver, call 999.

I need to report a dead body. I need to report a dead body. I need to report a dead body.

When the bored operator asks me which emergency service, I take a short breath and say, 'Police.'

I need to report a dead body. I need to report a dead body. I need to report a dead body.

When the police operator answers, I get to say it: 'I need to report a dead body.'

This operator also has a bored tone to her voice, like I should've dialled the number they save for bin fires and noisy neighbours. 'What's the address?'

A punch of panic in the chest, and I can't breathe. Stupid, should've sounded this out to myself. I fumble the address out of my pocket, can't see it properly in the gloom.

'Hello?'

My mouth is open, but sound refuses to come out. And I've got to say something soon, or else I'm sure they'll trace the call. And I'm nowhere near Sutpen Court now.

'Miles. Platting,' I say.

'Right,' she says.

'Sut . . . *pen.*'

The word comes out like a wet sheet. I put the receiver down, breathe out. That wasn't good. Should've practised more. The idea was when I called in the corpse, I would pass for a normal human being, that I wouldn't sound like such a fucking spastic.

That I wouldn't sound like *me.*

I shake my head, fight the rising urge to kick the phone off the wall with my good foot. Then I lean the door open, dig the address into my pocket and grab my cigarettes at the same time. I light one as I pick up the pace back to the Micra. Keeping an eye on the street as I limp along. I don't think anyone saw me, but the way tonight's been going, I wouldn't be surprised.

You can't afford to slip, Callum.

I know I can't.

Not now.

I know.

Too important to fuck up, mate.

I *know.*

Can't leave anything to chance, not anymore. Did that once, and look where it got me. So I need to plan, I need to wake up, and I need to be clever about this whole thing otherwise it's going to gut me. And if that doesn't happen, if the truth comes out, even some *version* of it, I'm sure Tiernan will have some special punishment he reserves for people like me.

I get back to the car, shove myself in behind the wheel. Lay my stick down on the passenger seat and look at it for a long time. Trying to think of all the things I may have fucked up because I was recognisable on the phone. Trying to work it all out when it feels as if my brain's already shut up shop for the night.

It's okay. It'll all be fine. Stick with the plan, and there's nothing I can't sort out along the way. I just need to be more careful in future. Not rely so much on all those handy little things I used to be able to do.

I twist the key in the ignition. The engine shakes into life.

Yeah, it'll all be fine.

That's why I can't see myself getting out of this alive.

PART TWO

My Brother's Man

My mum, for all her pinched Catholicism, wanted Declan buried. No son of hers, no matter what had happened to him (or, more importantly, what he'd done to himself), was going to be kept from a proper service.

So Kenny lied to the priest, told him it was an accidental overdose instead of a suicide. The priest played up to it, but he wasn't bothered how Declan had died. After all, you couldn't be a Leith priest for as long as he had without burying a few suicides, and he knew the grey areas better than anyone – there were council-owned needle bins on the gates to the graveyard. Like everyone else, as long as he got paid, he was fine.

From the way my brother talked about the people he knew at the Outreach, I expected more of them to turn up. Maybe the overdose scared them away; the few that did attend looked to have been dragged there by Declan's girlfriend, Rachel. I watched her, one hand on her pregnant belly, her head down the entire service.

In all other respects, the funeral was an almost-ran. My mum attempted grief, but only succeeded in pulling a series of tight faces. Kenny attempted to console her, but there was obviously no need. And the sky threatened to break open, drench us all in a traditional funeral downpour, but all we ended up with was the kind of drizzle that prompted a slow, sick feeling to spread through my stomach.

Once the priest stopped talking and we'd finally committed my brother to the ground, Declan's friends started to mill out towards the gates. Talking amongst themselves, noticeably less tense, glad the inconvenience was over. I stayed put, didn't want to draw attention to myself. When Kenny told me that him and my mum were heading back to the house, I nodded. I didn't need a lift. Had my own transport. And I didn't plan on going back to the house. Not yet, anyway.

I found Rachel by the needle bins, a cigarette in her mouth.

'Should you—'

'Don't,' she said.

'Okay.' I dug around for my Embassys. 'How are you?'

She blew smoke. Looked at me, one eyebrow crooked. 'Better than you.'

'Yeah. Suppose.'

We smoked in silence for a moment. Then she said, 'You'll want to know why he did it. That's what you're working up to, right?'

I nodded, but didn't look at her.

'Responsibility.'

I looked up to see her blow more smoke, one hand on her bump. 'He couldn't hack the responsibility, so he went back to the gear.'

'You know where . . . he got it?'

She smiled a little, but there was no humour in it. 'What difference does it make?'

'A lot.'

'What're you going to do about it?'

I stared back at the graveyard. Heard the thin crackle of cigarette paper as I sucked on the filter. 'I don't know. Something.'

'Dec told me you were a Scrappy Doo.'

'What's that mean?'

'That you spend most of your time looking for a fight.'

I shook my head, half-smiled. 'Nobody . . . *likes* Scrappy.'

'Exactly,' she said. 'So leave it.'

'I can't.'

A chill breeze moved her hair across her face. For a second she looked almost pretty, but she had a face that could never stay soft. Rachel finished her cigarette, dumped the butt. It bounced once, landed near the end of my walking stick.

'He wasn't perfect,' she said. 'In fact he was kind of weak. Probably because every time there was trouble, someone bailed him out.' She breathed out, and for the first time I noticed a sheen on her eyes. 'But sometimes, with some people, all that does is postpone the inevitable.'

'Still,' I said. 'Someone—'

'Please,' she said. 'For me? Just leave it.'

'Why?'

She didn't answer. Instead, she walked away, leaving me to chain another Embassy off the glow of the previous. I watched her catch up with one of the girls who'd come along from the Outreach, and the pair of them headed to a waiting taxi. I thought about going back to the graveside, but people didn't really catch any revelations in the company of corpses, not in this weather. Only thing they caught was a nasty chill.

And what Rachel said made sense. Because sometimes there was no big conspiracy. Sometimes people just couldn't hack it anymore.

But that didn't stop me from looking for someone to blame.

SIXTEEN

Donkin

Mo fucking Tiernan was dead.

He was dead, and there was bugger all I could do about it right then because I was stuck talking to our DCI. He hadn't said much, but I could feel a volley of shite coming my way any moment. I never bothered learning the bastard's name, because the way things were run around here – the words 'piss-up' and 'brewery' came to mind – he wouldn't be in the job come next Christmas, so it didn't matter.

Besides, you only needed to look at him to know how he got the DCI position. It wasn't because he was a good copper. More like it was because he was a *Paki* copper. What the Yanks called affirmative action, what I called taking the fucking piss. You asked me, it was those bastards causing all the trouble in the first place, but you'd have to ask us somewhere we knew we weren't being earwigged.

DCI Ali was one of the educated ones. Been to university, studied hard like his family expected him to, and ended up with a brass plate on his desk, which was the only reason I knew his name. I stared at that nameplate the entire time he was talking because I got the feeling that if I looked up and caught the expression on his face, I'd lose control and pan it right the fuck in. His voice was bad enough – like one of those sniffy twats on the telly who told people they were fat and ugly, about to give them a makeover, the 'I know what's best for you' spiel. Him tearing me a new arsehole, sounding like he was ordering fucking ice cream.

'I appreciate you've had some issues with some of your colleagues, Iain, but we can't have *anyone* acting out in the office.'

'Acting out?' I said.

'Demonstrating unacceptable behaviour,' he said. 'I mean, besides the fact that it's unprofessional, say it leaked to the press. How would it look for the force if people picked up the *Evening News* to find you on the front?'

'How likely's that?' I said. 'Really?'

'These things have a way of escalating. You know that.'

'It's only Kennedy. Nobody else I have any problems with.'

'Why Detective Inspector Kennedy?'

Shook my head. 'Just a difference of opinion.'

'Which is?'

'I think he's a cunt; he thinks different.'

'You see, that's something *else*—'

'My language,' I said.

'Yes.'

I let out a short breath. 'Tell you, if this is just going to be fuckin' random character assassination—'

'No,' he said, leaning back in his chair. 'I'm sorry, Iain. I didn't mean to sound as if I was judging you.'

'Course you did.'

He steepled his fingers on the desk in front of him. Probably reckoned it made him look important. It didn't.

'I'm not in the business of bringing people into my office to harangue them. But there are a number of issues I feel we have to address, okay?'

'Look, if I'm in here because you're going to bollock us, that's fine. I appreciate that you got a job to do. If someone made a complaint, you have to look into it, else you look bent. We both know Kennedy's a bastard – apologise for the use of language, but, y'know, if the fuckin' cap fits – and I appreciate that what happened yesterday probably got some of that lot's knickers in a twist. So here's what I'll do: I'll stay out of his way, do my job, and everything should be fine. That seem okay to you?'

There was this long silence. I'd said my bit, so I was just waiting on Ali to give us the wave, then I'd be out of there, back on with my day. Which, to be fair, was what I was desperate for, because I had a bit of a hangover and not enough time this morning to get some scran down my neck. So I had stuff I needed to do, and the only thing I wanted out of him sitting opposite was a thank you, come again.

Ali ground his throat, pulled a face that made his lips disappear. Then he looked at us with big, stupid cow eyes.

'We've had a complaint, Iain,' he said.

'I know. Kennedy complained because I raised my voice at him or something, right? Offended his delicate Scouse sensibilities.'

'No, this isn't internal.'

I kept schtum. I *wanted* to say, well, yeah, of *course* you had a complaint, then. People complained about coppers who did their jobs, it was a fact of life. You collared them for anything, they all cried brutality and didn't I have any real criminals to be chasing down? Course, when it was *their* motor that'd been nicked, then it was supposed to be red alert. So I reckoned, fuck it, it was nothing I hadn't already heard a million times before.

Ali grabbed a couple of stapled sheets of paper, frowned at it. 'Do you know the name Patrick Reece?'

It took us a moment – must have been the hangover fogging us up a bit – before it clicked and I burst out laughing. 'Oh Jesus. Oh man, you had us going there for a second.'

Ali turned the frown on me. 'Excuse me?'

'Paddy fuckin' Reece? He's the one that complained, is he?'

'I just told you that, yes.'

I leaned forward, grinning. 'Paddy Reece is a fuckin' *smackhead*. The lad's off his box three-quarters of the time he's awake. The rest of the time he's scratching so bad he'd swear you were the Milky Bar Kid if it meant he could spoon up.' I held up a hand, swore to tell the whole truth and nothing but. 'He's a good grass, don't get us wrong, but the bloke's hardly stable. Or credible, for that matter.'

The DCI's jaw was all knotted up as he stared at us. He looked back down at the paper. 'Mr Reece alleges that you accosted him on the street—'

'I talked to him.'

'Just that?'

'Yeah.'

'You didn't engage in a spot search?' He checked the paper again. 'Which included for some reason the man's shoes?'

I kept quiet. Tasted my teeth. But I was still smiling, still trying to see the funny side.

'These would be the same shoes that, after allegedly assaulting Mr Reece, you threw to places from which it would be' – he paused, poked at the words on the paper to keep them in place – '*dangerous to retrieve them.*'

Still nothing from me. I was just waiting to see if Paddy had dug himself any further into the shit. Ali smoothed the statement out on his desk, licked his lips quickly like a lizard.

'Do you have any response to this?' he said.

'When'd he say all that, then?'

'Mr Reece was brought in on a shoplifting charge yesterday afternoon.'

'Yeah, that's what I thought.'

'What does that mean?'

'It means, *sir*, that he's spreading shit to get off the charge.'

Ali raised both eyebrows. 'And the fact that he'd stolen shoes to replace those that you'd disposed of, that would be irrelevant, would it?'

'Well, considering he's fuckin' lying, yeah.'

'And the assault?'

'He didn't touch us.'

'Your assault on *him*.'

'And I didn't touch him.' I cleared my throat. 'Much.'

Ali let out this sigh, started to say something, but I leaned forward, got in his face.

'Wait a second,' I said. 'It used to be that you were well within your fuckin' rights to cuff someone round the lug if they were giving you gyp. And so what, suddenly that's out of order now, is it? Because you'll have to excuse us if *I'm* the criminal here. Y'know, as opposed to the smackhead with priors who's up on a fuckin' shoplifting charge.'

Another sigh out of him, and he was starting to sound like the most put-upon bloke in the world. He dropped his hands to the desk, looked at us with his chin down. 'We want to resolve this locally, Iain.'

'You're joking. You're going to take this seriously?'

'We have to.'

I shook my head. 'Can't fuckin'—'

'And we will resolve it at that stage. This doesn't go any higher than it needs to, Iain. I'm trying to keep the brass out of this.'

I wanted to tell him that he *was* the fucking brass.

'But I will not let it leave this station that one of my sergeants goes around beating up civilians. And if we go to the next level, that will most probably happen.'

'He's a grass.'

'Was he a suspect?'

'Paddy Reece,' I said, nice and loud, 'is a lying *cunt*.'

He ignored us. 'You'll have your chance to submit your version of events in due course. If there's anyone you'd like to have sit in with you – your union rep, someone like that – then it can be arranged.'

I didn't like the way this was going. Of course I'd been in the shit like this before, knew my wriggle room, but it'd never sounded this formal. There was always a wink before, something that meant that even if it was all written down, stamped and filed, there was nothing to worry about. In the end, it was all for the bureaucrats and easily lost, as long as I kept my head down for a bit.

But this Ali bastard, I realised I'd never been in the office with him before. And it looked to me right then that he was doing everything in his power to fuck with my job.

'Right,' I said, because there was nothing else to say. 'You do whatever you reckon's necessary. Now, if you'll excuse us, I've got work to be getting on with.'

'You know the procedure, Iain.'

'Yeah.' I got out of my seat, smiling at him. 'Old hat to us now, eh?'

'Still, it'll give you time to sleep off your hangover.'

I couldn't hang on to the smile then. 'You what?'

'When you go home. You've been through this before, so you know you're suspended until we reach a resolution.'

'You're fuckin' *kidding* us.'

'Standard procedure, Iain, when a grievance has been officially filed.'

'Well, how the fuck did he make it official? I mean, who took the complaint in the first place?'

'Iain, don't make this worse for yourself. It doesn't matter who took his statement.'

Of course it fucking mattered. If you couldn't trust your colleagues, who could you? I needed a ciggie, but I couldn't spark one in here unless I wanted the suspension to turn into the sack. I shifted my weight from one leg to the other, wanted to go out into the office and force them to tell us who'd taken Reece's statement, but then the rational part of us said that it wouldn't do any good. Better to make a show of calming down, and after a minute of slow counting in my head, I found a smile to give to the DCI.

'You're right,' I said. 'I'm just . . . How long d'you think it'll be before I can get back to work. There's a body that just came in—'

'Belongs to Kennedy.'

'You can't—'

'It requires a DI.'

'It's just a dosser. You give it to Kennedy, he won't bother his arse.'

'And you'll receive a letter about when you can return to work, if that happens to be the case.'

'Give us an idea,' I said.

'You'll receive a letter.'

I opened my mouth, couldn't find what I wanted to say, realised it wouldn't make a difference anyway, then went to the door. Didn't want to show this bastard any weakness, but there was a bubbling in my gut that meant I was close to either crying or tearing the place apart with my bare hands. This daft cunt might've given the Tiernan body to Kennedy – who probably didn't even know it *was* Tiernan – but I was the one with the only solid lead.

'One thing about the trainers,' I said. 'On the record, off the record, whatever you want, I didn't chuck 'em that far. If Paddy Reece had been in possession of a pair of balls along with all the illegal substances he had on his person, he would've bit the bullet and gone to fetch them. But lads like that, they're what us *coppers* term recidivists. His first instinct wasn't to look for his shoes, but to steal some more. And you can't be a recidivist like that *and* a victim. Hope you bear that in mind when it comes to your decision.'

There was a smile on Ali's face that belonged on a nursery teacher. 'Go home, Iain.'

I would've, but when I opened the door, I saw Kennedy striding into the main office like his balls were too big for his britches. I half-turned to the DCI.

'Aye, I will,' I said. 'Just need to clear out my desk.'

SEVENTEEN

Donkin

'You know what the uniforms are like,' said Kennedy, one buttock on the edge of the desk, talking at the top of his fucking voice for everyone to hear. 'They don't make 'em like they used to, do they? New lads coming on the force, they're squeamish. Now if it'd been *Iain* over there, he would've been in that building like a shot, wouldn't you?'

'Too right,' I said. I knew he was taking the piss out of us, but it didn't bother us so much because he was right – when I was a constable, I would've been right in there. I picked up the bacon barm from yesterday, took a bite out of it. It was cold and congealed, but it'd do for the moment.

'*These* lads, mind, they're educated. They've been to university. They don't want to go into some 'orrible block of flats looking for a dead bloke. Besides, right, they know as well as anyone in here, we've had calls from that neck of the woods before. Only bodies we ever picked up were our own uniforms.'

Couple of grunts of agreement from somewhere at the back of the room. I watched Kennedy pick up his mug, slurp some tea. Smug as you like, the kid at school everyone made a mental note to smack fuck out of, but somehow never got round to it. Thing was, he might've looked like he was just talking to the walls, but I could see the rest of them in the office, and they were watching him, waiting for him to carry on.

When I saw that, I didn't know who I hated more. Kennedy for being an obnoxious twat, or them for not seeing it.

'Anyway,' said Kennedy. 'They go in there, because they know if they don't they're going to get Brearley on their back if there turns out to be an honest-to-God case in there, and thank Christ they do, because there's our boy. And what a bloody mess he was in.'

Kennedy made it sound like he was on the scene quick-smart. I knew for a fact they had to bell him four times before he picked up. Took him two hours to get to the scene because the bastard was fast akip.

'Like I always said, someone like Mo Tiernan, he's going to piss off the wrong people one of these days, and those people, they're liable to be the dramatic sort.'

That was the first time I ever heard Kennedy say that. But he was the kind of bloke who seemed to know what he was doing because he was loud when he was right, and he could stick to his lies because he had a good memory. Looked at him, and all I saw were the talents of a street dealer, except this one wore a suit and tie, got paid a fuck sight less.

'How'd you know it was Tiernan?' I said.

He shifted on his desk, and I could feel people staring at us. He turned his head, played it like he was surprised I was still in the room. 'I recognised him.'

'Thought you said he was a mess.'

'Whoever robbed him dropped an ID card.'

'Handy, that.'

'Wouldn't have taken long, Iain. Made mince out of the lad's face, there are other ways. You know that.'

'That bad, was it?'

'Yeah. Nasty.'

'Well,' I said. 'There's no tears in this place, right?'

More grunts around the office. I saw Adams in the corner of the room, his arms folded. He nodded to himself. I opened one of my desk drawers, realised that there was nothing that I particularly wanted to take with us. I finished off the barm, dumped the bag in the bin.

'You know the Tiernans, don't you?' said Kennedy.

'Of them, yeah.'

'So, you got any ideas?'

I shrugged, sucked the sauce off my fingers. I had plenty of ideas about plenty of things, but there wasn't a single one of them I wanted to share with this twat. 'Could've been anyone.'

'Well, I'm sure I'll get a lead from somewhere.'

'Nothing yet, then?'

'Early days,' he said. 'And if we don't . . .'

He trailed off, smiling.

'And if you don't?' I closed my desk drawer, had a smile of my own going. Just like his, a real piss-taker.

'And if we don't, Detective Sergeant Donkin, it's not like we lost a cure for cancer, is it?'

'Right. No point in looking too hard, is there?'

'I didn't say that.'

'What did you say, then?'

Kennedy's eyes closed for a second, like he couldn't believe I still had the balls to get this close and talk this bolshy after what happened yesterday. He moved onto his other arse cheek, away from us. 'I said, if we don't find out who killed him, it's hardly a tragedy, is it? Said yourself that there were no tears shed in this office.'

'So that gives you a licence to half-arse it,' I said, making sure I was nice and loud.

'For Christ's sake,' said Kennedy.

'You're saying you don't care.'

'You don't *have* to care. It's a job.'

'You're saying you're quite happy to half-arse the case because you don't give a toss about the victim.'

'Iain.'

'Who you really working for, Colin?' I said.

He blinked, smiling. 'You what?'

'You're so up on your underworld connections, mate, I'm wondering if you didn't slip a little. You wanted to know if I had any ideas, I've got plenty. You know what they're saying about Morris Tiernan, don't you?'

'What's that?' he said, like he was humouring us.

I leaned forward. 'They're saying he's been a smug bastard for too long. That he's spent too much time playing the king and not watching his own arse. I mean, you can appreciate that. You know how easy it is to fall into that mentality, right?'

Kennedy didn't say anything, moved his head to one side.

'So what else d'you think they're saying? Maybe that Uncle Morris isn't keeping a watch on his own kids. And maybe the one person with the motive and opportunity to hone in on the Uncle's empire was his fuckin' son.'

Kennedy nodded, smiled like I was simple, then said, 'Who's *they*, Iain?'

'*They* is people in the *know*, Colin.'

'Right,' he said. '*Your* people. Like Conroy. Smackhead with a bag of stolen phones. These people are your eyes and ears.'

'You know me,' I said. 'Rather hear it from the street than the man himself.'

'What's that supposed to mean?'

'Means you're a bit quick to call this a closed case, aren't you? Means you want to watch how that looks. Because it *could* look like you're willing to drop an investigation for two bob and a toffee apple.'

He laughed, once and harsh, spit flying from his mouth. He moved off his desk. 'Right, whatever you want to think, Iain. Hey, you want to make a formal accusation, I'm not going to hold it against you.'

'Maybe I will.'

'Oh wait, no,' he said. 'You have to be active to make a complaint like that, don't you?'

I glared at him then, sucked my teeth. 'You took Paddy Reece's statement, didn't you?'

'Wasn't me, Iain.'

I saw movement out the corner of my eye. Saw Adams sneaking for the door again. Saw other people going back to the pretence of working.

'Sergeant.'

Ali. I half-turned to his voice. Then back to Kennedy, who nodded at the DCI over my shoulder, a sick little smile on his face. Because even before I went into the office, this bastard knew I was on a suspension.

'Finished cleaning out your desk?' said the DCI.

I sniffed, didn't move my gaze from Kennedy. 'Aye.'

'Okay, then.'

I stepped back, away from Kennedy, started towards the door.

'Send my best to Mrs Donkin,' he said. And then, with laughter in his voice, 'Oh, wait, sorry about that—'

I turned, stormed the cunt, grabbed him by his jacket and the whole place tightened up. He was all like, 'fuckin' gerroff us' all of a sudden, had a mouthful of shit that couldn't have made him look good in front of his gaffer. His face scrunched right up like he was going to do something. I heard Ali shouting my name at us, which stopped whatever Kennedy was thinking. But I'd already realised that this situation wasn't going to end well for us anyway, so I reckoned, fuck it, might as well follow through. I shoved Kennedy back against his desk, heard a thump that sounded painful, then saw his legs fly up in the air. Next thing I knew, half the world's paperwork went up with his shoes, and it started snowing A4. Then he disappeared from sight, hit the floor, bringing his chair down with him.

Except it wasn't his chair. Now it was upside down, I could see the part where I'd scratched my initials into the plastic moulding. I made a move towards him, found hands on us.

'C'mon, Iain. Don't be daft, eh?'

I shook them off. And stood still. The office dropped into a thick silence.

Kennedy broke it. Lot of breathing at first, a bit of a huff and a puff and I'll blow your fucking house down, working up to the hardcase he thought he was. Then I saw his face come up from behind the desk and he was bright red. Swollen, too, like all the blood in his body whooshed up to his skull when he went over his desk. Showing his bottom teeth, he looked like a proper steroid case.

I nodded at him. 'You alright there, Colin?'

'You're a fucking joke,' he said.

'Uh-huh.'

'Detective Inspector Kennedy.'

Kennedy looked across at the DCI and some of the blood went from his face. He tugged at his tie, tried to make himself look more presentable. Adjusted his expression, but the eyes were still the same when he turned back to us.

'Think you'd better go home, Iain,' said Ali.

I smiled. Everyone being all nice and polite, because they weren't allowed to do anything else. Conflict resolution training kept them all in check, and they certainly didn't want to rock the boat when the gaffer was standing there. Cowardly bastards to a man. And that was my point. This was what kept my arrest rate up. I wasn't scared to bend a few rules, and the likes of Ali had to appreciate that.

'Iain.'

'I know,' I said. 'I'm going now.'

I headed across the office, already heard the whispers starting up. I pushed through the door out into the corridor where a fresh breeze took the fighting sweat off my face. Pulled out my mobile, made sure I still had Adams' number on it. I might've been suspended, but that didn't mean I couldn't call in a couple of favours.

And the way I saw it, Derek Adams owed us big time.

EIGHTEEN

Innes

The call comes in early – Uncle Morris wants to see me.

Of course he does.

Not at the Wheatsheaf this time, though. And fair enough, I don't see Brian being too happy about an eight o'clock early doors for anyone. Besides, the faintest glimmer of an open pub round that way brings the drinkers out in force. Instead, Tiernan's told me to come round his house as soon as possible.

Which is a first, definitely. Even when my brother ran with Mo, it was invitation only to Tiernan's house, and anyone without that invitation was quick to find themselves blinded by their own blood.

When I arrive, a huge bloke with a shaved head makes a beeline for my car. I kill the engine as he approaches the side window. He takes one look at me and nods. Obviously I fit whatever description he's been given. He waves me out of the car and I comply, grabbing my walking stick and following him as he starts towards the house.

Tiernan's place is actually *two* houses – a couple of semi-detached ex-councils knocked through to make one large Ordsall mansion. He's lived here as long as anyone can remember, was dragged up on these streets. And the price he pays is this small army of bodyguards that hangs around outside the house. Of course, Tiernan wouldn't call them bodyguards, and they wouldn't acknowledge the job title, either. They'd be 'mates of Mr Tiernan', or *acquaintances*. Because the idea that Uncle Morris needed protecting was ludicrous, right? He was a bloke who could look after himself, thanks very much. That's if he needed protection. Because it wasn't like he was doing anything that could piss people off, so why would he need protection?

Morris Tiernan owns bars, pubs, clubs, snooker halls, a massage parlour on Lime Street, another one in the village. He calls himself a legitimate businessman because that's precisely what he is. And the reason he lives on the same sinkhole estate he grew up on is because he wants to stay true to his roots, put a little back into the community. And of course there are rumours flying about that he's somehow got his thumb wedged firmly into the urban regeneration project that's sweeping Salford, that he put up a thick pile of cash to build Quay 5, but what's the matter with that?

No, to all intents and purposes, the idea is that Morris Tiernan might be slightly rough around the edges, but he's truly a pillar of the community. Doesn't matter that I know for a fact he's killed people, robbed and extorted others. Doesn't matter that he had a drug-dealer for a son, and that Tiernan taught him what little he knew and a lot more he couldn't remember. If you have enough money in this city and invest it wisely enough, then you're forgiven a myriad crimes.

And it's obvious from the inside of the house that Tiernan isn't hurting for a bob or two.

I step into a massive living room, wooden floors throughout, buffed to a high shine. None of your laminate, either, which makes me think he's basically rebuilt the inside of these houses from scratch. Cream soft leather furnishings in solid geometric shapes, dark wood elsewhere. A huge LCD screen hangs on the wall above an obviously fake fireplace with a blue-flame pebble fire inset. The television's on, showing a muted BBC *News 24*. Looks like football highlights. Classical music, or something that sounds like it, comes from somewhere in the house.

'Mr Tiernan says take a seat, he'll be right with you.'

Trying to be posh, but the 'you' comes out like 'yoh', and the bloke still has the wide shoulder walk of a scally on the piss. But I do as I'm told, take a seat on a surprisingly comfortable cream couch and watch the ticker along the bottom of the telly screen. Before I get a chance to stretch out, the music dips in volume and I hear footsteps, the wet sound of bare feet on floorboards.

Behind me, one of the doors opens and the guy who showed me in tries to straighten up. I turn in my seat to see Morris Tiernan, bleary-eyed and pale as milk – possibly even slightly medicated, the way he's walking – clutching a mug and wearing a soft cotton tracksuit that looks a good couple of years older than me. I always thought of him as a menacing guy, but taking into account the fact that he's basically wearing his jammies, the wrinkles on his face look more like cracks in his armour.

'Callum,' he says.

I start to stand, but he waves me down.

'Don't bother. You want a cup of coffee or something?'

'No, thanks. I'm fine.'

'Okay.' He pulls on an easy chair, tugs it nearer to the sofa, and sits down. Then he leans forward and places the mug of coffee on the floor next to his foot. I inch towards him on the sofa. A closer look, and it's obvious that he hasn't slept. Tiernan reaches into his trackie bottoms, pulls out a pack of Rothmans and waves a hand at one of his bodyguards, who swings past a coffee table by the door, and delivers a small glass ashtray into Tiernan's hand. Tiernan balances the ashtray on the arm of his chair.

'You want to smoke,' he says, 'feel free.'

Another nod to someone behind me. Another ashtray, smaller than Tiernan's, appears by my side. I wasn't going to smoke, but now I feel kind of pressured to light one. So I do, and because it's the first cigarette of the day, I get a mule-kick of nicotine to the head that makes me glad I'm sitting down.

'Rough night,' says Tiernan, running one hand over his stubble. 'When did they call?'

'About one. Fuckin' police are quick to give you bad news. But then it's not like we didn't expect this, is it?'

I tap ash and don't look him in the eyes.

'It's alright, Callum. Obvious to anyone with a brain in their head that's what'd happen if he kept on the way he was. Just a matter of time.'

'I was there.'

Tiernan doesn't speak, watches me.

'I called it in.'

'Right.' He moves his hand, leaving a thick plume of smoke in the air. 'You called. Okay.'

'The police. I was the one . . . who found Mo.'

He closes his eyes for a moment, then opens them again. I don't buy it. He must've known already. If he didn't, it wouldn't be long before someone let him in on my telephone spaz attack, and then he'd wonder why I didn't tell him when I had the chance.

He says, slowly, '*You* found my son.'

I nod. Don't say anything else. Let it sink in. Tiernan clears his throat, then he reaches for his coffee. He takes a sip, replaces the mug on the floor, and returns his gaze to me.

'Why'd you call the police?'

'I had to.'

'You could've called me.'

'No.'

'Why not?'

'He's your son.'

'Which is why you should've told me first.'

'No. You're too attached.'

'What?' There's a flare in his eyes.

I tap the side of my head twice. 'You're too . . . *emotional.* If I told you.'

Tiernan's eyes narrow as he exhales smoke through his nose.

'You wouldn't think,' I say. 'Not clearly.'

I hear something shifting behind me and for a moment I think I've pushed it too far, reckon best case scenario is that I'm about to get my head kicked in. Worse case . . . I don't want to think about it.

'I did it . . . to protect *you*. If you knew Mo . . . was *dead*, you'd . . . *do* something.' I shake my head. Stop and think it through, try not to let the panic choke me now. 'Even if . . . it was right. It's still a *reaction*. And you needed . . . to stay *out* of this. Trust the police. Even if you don't.'

He's still staring at me. The expression on his face hasn't changed. I can't tell what he's thinking now, or even if he understood what I just said to him.

'Mr Tiernan.'

'You're right,' he says. 'I don't trust the police. They won't do their fuckin' jobs on this.'

I nod. 'I know. But they have procedures.'

He blinks as if he doesn't understand.

I take a deep breath, run through what I rehearsed last night. 'You can't care. Can't be seen . . . to care. Let the police work. It's easier for me . . . to find out. What *they* have. So you let *me* use them. But you're not . . . involved.'

Tiernan looks at me for a moment longer, then he picks up his coffee again. Takes a sip, lets the coffee linger in his mouth before he swallows. 'You have contacts in the police?'

'Yes.'

'Really?'

I want to tell him that I'm supposed to be legitimate now, but that word would never make it out of my mouth, so I say, 'I'm clean. I'm trusted.'

'Right, you're the local hero.'

'If you like.'

'Yeah, I heard about that.' He rubs his eye, half-smiling. 'And if they ask who you're working for?'

'Confidential.'

'And what do you have so far?'

That's the question I was brought here to answer. Now that he's aware that I found Mo, it's a question that must have some kind of answer, too. I take a long last drag off the Embassy, grind it out in the ashtray.

'Couple of leads,' I say.

'Already?'

I nod.

'Who?'

'Can't say.'

'Can't or won't?'

'Okay, won't.'

'Why not?'

'Same reason . . . I didn't call you. Nothing definite.'

'I should still know.'

'No,' I say. 'Not yet. Let me do this.'

Tiernan breathes out. He smothers his cigarette in the ashtray, keeps grinding even when it's long stopped burning. Then he lights another Rothmans. 'So that's you on this.'

'If you say so.'

He looks around at the two bodyguards, tells them to leave. He keeps silent until he's positive they're both out of the room, then he says, 'I appreciate you don't want to name names in front of other people—'

'I can't.'

'You want me to trust you on this?' he says.

'If you *trust* me . . . you trust me. You'll know when I *know*. Not when I . . . have a *lead*.'

'There's people talking,' he says, glancing at the door. 'You know that.'

'Yes.'

'People who think that maybe fucking up my son is a way to get their foot in the door, make some kind of statement of intent.'

I nod. 'I know that.'

'So if there's anyone I should be keeping an eye on, even if you're not entirely sure, you need to let me know.'

'There's nobody.'

He leans further forward, and I notice the coffee sloshing right to the edge of the mug as he does so. 'Look at me.'

I do. Tiernan doesn't blink.

'You're not daft, Callum. Your brother wasn't daft either. He just had some bad habits, some misplaced loyalty. But I'd understand it if you didn't see it that way. Like maybe you'd be harbouring some resentment towards my family on account of what happened to the pair of you.'

My jaw feels like it's locked. I want another cigarette, but I don't think I'd be able to smoke it. I breathe out through my nose and my sinuses hurt.

'But that resentment better be saved for Mo, not me. Like you said, this is an emotional situation, and I'd hate for another situation to crop up that tested your loyalties. Say if that contact you have in the force decides that I'm more of a career-maker than whoever killed my son. I'd like to think you'd do the right thing in that situation, that you wouldn't let your past interfere.'

I nod. Still can't speak.

'Yeah?' he says, a hard glitter in his eyes.

'Yeah.' Tough word to say, but it huffs out of my mouth in a single breath.

'Because this is delicate,' he says. 'Mo wasn't much fuckin' good when he was alive. He was a crack in the operation, and that hasn't changed much now he's dead. If people hear about it, they might get the wrong idea that they can fuck about with me. And that's not the case. Never has been.'

'I understand.'

'Good.' He gulps the rest of his coffee, then jerks his head at me. 'You let me know the minute you find anything out, and I'll get payment sorted for you.'

That's my cue to leave. I struggle to my feet. Tiernan calls for someone called Nathan to come back into the room. 'You need any help?'

Nathan arrives, and it's the big, bald bloke who showed me in.

'No,' I say.

'Nathan, you want to show Mr Innes out. Before you go, mind, Callum, just one quick thing.'

I turn to look at him.

'I'm sorry to hear about your brother,' he says.

I know I'm supposed to say something, but I shrug instead. Then I turn back to the door, where Nathan is waiting to escort me off the premises.

NINETEEN

Donkin

Adams wasn't answering his mobile. Probably already got wind of what happened in the office, so he was keeping a low profile.

Didn't matter. He couldn't duck us for too long.

There was this greasy spoon down Piccadilly – blink and you'd miss it – one of those places that looked little more than a front window and fluorescent star stickers with the specials written on them. But this place stretched way back into the building, further than you'd ever think. Kind of caff you could go into, eat your breakfast in peace. No way could anyone see you from the street, which meant Adams loved the place, and also that he wouldn't get a chance to bolt until I'd already made it clear that I'd seen him.

The scrawny little bastard was regular as clockwork. Bang on ten o'clock, he scuttled in for a late fry-up. By the time he managed to dodge round the people leaving the place, he was already spotted. I got out of my seat and shouted, 'Detective Sergeant Adams, what a surprise to see you here.'

He looked my way and nearly sighed his fucking shoulders off, then he looked at the door. Trying to work out if he could escape before I got to him.

He couldn't.

I put a hand in the centre of his back, and the impact forced him into a cringe. I nodded at the lass behind the counter. 'Whatever he wants times two, eh? We'll be over at the back there.'

Adams ordered like it was his last meal, and he was disgusted about it. I prodded him on to a free table at the back of the place.

'Glad I caught you,' I said. 'There's something we need to have a natter about.'

'I really don't have the time, Iain.'

'I know you don't, but you were going to eat anyway, so we might as well kill two birds with one stone, eh?'

I got him to the table, kept a solid hand on his shoulder until he sank into his seat. Adams pulled one hand over his mouth, glanced over his shoulder at the door. I sat opposite, put both my hands on the table, and stared at him until he looked my way.

'You know what just happened at the nick, don't you?' I said.

He turned to me, sighed. Turned his face down.

'I've just been in a meeting with the DCI.'

'Right,' he said. 'Saw you go in.'

'You know what it was about?'

His eyes got slightly wider, but he didn't look scared. Interested, maybe.

'Paddy Reece,' I said. 'Amongst other fuckin' things. But Paddy Reece was the main topic of conversation. How some daft cunt let him make a formal complaint.'

'If he wanted to make a complaint, he was entitled.'

'Even if the upshot is me getting fuckin' suspended?'

Adams shifted his hand across his mouth again. 'Hmm.'

'Hmm? Fuckin' *hmm*? It's your fuckin' fault, Derek.'

'My fault?'

'You talked to him, didn't you? I mean, you're the only stupid bastard in that place who still deals with the shite.'

'He wanted to talk to someone in charge.'

'And you were the closest they had at the time, right?'

'I was the only one who didn't run out of the office, yeah.'

There was a look in his eyes, a flash of something that he wanted to say, but he didn't have the stones to follow it up. Instead he puckered up his mouth.

'You let him make a formal complaint, Derek,' I said.

'I did my job.'

'Didn't fuckin' think about what it'd do to *me*, did you, mind?'

'He was—'

'I mean, yeah, fuckin' hell, they're *entitled* to make a complaint, *entitled* to make it formal, we all know that, but here's the way you're supposed to run it: make out like it'll be a long, drawn out process, that you can't be arsed and that they *shouldn't* be arsed because it'll probably end up doing fuck all except getting a copper pissed off at them. That's the way I was taught to handle it. That's the way you should've handled it.'

'He was well within his rights to make a complaint, Iain. You assaulted him.'

'So then you come to *me*,' I said, trying to keep my voice down. 'You talk it out with us, you give us a heads-up, and I tell you what to do from there.'

Adams' eyes dropped half-closed. 'You don't outrank me.'

'I don't give a fuck about *rank*, Derek. Just common fuckin' courtesy to let a bloke know when he's going to get fuckin' chewed, give him a head start on it.' I pointed at him. 'What you did was play the fuckin' cunt. Put us out to the brass.'

'You put yourself out.'

'No, you made a mistake, Derek. You admit that, and that you owe us, and we can—'

'I don't owe you anything.'

'Alright, and I'm not asking you to do anything for us, am I?'

'Right.'

'I'm *telling* you to do something for us.'

The lass from behind the counter came over with two breakfasts, the full whack. We didn't say anything to each other as she put the plates down in front of us. Adams looked down at his food, the blood gone from his cratered face. As soon as the waitress left, he picked at a fried egg and his gut made this long, loud gurgling noise.

'Better get something in you,' I said. 'Sounds like you're digesting yourself.'

'You can't bully me, Iain.'

'Bully? Nah, I'm not trying to bully you, Derek old son. Don't get us wrong on this: you can keep your fuckin' dinner money. But you do need to help us out.'

'I did my job,' he said again. Starting to sound like a broken record here as he muttered, 'Paddy Reece had every right to make an official complaint in the event of his assault, and I had to treat any such complaint as a priority.'

'What if it'd been Kennedy?'

Adams poked harder at his fried egg. Broke the seal on the yolk and the runny yellow mixed into the bean juice. Between that and his face, I was starting to lose my appetite.

'I would've done exactly the same thing,' he said.

'Like fuck. You and the rest of 'em in there, you're so far up that Scouse bastard's arse you can read his collar size. Paddy Reece came in with a complaint against that twat, you'd have gone to him straight, would've warned him at the very fuckin' least. But because it's *me*, I get the shitty end of the stick.'

'DI Kennedy's not known for assaulting people in custody.'

'Not here, but c'mon, he's only been here five fuckin' minutes.'

'And maybe it was about time someone called you on your methods.'

'My *methods*?' I had trouble thinking straight. Here was me, I'd gone out of my way to be courteous to the fucker, even bought him the breakfast he was prodding, sat him down and talked to him like a man, and he had the balls to call us on this? This whiteboard copper, facts on fucking index cards before he felt a collar, suddenly thought he had the right to grass us up.

Which meant he had an inflated sense of self-worth, and I had the fucking pin.

I grabbed him by the tie. He couldn't do anything about it but fold his face.

'Iain, for fuck's—'

I pulled tighter, pushed the knot into his Adam's apple. 'You know better than that. Call us on my fuckin' methods like you're some kind of fuckin' supercop, you daft twat. Got to expect I'm going to get wound up by that.'

Pushed him back in his chair, which scraped loud against the floor. He grabbed hold of the table before he went arse over tit, pulled at his tie with his other hand. He was starting to draw stares from the rest of the arseholes in here, so I gave as good as I got until they shrank back to their tea and toast.

'If you think that grassing us up is a way to get on in this job, Derek, you're going to get your tie mangled.' I pushed my plate out of the way; wasn't hungry at all now. 'And if you continue to act the arse, I'll smack you like one.'

'Don't talk to me like I'm one of your grasses,' he said, his voice scratchy.

'But you are, Derek. Because it if wasn't for you, that body that came in this morning would be mine, not Kennedy's. As it fuckin' turns out, I wanted that case and it's rightly mine, so what you're going to do is let *me* know what Kennedy knows.'

'You can't investigate—'

'Not that it's any of your fuckin' business, but someone has to. You reckon Kennedy's going to do a decent job of it, the way he was talking? This Tiernan thing isn't something that concerns him. His first dead end and he'll chuck it in, and you know why?'

'Because nobody gives a shit about Mo Tiernan,' said Adams.

'Because Detective Inspector Colin Kennedy is bent as all fuck.'

Adams shook his head, his bottom lip putting a move on his top. 'I don't think so.'

'You reckon he's clean, and I know why.'

'Because he is.'

'Because you can't see anything but the inside of his arse. You ever wondered why he transferred over from Liverpool? Why he never fuckin' talks about it?'

'If DI Kennedy doesn't want to make the Tiernan case a priority, then that's his problem. If and when he jacks it in, and if you don't think the investigation was handled correctly at that time, I'm sure you can put a formal complaint in to the DCI.'

'And how do I know how well the investigation was handled if you don't help us?' I sat back in my chair, looked at Adams. I kept my voice low and friendly. 'Okay. Tell you what, Derek, I fully appreciate I've put you in an uncomfortable position here. I'll just take my suspension, watch Fern and Phil, let the bent coppers breed through our nick. But just so's you know – so there's no fuckin' misunderstandings about this further on down the line – this thing here? It's not about putting one over on Kennedy. It's about finding out if what I hear about him is true.'

'And what's that?' said Adams, a new smile pushing his mouth wide. 'That he's bent? You heard that from your grasses?'

He was laughing at me on the inside. Just like the rest of the twats I came into contact with. I wanted to ram his face into that free breakfast, going cold in front of him. And the truth was, I didn't know that Kennedy was bent. He just *felt* bent to me, and it was a good enough justification to get Adams to grass him up. But something had happened to the skinny fuckwit. Someone out there had promised him back-up if I ever put the strong arm on him. I could guess who.

'Fine, right.' I pushed away from the table. 'You watch him, Derek. If anything crops up that brings this conversation back to fuckin' mind, you've got my mobile number. Don't let him drag you down with him.'

Then I pushed my way past the tables to the front door.

I didn't look back, knew that Adams would be chuckling to himself about this. Probably tell Kennedy about it, and I suddenly felt utterly fucking stupid. It didn't matter what he told Kennedy, mind. They'd have a laugh about it. But at the end of the day, I'd be the one laughing at the pair of them.

Because there was no fucking way I was going to drop this investigation, not when I had a chance to one-up that Scouse cunt.

TWENTY

Donkin

I wasn't in the mood to play kiss-chase with Innes, so I went straight back round the poof's club. And as soon as I got through the doors, that was it. The poof was out and almost running at us.

'He's not here,' he said.

'I know he's not here. I can see he's not here. He's never fuckin' here, is he?'

The poof stopped in his tracks. Behind him, I saw the door to the IC Investigations office standing open. The big jailbird was in there, looking at some papers. The poof moved to one side, blocked my view. 'So what are you doing here? I thought we discussed this.'

'I need to know where he is,' I said.

'If he's not here, then I don't know.'

'Maybe your big friendly giant in there knows something.'

'The fuck is the matter with you?' he said. 'Seriously, I mean, are you fuckin' retarded in some way?'

'You don't need to talk to us like that,' I said, frowning at him. 'Hurts my fuckin' feelings. I just need to talk to Innes. It's important, otherwise I wouldn't have come back, would I?'

'Well, he's not—'

'Then I need his mobile number.'

'No.'

'Oi, look, I'm trying to be fuckin' nice about this, aren't I?' I took a few steps up at him, gave him my brightest smile. 'I haven't got handy with you, haven't asked your jittery mate in there any more fuckin' questions, so I reckon that's got to count for something, doesn't it? So how's about this, you go and get us Innes's mobile number, right, and I won't bother coming round anymore.'

The poof didn't say anything for a long time. He was staring at us like he was waiting for us to carry on, give him some more reasons to help the police with their enquiries. Then, when he realised I didn't have nowt to give, he said, 'No.'

'What exactly is your fuckin' problem here, Nancy?'

'If he doesn't want to talk to you, he's not going to talk to you on the fuckin' phone, is he?'

'It's in his best interests to talk to us,' I said, the smile gone. 'Seriously, no fucking about anymore, I need to talk to him.'

'Then how about I take *your* number and get him to give you a call as soon as I see him?'

I rolled some spit around the inside of my mouth. 'I understand that you don't trust us, Mr Gray—'

He got in so close I thought he was about to kiss us. 'Too fuckin' right I don't trust you.'

'And you'll forgive us if I don't exactly trust *you* to pass on the message.'

'Not a problem,' he said. 'You can go sniffing for him by yourself.'

'Or I bet your man Frank can help us out.' I pointed through to the office. Frank looked up at the sound of my voice, caught us pointing, and his mouth got tight as a cat's arse. 'Y'alright there, Frank? Coming in there in a minute, have a little word with you.'

'How about I report you for harassment?' said the poof.

'How about I put a finger on you to the NSPCC?'

'Right,' he said. 'Here we go.'

'Yeah, why not? I mean, even if you don't measure up to my suspicions of you being a fuckin' arse bandit with a taste for the young 'uns, something I'm learning is that every complaint officially filed has to be investigated thoroughly, doesn't it?'

'I've already had police checks.'

'So did Huntley, mate.' I took a deep, crackling breath in, fixed him with my copper stare. 'Only shows the convictions, though, eh? Might not come to anything, they might not lock you up, but you know as well as I do that they're judgemental pricks round here, and I'm guessing that your status as local poof has done you no fuckin' favours, am I right? Mind you, that's preferable to being the bloke investigated on suspicion of kiddie-fiddling. Doesn't matter if you touched 'em or not, either. And when that happens – because you know if there's the slightest fuckin' sniff, they'll be out with the flaming torches, come to burn the monster's house down – you're going to have to ask yourself if it was all worth it. Because I wouldn't be talking this serious unless it was fuckin' *imperative* that I talk to your mate right the fuck now.'

The poof blinked at us, worked his mouth. Yeah, he knew I was serious now, and he was fucking boiling that I was able to keep walking back into his place. He also knew Innes better than most, and I guessed that there was a large fucking part of him that knew he was in the shit. And he was in the shit purely because of Innes.

'So you know,' I said, 'I'm not just round here to mess him about.'

'Yeah, right, you're not,' he said quietly. 'That's all you ever—'

'I'll admit, right, that's what I was after yesterday. Wanted to get a gander at the freak, give him shit about being a mong an' all that.' I moved my shoulders back. 'But I already did all that last night.'

'So?'

'So, Mr Gray, I'm here in a more official capacity.'

He was hesitant when he said, 'How?'

'Can't divulge the details,' I said. 'Y'know, considering it's an ongoing investigation. But here's the thing: I don't want to *have* to get nasty with you, Mr Gray.'

'Course you don't.'

'I mean, I *could* do you for obstruction, wasting police time, all that bollocks, but it's petty. Besides, I don't want you, I want Innes.'

'And you can't tell me anything about it.'

'Only that it involved Mo Tiernan,' I said, 'and a body we found last night.'

The sarcastic smile leaked from the poof's face right then. Some of the colour in his cheeks went along with it. I hadn't expected that reaction. If anything, I was waiting for the usual Innes-is-innocent bollocks that usually followed an implied accusation. Expected him to be raging at us by now, telling us to get out, that he didn't care about any threats, that in fact, it was just fucking texture for his eventual harassment complaint. Which, to be honest, was the last thing I needed, but I couldn't let the poof think he was better than me.

Still, he was stunned, almost looked fucking caught, truth be told. So rather than look a gift horse in the gob, I hitched up my belt and said, 'You know anything about it?'

The poof looked straight at my gut for a few seconds, thinking about his answer. 'No.'

'You're sure?'

'Yes.'

'He never told you.'

'No.'

'Well, consider yourself told now, then.'

He scratched his top lip, looked like he'd stray up to his nose. 'He's dead?'

'I said there was a body. Didn't say who it was.'

'But it's Mo, isn't it?' he said, squinting at us.

'I'm not at liberty—'

'How?'

'Again, I'm not really at liberty to tell you that.' I sniffed.

'And how's Cal involved?'

I looked around the club. It was a nice enough gym, better than it used to be, but I wasn't really all that interested in what I saw. I was just doing something other than answer the poof's question, because he was bricking it about something, and it couldn't do any harm to let him sweat a little longer. In the end, I winked at him. 'I don't know that he *is*. But I don't know that he's not, either.

I've evidence to tie him to the scene, and I've yet to eliminate him from my enquiries.'

'You're not actually treating him as a suspect, are you?'

'Here, you know how it is. Everyone's a suspect until they're cleared, right?'

'You've *seen* him recently, though.'

I nodded. 'And I know what you're going to say – he couldn't have done it, look at the state of him, he can barely get around by himself, how the fuck could he be responsible for killing someone?'

'I wasn't going to say that.'

'Either way,' I said, 'you never fuckin' know. Which is why I need to talk to him.'

I wasn't about to tell the poof that, yeah, it was Mo Tiernan who was dead. I wasn't going to tell him that the lad's face was a mess, either. And I wasn't going to ask him what he thought about Innes being on the crime scene an hour before it was called in. Just would've complicated matters, and from the look on the poof's face, he didn't know anything about it. And the idea was to keep as much information about this to myself, let other people give it out. This bloke knew something, mind. He was feeling guilty about something, came off him like a bad smell.

But it would have to wait until I came back. And I was going to come back, there was no doubt about it.

'If I don't get to talk to him soon,' I said, 'I guarantee you it won't be long before the whole of Serious Crimes are down here to wait for him, and it won't be pretty. So how's about you break the lock on your fuckin' jaw and give us his mobile number before all this gets so dramatic even someone like you won't be able to handle it?'

He worked his mouth again. Then he came to a decision.

'Hang on a second,' he said.

The poof headed back to the IC Investigations office. I followed him to the door, saw him writing something down on a piece of paper. He ripped the sheet from the pad, came over and slapped it into my hand. Frank watched the pair of us with large eyes.

'There,' he said. 'But that's it, right?'

'Yeah, alright. But if your boy's got anything to do with this—'

'Get a grip, Detective. You saw him. He's not capable of something like that.'

I pointed to him as I walked towards the exit. 'You don't know *what* that lad's capable of.'

TWENTY-ONE

Innes

I'm sitting in the corner of my local watching the inside of a half-empty pint glass. Joe's over by the television, staring up at the scores as they come in on Sky Sports. Waiting for Man City to come on, and he'll be there for a while, considering I saw them announce the score just now when he went to the toilet. As I watch the sports news scroll along the bottom of the screen in primary colours, I can't help but think of Morris Tiernan.

And that's when my mobile rings.

Pull the phone out of my pocket, look at the display. It isn't a number I recognise, so nobody I know, which makes me automatically antsy about answering it. The mobile's become an emergency tool only these days – anyone who knows me knows that I'm not at my best on the phone.

Still, I connect the call.

'Guess who?'

'How did you get—'

'How the fuck d'you think?'

I breathe out, look around the pub. Paulo. 'I have an idea.'

He sounds like he hawks and spits. 'So I'm thinking we should have a word in person, what d'you think?'

'Alright.'

I can almost hear the double-take. 'You what?'

'I'm in the Long Ship. You know it? If you're at the Lads' Club, it shouldn't be too much of a hike.'

Kill the call, put the mobile on the table and stare at the dregs of my pint. Then I knock them back, get to my feet and leave the glass on the bar as I order another. It arrives just as Donkey does, making a blustering entrance, as if he's not sure I haven't already done a bunk. When he sees me, he tugs at his jacket, takes long steps towards the bar. He already has the landlord's attention, but I beat him to the punch.

'Pint?'

He regards me through narrowed eyes. Came in here, expecting to see me gone. When I wasn't, he expected a fight. So when he gets neither, and I offer to buy him a drink, I can almost hear the alarm bells ringing inside Donkey's head. He leans against the bar, pulls at his face as he looks at the pumps. If the man's on duty, he should really turn it down, but then I'd be surprised if Donkey turned down a free drink in his entire life.

'Whatever you're having,' he says.

I order two pints of Kronenbourg, Landlord pours them out, and I remain as relaxed as I can be with a copper standing next to me. I jerk my chin at the corner table, let him lead the way as I pick up my pint with one hand, hold the walking stick in the other.

Once we're both settled, Donkey says, 'You happy to talk to us?'

'Depends. You arresting me?'

He puts his elbows on the table. 'Should I?'

I shake my head.

'Then we're just talking.' He looks at his pint. 'Thought you'd have done a fuckin' runner, mind.'

'No point, is there?' I say. 'You always . . . find me. In the end. Might as well . . . get it *out*. In the open. Right?'

He chuckles, then wipes his mouth. 'You wouldn't believe the shite I went through to get your number, son. That poof's really protective.'

'He is, yeah. He's a mate.'

Waggles a finger. 'You two . . . ?'

'No.'

The finger turns into a hand, palm out. 'Just asking.'

'You wouldn't be . . . the first.'

'So,' he says, wrapping that hand around his pint. 'You going to tell us what you were doing round Sutpen Court last night?'

'Already told you.'

'Tell us again.'

'A job. Looking for Mo. And I found him.'

'You call it in?' he says.

I nod.

'Why?'

'Let you lot . . . handle it. I'm not Jessica . . . fuckin' *Fletcher*.'

Donkey laughs. There's a slow wheeze attached to the end of it. He drinks some of his pint, happy in the knowledge that I'm not about to slam the glass into his face and bolt out the door. He replaces the glass on the beermat, sucks his bottom lip. 'So you're willing to tell us what you know, eh?'

'Yeah. Why not?'

'Who d'you think did it?' he says.

Right off the bat. Kind of surprising. Makes me think that Donkey doesn't have the first fucking clue about this, which is interesting. Means he's reliant on my information. I'd hoped that was the case. Now it is, I feel like buying him a short to go with that pint.

'Don't know,' I say. 'It was definitely . . . *murder*, mind.'

Donkey shakes his head, but he doesn't believe what he says: 'His wallet was missing. We're supposed to be looking at it like a robbery.'

'Wasn't robbery.'

'His wallet—'

'Anything left?'

His lips bunch up as he breathes in through his nose. 'Yeah.'

'ID card, right? Fallen on the floor?'

He nods.

'Right. Wallet was taken . . . to avoid identi-fi*cation*. Card fell out. Bad luck. It was dark. They didn't see it. Besides, you saw . . . the *mess*.'

Donkey keeps nodding. 'Face was fuckin' minced.'

'Lot of anger.' I tap the side of my pint glass. 'Probably asleep . . . when it happened. Right?'

'We don't know that for sure.'

'He's lying down. So he's relaxed. You rob a . . . sleeping man. You don't do that. Don't beat him. No need.'

'You just take the wallet. Or he woke up.'

'You saw him,' I say. 'He was still asleep. I'm sure.'

Donkey sits back in his chair. I can tell he'd love a cigarette about now. So would I. But he's not about to break up this conversation, give me a chance to second-guess myself, change my mind. As far as he's concerned, I know he thinks I've always been jittery when it comes to sharing information with him. And getting it on a plate like this is starting to make him a little suspicious. I should tone it down, put it back on him.

'You know it wasn't . . . robbery,' I say. 'If it was, you . . . wouldn't be interested.'

'Alright,' he says. 'Okay, so someone killed him.'

'Took his wallet. So you lot . . . wouldn't ID.'

'We'd still ID.'

'In time. And he'd be . . . end of the queue. It's a delay. All you need. Treat it like a robbery . . . watch it grow cold.'

Donkey runs a hand over his mouth, looks at the bar. Behind him, I can see Joe giving us worried glances. He's already clocked that Donkey's police, probably wondering what kind of trouble I'm in. Joe's the kind of bloke who'd help out if he could. Just as soon as that Man City result comes in.

'I knew it wasn't a fuckin' robbery,' says Donkey, nodding at me. 'I knew it, told them it wasn't.'

'They?'

Waves his hand. 'Some twat running the show.'

'You're not . . . investigating?'

'Course I am. Just not *running* it. But he's a twat, doesn't know his arse from a hole in the ground.' His face takes on a purple colour around the jawline. 'Don't think for a fuckin' second that I'm not in charge on this.'

'I don't. You said—'

'Because if I hear you're going elsewhere, I'll fuckin' carve you up.'

'I'm doing you . . . a *favour.*'

He leans forward again. I can smell the beer on his breath, even though he's barely made a dent in his pint. 'You're not doing us any favours, you're helping with enquiries, you get me?'

'Okay.'

'I'm the one in charge here. You're *my* fuckin' boy.'

I look at the surface of the pub table, my head down. Wait for him to stop breathing so hard. Yeah, I'm his fucking boy. That's precisely the way it needs to be, and for all my instincts crying out that this is a bad idea, I told Tiernan I had a contact on the force, and I intend to make Donkey that guy. The only way to do that is to play nice, even if that's the last thing I'm used to with Donkey.

'So, you know the Tiernans,' he says finally. 'You know who's likely to have a pop?'

'Nobody—' I stop, take a drink to wet my throat. 'Nobody has . . . the balls.'

'I don't know, I'm thinking Tiernan's getting lazy, there's somebody maybe moving in, know what I mean?'

'Maybe.'

He looks at me. 'You don't think so.'

'I don't *know.*'

'But what do you think?'

I look at him across the table. He's not drinking, seems genuinely interested. And there's something different about him, not so quick to jump to the aggressive, maybe because I'm the one that's invited him here, and he's still wondering what my game is, especially now the information I'm giving him seems plausible enough. Of course he'll check all this stuff out, most likely behind his gaffer's back, take the credit if it pans out. But I still need to be careful here. The way he's been lately, he's quick to rile if things don't look like they're going to go his way.

'Not a bloke,' I say.

His eyes drop to slits, his mouth the other way. 'You what?'

'Might be nothing. The hair.'

'What hair?'

Possible that Donkey hasn't been privy to the forensic reports or whatever yet. And even if he has, and they've missed out, he needs to know.

'A long hair,' I say. 'On the body. In Mo's hand. Rules out most of the . . . *blokes* I know.'

Donkey doesn't say anything for a while. He's chewing his bottom lip.

'And if he *was* asleep . . .' I try to catch his eyes, see what he's thinking.

'Then it was a probably a bird,' he says.

'Maybe.'

'Only way she'd be sure not to get overpowered, she'd wait until he was asleep.'

'Or nodding. There was a needle.'

Donkey looks back at me. 'He was using?'

'Only a matter of time.'

He takes a long pull on his pint, wipes his mouth. 'I don't know. Don't buy him as a smackhead. Why the fuck are you telling us all this, anyway?'

'Sick of running.' I shrug. 'Tiernan asked me . . . to *find* his son. Not find his killer.'

Behind Donkey, the score's just come in for Joe. He moves away from the television looking for all the world as if someone's just kicked him in the gut. He orders a single malt and stares at himself in the back bar.

In front of me, Donkey has a similar expression. It's weird. I thought he'd be over the moon.

'But you have an idea who it is,' he says.

'No. No answers. Only questions. Sorry.'

'What's that supposed to mean?'

'I don't know . . . who did it. I'll try to help. But I don't have . . . your *resources*.'

'Or my fuckin' skills,' he says.

'Or your . . . fuckin' skills.'

Another long pause. If he's still trying to work me out, he's long since failed. He drinks his pint down to the quarter mark.

'Y'know, your brother,' he says, 'he was a good grass. Always gave it up, but always took just enough punishment to justify the information, like he wasn't comfortable with it. Reckon he was a decent bloke underneath all that fuckin' baggage he was carrying around with him.'

'Don't,' I say. 'Don't bother.'

He looks up at me. Finishes his pint. 'What?'

'You didn't know him.'

'You think?'

'I know.'

'Spent more time with the bastard than you did, if I remember rightly. Once a week at least while you were inside, and what was that? Two years? Bit more, you think?'

'What you doing?' I say.

He grins wide. 'I'm just wondering what you're playing at.'

'Well,' I say, shifting out of my seat. 'You're the copper. You work it out.'

TWENTY-TWO

Donkin

Innes pulled himself out from behind the table. For a second, I reckoned he was going to get some more beers in, but he stood there waiting for us to stop him.

'You leaving, then?' I said.

'Thought I might.'

'Okay.'

'Okay?'

'Yeah, don't change your phone or anything, mind, or else I'll fuckin' batter you.' I pointed at him. 'You're my eyes and ears now, aren't you? I mean, we're fuckin' clear on that. You get any other ideas working for Tiernan, you let them come my way, I'll see what I can do for you.'

'I won't need any help.'

'Innes, someone like you will always need a friendly copper. Don't bite the fuckin' hand, alright?' Talking of which, I held mine out to shake. He looked at it like I'd offered him a lolly stick with a dog turd on the end. I wondered what the fuck was the matter with him until I realised, that was the hand he was using to hold onto his walking stick. I put my left out. He shook it, and pulled this half-a-smile.

'Right.'

'Keep in touch,' I told him.

And then watched him gimp his way out the door. When the doors shut behind him, I pulled out my mobile, turned it on. One missed call from Annie. She would've left a message, but I didn't want to listen to it right now. Instead, I called Adams.

'Derek, you got anything for us yet?'

'Iain, is that you?'

'Yeah.'

'Why are you calling me?'

'I just said. Wondering if you had anything for us.'

'I'm sorry, I thought I made my position clear. I can't help you out here, Iain.'

'I need you to check on something for us, then. Might change your mind.'

'No.'

'Buy you a drink next time I see you, alright? Check to see if anyone picked up on a long hair on the body. Then let us know what Kennedy's thinking about it.'

'You're joking.'

'I'm fuckin' not.' I got to my feet, nodded at the landlord as I headed for the door. 'Listen to us, Derek. You check into that, I guaran-fuckin'-tee you he's dropped that evidence, still playing this like it's a robbery.'

'And it's—'

'Can't be a fuckin' robbery, alright? First off, who the fuck robs junkies except other junkies?' I let the doors swing shut behind us, pulled at my jacket as I headed out to my car. 'Second, who the fuck beats the shit out of someone who's just lying there? Something else you might want to check – his fuckin' blood work. Got a feeling that Mo was nodding at the time, so check for smack.'

'Wait a second—'

'I'm telling you, check this stuff, I bet Kennedy's doing fuck all with it.'

'Iain, hang *on* a moment.'

I reached the Granada, unlocked the door. 'What?'

'Do you even realise what you're asking me to do here?'

'Yeah. Absolutely.'

'And what in God's name makes you think I'm going to do it?'

'Because you know as well as I do that Kennedy's a bad copper.' I put one hand on the roof of the car, a quick check behind us to make sure I wasn't being watched. 'You know he's bent. I told you he was bent. And I'm telling you now that he's fucking this case up on purpose.'

'You don't have any proof, though.'

'That's what you're going to get me.'

Adams let out this long, noisy sigh into the phone. 'No.'

'The fuck you mean, no?'

'I mean, you're already suspended, Iain. You're not a copper. You're a civilian who's looking to get arrested if you keep on at this. And even if you were a copper, you don't rank me, so I'm not duty bound to do whatever you tell me to do.'

'Alright,' I said. 'Okay, maybe my tone was a bit—'

'I don't give a fuck about your *tone*,' he said, and he was a fine one to talk because he came off right snippy just then. 'I'm warning you. Stay away from this case. Stay away from *any* case.'

'Come on, Derek, don't play that game.'

His voice dropped in volume. 'There's people at this nick who're *waiting* for you to fuck up, Iain.'

'Yeah, I know,' I said.

'No, you don't know. Because if you *did* know you wouldn't be acting the way you are. You're fucking *this* close to losing your job, did you know that?'

'Thanks to you, you fuckin'—'

'You think that's it? You think the brass haven't been keeping an eye on you all this time? The only thing you should be worried about right now, Iain, is preparing for your meeting with Ali. Because you'll be fucking lucky if you just lose your job. There's whispers round the nick that Reece is going to press charges.'

I looked at the ground, suddenly dying for a fucking ciggie.

'Right,' I said. 'I get you.'

'You understand what I'm saying, Iain? Don't be bullish about this. I mean, I appreciate you've got problems at home—'

'I don't,' I said. 'Everything's fuckin' dandy round mine.'

'I meant the divorce,' he said.

'I know what you fuckin' meant, and it's not a problem.' I scratched the back of my neck, felt the cold creep in under my jacket.

Fuck it.

'Look, you're right,' I said, as convincing as possible. 'I need to get this thing with Ali sorted first. Makes sense to put a pin in that, right? In the meantime, all I'm asking is keep an eye on Kennedy.'

'I can't.'

'Then do what you can.'

I disconnect, pop the phone back into my jacket pocket. Then I get into the car, crank the heater up until I can feel my fingers again. Once the circulation's going, I root around in my tin for a cigarette. Get that smoke going, warm up the old lungs.

I didn't know they were pushing Reece to press charges. Adams was right; there were plenty of wankers at the station who'd happily see us on the dole or, even better, in prison, but I never reckoned they'd be so fucking proactive about it.

Well, they weren't the only ones who could turn the fucking screw.

I drove out to where I cornered Paddy the last time, cruised around the estate. By the time I got there, it was already getting dark. Paddy had a mate who lived round here, and I wouldn't have been surprised if that mate happened to be a fucking dealer, judging from the company that Paddy used to keep.

As I drove, I pulled out my phone. Called a grass I knew, Coldfeet. The lad was like a Yellow Pages for dealers. Gave him the area I was driving around, he gave us three addresses.

'You know these people?' I said.

'Like, am I bothered if you nick 'em?'

'No, as in have you ever bought from them before?'

'Yeah. Off and on. You know me.'

I did know him. He had a habit as long as the A1. 'Any of 'em have a lady friend?'

'Funny question, that.'

'Just fuckin' tell us.'

'Just funny you should mention it. Daryl Goines. His missus is something fuckin' special.'

I already had the address, and it all fit together perfectly. See, Daryl Goines was a black bloke, moved up from Birmingham because he thought he'd have plenty of easy trade routes further north. Stood to reason that his missus would be a black girl, and she was. A fucking looker, too, by all accounts.

I parked outside the house, watching the front from across the road. Paddy, as long as I'd known him, was a sucker for the dark meat. And if this woman had even been slightly nice to him, that would be him thinking he had a fucking chance. Even though, from what I could find out about Daryl Goines, he was a nasty piece of shit who'd rather cut you up than shoot you. There were stories of pig farmers and plastic bags, people going missing and ears turning up in the post. And yet, there was Paddy, still reckoned he could, what, get his end away? It explained why he wasn't off his tits when I grabbed him on the street. Explained why he didn't want to tell us where he'd been, too.

So, what was the plan? I could sit in my car, listen to my Dido CD, and wait until Paddy showed his face again. But there was no real certainty of that happening. For all I knew, he'd been and gone. Or I could get out of the car, march up to the front door and kick it in. Announce to Goines and his woman that if they saw Paddy Reece again, he better give us a ring. Then, course, there'd be the chance that Goines would carve us the fuck up, or else expect to be arrested. Because who the fuck was I but a fat bloke with a temper right now?

I dug into my jacket, pulled out my wallet with my identification in it. Stared at the picture of myself.

A good copper would have left it well enough alone. But then a good copper wouldn't have found himself in my position.

I snapped the ID wallet shut and looked out at the house again. If I collared Paddy, what was I going to do? Beat fuck out of him? To be fair, that was what'd got us in the shit in the first place. So, what, then go in and maybe get Goines to do my dirty work? After all, a quick word to Goines about Paddy's little crush on his missus would be enough to put the cokehead wog on the offensive. And Paddy wouldn't stand a fucking chance.

Shook my head. I was headed for a dive if I did either one of them things. They had us on Paddy; no getting around that. Better I kept it filed away, get the fucker later when he wasn't expecting it. Right now, the best thing I could do was carry on with the investigation, act like the copper I knew I was and not get fucking sidetracked by personal errands.

So I turned the key, started the engine, headed home.

Because, after all, Paddy Reece wasn't the target here, was he?

Nah, that role belonged to Innes.

TWENTY-THREE

Innes

My hand shakes as I pour another drink.

Even now, when I'm at home, with four or five good stiff vodkas inside me, half a pack of Embassys smoked and ground out, there's still a tremor that's not a side-effect of the stroke. I'd get up and walk it off – probably the closest I could come to home physiotherapy – but there's the chance that moving around might make it worse. So I keep parked on the sofa, drinking. Light another cigarette. Wonder why the fuck Morris Tiernan just called.

On the face of it, I already know – he wants to see me again. Yeah, I saw him this morning, he wants to see me again. For an 'update' he says. I don't know how much of an update I'm likely to give him, to be honest.

Which gets my mind rolling on other things.

Like, he's picked up some information I don't want him to.

Like, he's suspicious.

The way he was talking to me this morning, all that shite about loyalty, hypothetical situations, my brother. He's got other things on his mind, definitely, not sure if he can trust me yet.

Fuck it, not sure if he can trust *anyone* yet.

My mobile rings. I put down the glass of vodka, check the display.

Paulo.

'Y'alright?'

'I'm okay,' I say.

'Where are you?'

'Home.'

'Doing much?'

I tap ash. 'Going out soon.'

'Right. Look, there was something—'

'How's Frank?'

I hear him shuffling on the other end of the line. 'Yeah, he's fine.'

'Still working?'

'He's out every night, keeping an eye on the Sadler house. You know what he's like, thinks he has to keep the place on a twenty-four-hour surveillance.'

'Nothing happened yet?'

'Not according to Frank, no. Any day now, he says.'

'Right.'

'You ask me, he needs help. He can't be sitting out there all night by himself.'

'He's a grown up.'

'That's not what I mean. He's not sleeping. You know how he's like.'

'Like I said . . . he's a grown up. He can handle . . . himself.'

'Wouldn't hurt for you to help him out, though, would it?'

'I'm busy.'

'On what?'

I blow smoke. 'You know what.'

There's a long silence at the other end. A year ago, I'd have been scared of that silence. It meant Paulo was thinking, probably about my situation. Now, though, he's not thinking about me. He's thinking about himself.

'That paying, is it?' he says.

'Not yet.'

He sighs down the phone at me. 'Look—'

'Doesn't matter.'

'It fuckin' does matter. I want you to—'

'No.'

'Callum, I know what you're doing here. And, y'know, I've been thinking about it. You have to stop it. Right now.'

'You don't . . . make that choice. Not for me.'

'You're doing it for all the—'

'Leave it, mate. I talked to . . . Tiernan.'

'When?'

'The other morning. It's a case.'

'You don't have to do this.'

'I do.' I shift position on the sofa, stretch an aching leg. 'When this is . . . finished. I'll help Frank. You're right. It's not fair.'

Silence at the other end.

'How's it going?' he says.

'Fine.'

'Donkey was here.'

'I know. You gave him . . . my number.'

'I had to.'

'I know,' I say, nodding despite myself. 'It's fine.'

'You talk to him?'

'Yes. It's sorted. He's fine.'

Another sigh. 'You're not going to tell us anything, are you?'

'No.'

'Why not?'

'Because it's not . . . in your best *interests* . . . to know.' I check my watch, and get a sick, fluttery feeling against the pit of my stomach. 'I've got to go.'

'Okay,' he says.

'It'll be fine. Don't worry.'

And I kill the call, put my mobile back on the coffee table. Stare at it, then finish my drink. I probably shouldn't be driving, not with all this alcohol in me, but what the fuck. There's a good chance I'm going out to the Wheatsheaf to my fucking death anyway, right?

I struggle upright, grab my stick. Look down, and I can see the dried blood still on the handle. I bring the stick closer, pick at the blood furiously until it's all gone. I've got to be more careful. You never know what disparate things people like Morris Tiernan is likely to connect, and even if they're just thrown together, there could still be a grain of truth in there that I can't possibly deny. And if that happens, I'm fucked.

I close my eyes for a moment, concentrate on taking deep breaths. I can't go in there nervous. It won't look right. I'll look like I have something to hide, which won't be good. When it feels like my heart rate is back to a normal level, I open my eyes again, limp across to the door, and then I'm gone.

TWENTY-FOUR

Innes

The Wheatsheaf looks different when it's dark and the place is locked down. Nobody on the streets when I pull up in the Micra, which just adds to the desolate look of the place, broken by a single light in the lounge bar, burning yellow. I finish my cigarette in the car, watch the light cut out as someone moves in front of it.

Tiernan's in there. He's not alone.

I try to swallow. Can't, because my mouth is too dry. I flick the cigarette out onto the road as I struggle out of the car.

When I get to the front doors, Brian's already there waiting for me. He stands to one side to let me in, and I see the bloke, size of a fucking house, standing in front of the door to the lounge bar. The house looks at me evenly, then nods to where Tiernan is waiting.

'You want to leave us alone,' says Tiernan to the big guy, in a voice that sounds like he's gone through a pack and a half.

The house leaves, closes the door quietly behind him.

We're alone in the lounge bar, right enough. The shadow must've been Tiernan himself. Now he's settled, watching me, and looks like he's aged five years in twelve hours.

'What do you have?' he says.

'It's been a day.'

'And?' He doesn't take his eyes off me now. Already used to my face and what happens to it when I speak.

'And . . . nothing.'

He remains still. 'You were talking to your copper friend.'

I close my mouth. Rethink my current situation. I can't lie to him, can't say that nothing's happened. So I have to step this up, tell him stuff *has* happened that he needs to know about, that I didn't want to tell him before I had all the facts. Also, I need to watch my fucking back from now on, because he's got people out there following me.

Which makes me wonder how much he already knows.

'I talked . . . to him. Yes.'

'You want a seat?'

Shake my head. 'Rather stand. If you don't mind.'

'No.'

'Can be a little . . . *difficult*. To get up again.' I try a smile, defuse the tension, but it doesn't work. Clear my throat. 'I saw my . . . police contact.'

Tiernan moves one hand like I should continue.

'He told me some things.'

'Which were?'

I look at the floor. 'They have leads.'

'Who?'

'Wouldn't tell me.'

'Then what the fuck good is he?'

I look up. Tiernan's hands have started moving on the table. Tiny little lurches, the fingers tapping each other once, twice.

'They found a hair,' I say.

He stops moving. Then he shakes his head once and quickly, pats his pockets. Brings out his Rothmans and shakes the pack: there's only about five left. 'Do us a favour, hand us one of those glasses over there, would you?'

On the lounge bar are stacks of pint and half-pint glasses that Brian hasn't bothered to shelve yet. Behind the stacks is a dark bar, deep shadows that could hide anything.

Maybe this is it.

'You need to stop,' I say, not moving.

'Excuse me?'

'Having me followed.'

'I didn't.'

'Someone saw me? Talking to my contact?'

'No. You said you were going to do it.' Tiernan has a cigarette in his mouth, a lighter in his hand and he nods towards the glasses. 'Not supposed to smoke in here. Fuckin' law says so, but then the fuckin' law says this place isn't supposed to be open right now.'

I move painfully over to the bar. Stop when I'm at arm's length and grab a half-pinter.

Nothing happens. There's no one behind the bar.

'Callum,' says Tiernan.

I turn. He moves his chin.

'The glass?' he says.

Look down and I'm still holding the half-pint glass. I put it down on the table in front of him, and he lights his Rothmans.

The first drag makes his voice thick. 'You said they found a hair.'

'A long hair,' I say, moving away from the lounge bar. 'Female.'

His eyes flicker narrow for a second. 'Female.'

'Just an assumption. Could be male.'

'How long?'

'I don't know. Shoulder?'

Tiernan visibly retreats into himself for a moment, blowing a long, steady stream of smoke into the air. I stand there, too tense to move, wondering if that'll be enough for him right now. Looks like he's on the right track with it when he asks, 'He have a girlfriend?'

'Only one. That I know of.'

He looks up at me. Shakes his head, but it's a warning. 'No.'

'You asked.'

And as it turns out, the hair *does* belong to Alison, but I'm not going to push that. Not yet. Still, it might be worth sowing a few more seeds.

'I have to tell you . . . when I'm *sure*. At the moment . . . Alison—'

'She's not involved.'

'I know. She told me.'

Tiernan shows his teeth, then moves his attention back to his cigarette. Appears to smoke half of it in one draw. 'When did you see her?'

'Yesterday.'

'What for?'

'Needed to check . . . see if she'd seen Mo.' I wipe my nose and sniff. 'Had to check . . . *everyone*. Didn't I?'

I let that hang in the air between us for a minute or so.

'Was I wrong?'

'She doesn't have anything to do with this.'

'You sure?'

There's an angry glint in his eyes when he looks at me again. 'I'm fuckin' positive. Don't push this.'

An after-growl in his voice, like the roll of thunder after a flash of lightning.

'She said she . . . hadn't seen him. So it doesn't matter.'

'You should've told us you were going to see her.'

'I didn't know I needed . . . *permission*.'

He moves in his chair suddenly. A split-second, and he's a scrapyard dog on the end of a short, thin chain. I flinch.

'Sorry,' I say.

He seems to settle a bit, repeats himself in a tired voice: 'She doesn't have anything to do with this.' He runs a hand briefly over his eyes, as if the glare in here is too much for him. 'She couldn't have. She's working. Did she tell you that?'

'No.'

'She's working. Not much, like. I mean, her age, there's not a lot out there. Working at a salon in Oldham. My day, they were called barbers, but not anymore, right? Don't think they even cut the hair anymore. Not much money, but I help her out, whatever she needs for the kid.' He makes a show of clearing his throat, then swallows whatever he's brought up, takes another drag off the Rothmans. 'She doesn't come into Manchester. That's the deal. She works in Oldham, she lives in Oldham. Whenever she needs something, I go out to see her.'

I nod at him. 'Okay.'

'So she wouldn't come to Manchester for anything anyway. Least of all to kill Mo.' He pulls a quick, disgusted face, and plants the cigarette in his mouth. 'Not without telling us. She wouldn't do it. So there's no point in telling her about . . .' He looks up at me, staring hard. 'She know about him?'

'Yes.'

'You told her?'

I pause for the count of three, as if I'm trying to remember. 'Don't think so.'

'What's that mean?'

'She already . . . seemed to know.'

Tiernan returns his gaze to the pub table. Removes the cigarette and replaces it with his thumbnail, which he nibbles absently. 'Right.'

'Someone must've . . . told her.'

'Yeah. That's what happened.'

The room falls into silence, apart from the slight, quiet click of Tiernan's thumbnail against his teeth.

Then he stops. Looks at the cigarette that's almost burned down to his fingers, and disposes of it in the glass.

'Anything else for me?'

'Not yet. When I find out . . . you find out.'

'You have my number.'

'Yes.'

'Good.'

He nods, sucks his teeth. 'Okay. Then you can go. Keep me up-to-date.'

I head for the door.

'Do yourself a favour, Callum,' he says as I reach the exit to the lounge bar.

I turn to look at him.

'Leave Alison out of this.'

'And if she's . . . involved?'

'She won't be.'

'But if she is?'

He fixes me with a stone glare.

'She isn't. And even if she is, according to the police, she isn't. You understand me? Something comes up in that vein, you come to me, I'll sort it.'

I smile with half my face and indulge him with a slow nod, one hand on the doors to the hall. 'You can trust me.'

'Yeah,' he says. 'I better.'

TWENTY-FIVE

Donkin

Crack of dawn, I was out and about. I had the scraps of a hangover, but I didn't drink that much the night before to put us in a slow mood. A coffee and a sausage and bacon from the dirty van in Levenshulme, and I was ready to get to work.

I couldn't do anything about Paddy Reece, so I just had to fucking suck it up, hope it all went for the best. Maybe if I got a head start on this Tiernan thing, got that wrapped up all nice, I could use it as a cudgel when it came to Kennedy thumbing his fucking nose at us. Either way, when I got the bastard in cuffs after that Scouse twat already jacked in the case, it would look good for me. And I had come to the understanding that anything that made us look good would have to offset that six-storey pile of shit that was looming over us right now.

The only way for us to get in there, though, was to verify what Innes was telling us the other night. When he was talking, I reckoned I played it off alright, acted like I knew what I was supposed to be doing, knew about any scene evidence that he brought up. But the problem was, if it ever came to an arrest, I knew I'd need more proof than the word of a mong jailbird.

Which was why I was in Levenshulme nice and early, and hammering on the door of a bloke called Mickey Watts. About five years ago, the bastard was mixed up with some of the nastiest fuckers in Manchester. He'd always been a bottomfeeder, nothing worth getting too het up over, and mostly forgotten by the dangerous people. But he was still paddling in the same pool, privy to some of the same information. So he was close to being the perfect grass.

Especially now he was straight, working the night shifts down the local Aldi.

Banging on his door now, I reckoned the fucker should still be up. It was early enough, and I remembered when I worked nights, the last thing I wanted to do when I got in was sleep. Normally stayed up for a couple hours drinking, just so's I *could* sleep.

I heard some thumping from behind his front door, and then his mug close to the frosted glass, giving us the eye. He must've seen the suit, not recognised us, because he opened up and pulled a face like he was expecting someone important. Mickey wore an old Sabbath T-shirt, boxer shorts that were hanging a little bit too open in front, and three days' worth of stubble on his face, surrounded by a wiry shock of metaller hair.

First thing out of his mouth was, 'Shit.'

Might as well have been 'good morning' the amount of time people greeted us like that. I grinned at him. 'Need a word with you.'

'I just got in.'

'You work in your skivvies, then?'

'You know what I mean.'

I waved him back inside, stepped into the hallway. As I was closing the door behind us, blocking out all the light that came into this place, I said, 'Won't take a minute, I promise.'

He was already heading up towards the kitchen. 'You'll want a brew.'

'Wouldn't say no.'

Thing was with me and Mickey, there'd never been any real aggro between us. Like I said, he was a bottomfeeder and, as such, he never really gave a fuck for the people he helped put in the jail, just as long as he wasn't fingered as a grass. All Mickey Watts really cared about was that expensive stereo system I caught a glimpse of as I was walking up the hall to the kitchen. He loved his music, did our Mickey. Fucking right headbanger he was an' all. That Sabbath T-shirt was a rare nod to the fucking mainstream for Mickey. Norwegian death metal, speed and thrash from places I couldn't point on a map. The bloke was only a couple years younger than me, made us feel like his dad.

Mickey put his back to the kitchen counter, pointed at the table and chairs. 'You still milk and four?'

'Three.'

'Cutting down?'

I patted my gut. 'Yeah.'

'So what is it, Detective? Who's pissed you off today?'

'No one.'

The kettle bubbled behind him. Mickey grabbed two mugs, dropped tea bags into each. 'Aye, right. You want information on someone so's you can fuck them over.'

'Just need to ask 'em a few questions,' I said, sitting at the table. I held out my baccy tin. Mickey shook his head. I rolled a cigarette. 'Need to talk to one of Mo Tiernan's lads.'

'Why?'

'None of your fuckin' business.'

He poured water on the tea bags, went to his fridge. 'Just wondering. Because what I heard was that Mo was out of the game, and so were his boys.'

'Yeah?'

'Nobody's seen Mo for a while.'

'What about his lads? Which ones do you know are straight?'

Mickey dumped tea bags, started shovelling sugar into my brew. 'Don't know anything about Baz, but I think Kevin Ross is working out at the Trafford Centre.'

'Doing what?'

'Currys. Selling tellies for a living.'

'Right, get us the Yellow Pages, then.'

Mickey stopped making the brews, shook his head at us, then trudged through into the hall. Came back and dumped the Yellow

Pages on the kitchen table. I blew smoke and pulled it open. Looked for Currys' number. When I found it, I pulled out my mobile. Rang for ages before someone picked up. Nice and lazy did it.

'That Currys?' I said.

'Yeah.'

'You got a Kevin Ross working there?'

'Who's calling, please?'

'Just answer the fuckin' question.'

There was a cough, and I could tell whoever this arsehole was on the line, he was wondering who the fuck I was, and whether he should hang up. My guess was Rossie worked in a place where they had an idea of his past, which was why this conversation was still taking place. Nobody wanted to be the one to hang up on the bloke who'd come round and take their fucking kneecaps.

Then again, nobody wanted to be the bloke who grassed out a colleague.

Rossie couldn't have been employee of the month, though, because this bloke said, 'Yeah, he works here.'

'He in today?'

'You want to speak to him?'

'In person. Who're you?'

Another pause. Wondering if he should give a false name.

'Don't fuckin' lie to us, son.'

'Kyle,' he said.

'Kyle? That your real name?'

'Yeah,' he said. 'I'm the manager.'

'Good.'

And I hung up. Mickey put a brew down on the table next to us. I looked up at him. Slammed the Yellow Pages closed and flicked ash into the brew he made us. 'No time for that, Mickey. Ta, anyway.'

'Don't know why I fuckin' bother,' he said.

I stood up and patted him on the cheek. When I did, more ash fell off my ciggie onto the table. 'Because you fuckin' love us, you old tart.'

'You know how much milk costs?'

I stuck my cigarette back in my gob, reached into my jacket. Wasn't usual, but I pulled out my wallet, chucked him a twenty, squinted against the smoke. 'Any more than that?'

'You never paid us before.'

I tweaked the ciggie from my mouth again, prodded the twenty. 'Times are changing, Mickey. Can't go around being a tightarse my whole life. Better I pay you lads every now and then, compensation for putting you out if the information's any good.'

He was smiling at us, his eyebrows high. 'And if it isn't?'

I was already halfway down the hall. 'If it isn't, Mickey old son, I'll come back and I'll beat seven shades of shite out of you.'

That got him nodding. Some things never changed. But I did want to treat my grasses better if I could, maybe get the rep for being a fair copper. It was a new leaf, and probably only turned because I was in a good mood.

We'd see what Rossie had to say for himself. Because the thing about good moods was they had a habit of changing if someone started playing the cunt.

TWENTY-SIX

Donkin

Normally the last place I wanted to go was the bastard Trafford Centre. Swear to God, it was the kind of place that'd send anyone loopy if they were of a mind. Part of me reckoned if I ever did enough bad stuff in my time to be sent to Hell, it'd look something like that place. Maybe a degree or two colder, seeing as they always kept the heating ramped right the fuck up.

But work was work.

I swung off Junction 9, headed right for the car parks. But because this was the Trafford Centre on a Saturday fucking morning, the place was heaving. Took us a good fifteen minutes of aimless driving before I found a space close enough to the shopping centre and not flanked by arseholes. I parked the car between a Corsa and a Ka, couple of bleeding heart liberal motors, and their owners easily scared if need be. Nobody would dare scratch us up there.

As I walked out into the main mall, I was reminded why I hated this bastard place so much. Not even double digits into November – not even fucking bonfire night yet – and they already had their Christmas decs up. More than that, over the railing I could see a Santa's grotto laid out on the ground floor. A sign outside that said it cost nine quid to see Santa and get a present. Ya fucker, it made us sick. Wouldn't have minded so much if the grotto looked like a fucking grotto, but I'd seen bus shelters look more festive. I supposed it didn't matter. Wasn't like I was going to take Shannon down there. Not that I would've. My experience was, you didn't want to know which itinerant swine they got in to play Santa. Fucking gypsies looking for a Christmas job, and none of them police-checked like they were supposed to be.

Went up to one of those big mall maps, took us about five seconds to find the Currys on it. Took about an hour to find it in real life. By the time I got there, I was knackered and ready to twat the first person who gave us any grief. Which, considering my new leaf and everything, was a bit unfortunate. Even more unfortunate as I was bombarded by these arseholes who'd had their peripheral fucking vision removed. I pushed my way across the concourse, got myself a couple of swear words into the bargain, but they were gone by the time I'd managed to turn.

I kept a tight face as I went into Currys. Looked around for Kevin Ross. Been that long, and I only really knew him in passing, so I didn't think I'd recognise him right off the bat. Didn't matter, though – all I had to do was look for a bloke with the word KEVIN on his tit.

'Help you, sir?'

Now there was someone I did recognise. Kyle. Supposedly the manager, though he couldn't have been much older than the wank I had the other night. I showed him my ID. 'We talked earlier.'

He blinked, tried to smile. Obviously didn't place us.

'Kevin Ross?' I said.

Kyle opened his gob wide in an O, rolled his narrow shoulders, trying to add another couple of inches to his height. It didn't work. 'I didn't know that was you. Was there something in particular you wanted to talk to him about?'

'I'd need to talk with him about that.'

'You can tell me.'

'It's confidential.'

Pulled this face, like, did I not know who I was talking to? 'I'm his manager. If he's done anything—'

'You're fuckin' joking us.' I wondered how much of a fucking loser you had to be in order to have a manager that was half your age. Then I remembered DCI Ali, and rethought the situation. 'Alright, if you're his manager, then you can point him out to us.'

'Yeah, but—'

'Here,' I said. 'Three choices. Point him out, fetch the lad, or I'll go looking for him. Up to you.'

Kyle looked behind him at the back of the shop, a door marked STAFF ONLY, and I saw this quick pull on his face that made us think he'd been through this before.

'Back there, is he?'

Kyle nodded.

'Anyone else been around here I should know about?'

'No, officer.'

'Detective. You saw the fuckin' ID.'

'Sorry. *Detective.* Nobody's been talking to him. Just, if you could try to remember that we're running a business out front.'

Which meant, try not to batter him so hard he makes a lot of noise and scares off the punters. I grinned at Kyle, put a finger on my lips, then went for the back office. Rolled my head, then kicked open the door. It bounced off the inside wall. I could hear Kyle start to say something as I strode into the staff room.

Ross was in the corner, sat reading some film magazine with his legs propped up on a plastic chair. He was already staring at us when I came in. The other bloke in there, black fella with the wide eyes on him like he thought I was there for him. He didn't know what to do; I was blocking the only exit to the room. I clocked his name tag – KWAME – and made a quick mental note. Probably a fucking illegal, so it never hurt to remember the name and the face.

Showed Kwame my ID. 'Take it outside, mate.'

He did as he was told. Ross put down his magazine.

'Aw, fuck,' he said. 'It's me you want to talk to, is it?'

Waited until Kwame was well out of the room, then I closed the door. 'Kevin Ross, is it?'

He looked like he wanted to shift his feet from the chair, like he was suddenly uncomfortable, but I'd already got too close to him. If he moved, he'd have to do it slowly in case I took a sudden movement to mean resisting arrest. The lad had been through all this before, knew the tune. Knew that when someone kicked in the door and called you by your court name, you had to take things easy or else have your arse handed to you.

'Detective Sergeant Donkin,' I said, holding up the ID. 'Need to ask you a few questions, Kevin.'

His arse got busy gobbling his skivvies. 'What's this about?'

I reached forward, took the magazine from his lap, dumped it on the bench next to him. Then I tapped my ID wallet against his knees. That gave him the permission he needed to move his legs off the chair so's I could sit down. I grabbed the seat, pulled it in close and backwards, so I was riding it with the hard plastic bit in front of us. A bit of protection, just in case, and I was so close there was no way around us. I looked at Ross for a long time, one of those big stares that make them feel like I'm staring right into their brains.

'So,' I said. 'Rossie.'

Rossie kept it shut. But the sound of his old name made him swallow. I reached into my jacket pocket, pulled out a piece of paper with Mo's address written on it. I'd written it earlier, and now I held it up to Rossie like it was valuable evidence.

'You know this address?' I said.

He started to shake his head.

'Don't fuckin' lie to us already, mate.'

'I don't know it.'

'You didn't look at it.'

He made a show of reading the address. 'I don't know it.'

I smiled. What the fuck. I tried, didn't I?

I reached out quick, grabbed Rossie's face with my free hand and squeezed his cheeks up so he looked like a Cabbage Patch Kid. He couldn't deny anything now I had his jaw pinched. He struggled a little bit. Not too much. Didn't want the situation to escalate. In the end, and because I didn't want to laugh at the stupid face he was pulling, I had to let go. He turned away from us, rubbed his cheeks.

'You know the address,' I said.

'Yeah, alright.' Wondering what that meant.

'So who lives there?'

Narrowed his eyes when he said, 'It's Mo, isn't it? What the fuck's he done?'

'Died,' I said.

The look on Rossie's face told us he didn't know about it. But it wasn't necessarily news to him, either.

'So your involvement in this now looks suspicious, son.'

He shook his head. 'I didn't have nowt to do with it.'

'You've been to his last known, though.'

'No.'

'Aw, Kevin, we were doing so well.'

'Alright, but only like fuckin' *once* or something.'

'That's all it took.'

'I didn't do nowt, man. I didn't touch him.'

'Touch him?'

Rossie closed his eyes and his mouth at the same time. I saw the muscles working in his jaw. He repeated himself like he was already self-editing. 'I didn't do nowt.'

'You know someone *touched* him, though, right? I mean, I only said he died.'

'No.'

I pointed at him. 'You said *you* never touched him.'

'Figure of fuckin' speech.'

'And you know where he lived. So let's just say for sake of fuckin' argument that we found Mo Tiernan beaten to death at that address. How would you join the dots, son?'

'I . . . didn't know that.'

'That he was dead or that we found him?'

'Either one, man.' Rossie stared at us. 'I'm not involved. You know I'm not involved, this is a fuckin' put-up job. I'm straight now, you ask anyone. Got a girlfriend, got a kid, the last thing I'm—'

'But you were hanging round a shithole like Sutpen Court.'

'Here, Mo was living there for a while, alright? You want to talk to someone about this, you talk to fuckin' Baz.'

'I don't want a word with Baz, Kevin.'

'I didn't fuckin' *do* it.'

'Here, keep it down. Your man Kyle out there, he's this close to handing you your P45. He hears you kicking off in the break room, upsetting the fuckin' customers and talking back to a copper, he's going to think you're not as stable as you've been letting on.'

Rossie fell into a sulk. 'I got a girlfriend—'

'You'll be lucky to keep your right hand in a minute, son.'

'I got a flat. I got a mortgage. It's different for me now. I didn't want Mo dead. Couldn't give a fuck. He's not in my life.'

'Because he's dead.'

He frowned hard at us, like he didn't know if he was playing this right. Or wondering what the fuck he thought *I* was playing at. Because he was catching on to that idea that I was trying to fit him up for Mo's death.

'Wait a second—'

'I'm just joking,' I sat straight on the chair, smiling at him. 'Reckon I can smoke in here?'

'We have to go outside.'

'Fuckin' pansy rules, eh?' I pulled out a pre-made, lit it up. Blew smoke and waited for the alarms and sprinklers to go off. After about thirty seconds of nothing happening, I nodded at Rossie. 'Tell you, you *do* know something about this, Kevin. Might not know anything about, say, the circumstances of the lad's death, but you could know something important about his *life*.' I blew smoke at him. 'You get me?'

'I don't know what you want to hear.'

'Well, let's try this for first up: who'd want to kill Mo Tiernan?'

He shrugged. 'Take your pick.'

'I already did.' I stared at him, waggled one finger at him. 'Came up with you.'

'Then talk to Baz. He's still involved.'

'Where?'

'The Harvester.'

'The one on Gibson?'

He nodded. I took a drag. Fucking hell. I thought they'd pulled that shitheap down years ago.

'Right,' I said. 'Anyone else spring to mind?'

Rossie looked at the film magazine. The front cover had some skinny bloke with a gun in his hand, looked bigger than him. 'You talked to Innes?'

'You think he has something to do with it?'

'Wouldn't put it past him. If he's the one told you to come to me, then he's trying to pin it on someone, isn't he?'

'You spoke to him recently?'

'Not in fuckin' ages,' he said, looking up at us now. 'Fact, the last time I remember seeing him, he was beating the shit out of Mo. Threatened to kill him if he ever clapped eyes on him again.'

'Fuck off,' I said.

'Pub full of witnesses.'

'What happened?'

Rossie blinked hard. Like, *who the fuck are you if you don't already know this?*

'What, you don't want to tell us?' Getting wound up now. Not one of my fucking grasses thought to tell us this whenever it happened, and I hated getting old news. 'Because we don't have to carry this on here, y'know. You can even get yourself a fuckin' brief.'

'We burned it.'

'Back up. I need specifics. Who burned what?'

'Me. Baz. Mo. Mostly Baz. Burned the club.' And then, quickly, 'But it was Mo's idea, man. Had this thing about the poof who owned it on account of the poof broke his finger ages ago. And you know Mo could hold a grudge forever.'

'Right, and Innes and the poof are close.'

'You ask me, they're more than that.'

'How so?'

'Seen that poof, he *moons* over Innes. And you should've seen Innes when he started in on Mo.'

I watched Rossie. When I heard stuff like this, stuff that sounded too good to be true, most of the time it *was* too good to be true. But if it held up . . .

'And that's just the last time I saw him,' said Rossie. 'There's all that shite with Mo's sister an' all.'

'What, he fucked Mo's sister?'

Rossie laughed so hard, I moved without thinking and back-handed the cunt across the face. He snapped to one side, breathed out like he had something hot in his mouth.

I backed off, straightened up, and waited for the red to fade from his cheek.

'Don't fuck us about,' I told him. 'Now, what about Mo's sister?'

'He went to Newcastle to get her back.'

Far as I knew, Innes went to Newcastle to avoid a fucking murder collar. Because I was tagging him on this stab case I was working. That was what I thought at the time, anyway. I pulled the rollie from my mouth, dropped it on the floor and stepped. Dug around in my pocket until I found my old notepad, moved my chin at Rossie.

'Right, Kevin. Looks like I've been out of the fuckin' loop, doesn't it? So why don't you fill us in about what happened in Newcastle then, eh?'

'I should really be back on the floor by now.'

Rossie looked at the exit. I caught his eye.

'Here, don't worry about your manager, son, worry about me.' I flipped to a clean page. 'Now, don't fuck about, start at the beginning, and I'll chip in if I have any questions.'

TWENTY-SEVEN

Donkin

As Rossie talked, it turned out that I had *plenty* of questions. At one point, that twat manager came in to check up on him. I think he saw the mark on Rossie's face, because he gave us this sickly smile, and then made his excuses. Once he'd gone, I nodded at Rossie to continue.

And what a fucking story. Gutted us that I didn't know any of this. You think you're in the fucking loop and then something like this crops up. And it hacked us off no end, because if I'd known all this shite about Innes and Mo Tiernan up in Newcastle, if I'd known about what'd happened to the poof's club, I would've had motive from the fucking get-go. So instead of having to chase it round the houses now, I could've had Innes on the scene with the body, before I got myself fucking suspended.

When I finished with Rossie, he looked relieved. I was getting up when his mobile rang. The ringtone was some kid singing 'Kyle's Mom's A Bitch'. Obviously this lad felt the same as I did about his manager.

'Keep your nose clean, Kevin,' I said.

He didn't reply, just nodded and slowly removed his phone from his jacket pocket, waiting for me to leave so he could answer it.

When I got to the door, he said, 'Alright, babes?'

I glanced at him with one eyebrow raised, but he was already caught up talking to his missus. Then I snorted a laugh and left.

Amazed us how blokes gave themselves up to women like that, all twisted up because they know they haven't answered the fucking phone quick enough.

Anyway. I had work to do.

Once I got back to find my car still pristine, I drove out to the Harvester.

Christ, when I thought it'd been pulled down, I wasn't all wrong.

The place had that ingrained stink of sweat, booze and piss from the gents. The women's toilets were there for show only. Maybe for the fifteen-minute brassers to wash their mouths out after a five-pound blowjob. I corralled the three blokes who looked like they spent the most time in here, bought them all a pint and a chaser each, sat them down and asked about Innes.

Yes, he'd been in. Yes, he'd done what Rossie told us he did.

'Just come in, son. Grabbed yon young lad and yanked him over the table, like.'

'Aye, beat shite out of him.'

'Horrible. I had to have another short.'

Not only that, but Innes had been in recently, too. Talking to some lad called Baz. Guessed it was the same Baz that Rossie was going on about, one of Mo Tiernan's mates. But this lad wasn't close to being suspect in my mind, despite what Rossie might've alluded to earlier on. Because when they mentioned Baz, again it was in the context of him being at the mercy of Innes.

Innes was the key. Innes was the fucking dangerous one.

'Came in,' said this bloke in an anorak that was stained yellow down one side, 'and he wanted to talk to Baz. Then they talked for a bit, but Baz wasn't having none of it, because he's a fuckin' miserable cunt sometimes, so he went off to the bog. And when he came back this lad just went mental.'

A bloke in a tweed jacket barked something at us from the corner of the room.

'Don't mind Hamish. He's harmless.'

'I don't,' I said. 'How d'you mean, mental?'

And I got the whole story. Baz ordering a pint, Innes lashing out at him. The mess, the confusion and then Innes shouting that he was working for Morris Tiernan.

I nodded, took it all in. Bought another round for the barflies before I left the pub. Then I took a nice big deep breath of fresh air soon as I stepped outside.

If I was pissed off at not being kept in the loop, this was a bit more cheering. There was no way Kennedy'd have this information, and he wouldn't bother his arse to find it out. Which meant I was still working on an advantage.

Except for one thing: I hadn't looked at the scene.

On the way to Sutpen Court, I thought about calling Adams, see if he could get us any information on the people interviewed around the scene. Then I remembered that there was no way he'd help us out. No, that avenue was pretty much fucking bricked up as far as I was concerned. There were some blokes out there, they were blinkered to the truth about their colleagues. And it was easier, obviously, for Adams to side with the common view of us, which was that I was a fuck-up and not to be trusted.

But that was the problem with following majority opinion. It was general, and most times wrong.

Got to Miles Platting, and I left the Granada out in the open. As I passed the bonnet, I noticed the dirt. I wrote UNMARKED POLICE CAR in the shit. Better than any fucking car alarm round here, because this lot knew better than to fuck with a CID vehicle. Especially mine.

I took the lift to the sixth floor. When the doors slid open, I was gasping for breath. It smelled like someone had died in that fucking box and the council hadn't scrubbed it out properly. I coughed, sent the lift back to the ground floor. Wiped my nose and looked around at the corridor that led down to Mo Tiernan's last known. There was still tape on the door even though the SOCOs were long gone. I bent under the tape, pushed the door open and onto a crime scene. Typical of Kennedy, he'd left it open apart from the tape. The bastard really didn't care.

The flat was a four-room shithole: bathroom, kitchen, living room and bedroom, or at least what I thought was supposed to be a bedroom. Mo had brought a mattress out to the living room. What looked like shit smeared on the wallpaper in here, the stink of death and more. The mattress had a deep red stain and indentation where Mo's head had been. I looked closer, saw the splatters on either side, tracked out onto the carpet. I wanted to open the window, but couldn't touch anything, just in case.

Something wrong about that blood. A lot of it stained deep in one place, the rest light and splattered. Didn't know what it meant, but I did know it looked weird. I knew that Kennedy should've picked up on it, and he had the resources to tell us what happened. But there was no way he'd share, especially if he already had it in his head that this was something other than a fucking murder. He was making his case, not finding out the truth.

I turned back to the door. Ducked under the tape as I left, heard noises coming from behind one of the doors. Sounded like Jeremy Kyle, the cunt. I went straight up, looked for a doorbell, put fist to wood when I didn't find one.

Yeah, it was definitely Jeremy Kyle. Chucking shit at some errant dad, or some dirty fat slut who got herself knocked up sixteen times, lived solely on benefits and didn't have no regrets about the way her life turned out.

Another battery, louder this time. And somewhere inside I heard someone swearing loud. Questions asked in a high, trembling voice that couldn't have been younger than eighty, and then the heavy footsteps of a fat person coming my way.

'Who is it?' came through the door.

Held up my ID to the peephole. 'Police.'

'*Fuck's* sake.'

'Open up.'

'Fuckin'—'

'You want me to kick the door in, son?'

'*No.*' There was the sound of someone jerking at chains, smacking deadbolts and generally acting like a pissed-off kid. 'Hang on.'

I hung on. A couple more sounds like someone scraping rusty nails together, and the door opened a crack.

'Let's see that again,' said what appeared to be a fucking toddler, but six foot and morbidly obese.

Showed him my ID again. He squinted at it, looked like he needed glasses. Then he shook his head.

'I already told you lot what I seen,' he said.

'I understand that.'

'Nowt you can ask us, I haven't already been told.'

I looked behind him, caught a draught that smelled like pizza. Made us hungry and pissed off at the same time. 'You told me personally, did you?'

'I don't—'

'Because if I didn't hear it personally, it doesn't matter.' I smiled, but made it obvious that I didn't mean it. 'Sorry to tear you away from Jeremy.'

'My mam likes it.'

'Bit loud for me, like.'

He puckered his lips, had dimples in his cheeks when he said, 'She's deaf.'

Then it wouldn't matter how loud it was, but I didn't say it. Instead, I squared my shoulders and gave him my best copper look, made it clear that I wasn't going door-to-door making fucking small talk. 'So what did *you* hear?'

'Nowt much,' he said.

'But something.'

He stuck his head out from the door, nodded it at Mo's squat. 'Heard someone go in there.' Back to me. 'That's all I heard.'

'Someone go in? You never heard them come out?'

'Nah.'

'When was this?'

'Thursday night.'

'What time?'

'About halfway through *First Wives' Club*.'

'Which was?'

'I dunno. Halfways through.'

'And you just *heard* someone?'

'Yeah.'

'Were they limping?'

The toddler tasted his bottom lip, scrunched up his face. 'How'm I supposed to know?'

'It'd sound different.'

'I don't know. I heard someone.'

'Not limping?'

'Here, I don't go looking for trouble, know what I mean? I live here, I can't afford to start worrying about my neighbours, you get me? If he was limping, I didn't hear it, I didn't see it, I didn't have nowt to do with it. And I told all this to the other coppers, so unless you're wanting to take us down the nick, I'm going to close this door on you and get back to my mam before she worries where I am.'

He looked at us, waiting for a response that he could kick off to. I didn't give him it, buttoned my jacket, said, 'Thanks for your time.'

I headed back to the lift, thought better and switched to the stairs. Then I heard the soft snick of the door closing, and the barrage of locks slamming across that followed. I pulled out my baccy tin, took enough tobacco to roll a thin one as I took the stairs slow.

The rest of the flats up here were boarded up. Empty. Squats with people in them that shouldn't have been there. And the only other bastard up there only heard a couple of footsteps, couldn't even confirm that it was Innes. At the moment, all I had was my word against his that he was there. And as much as I didn't want to admit it, it looked like his word would win the day.

I stopped when I hit the next landing. Lit the cigarette. Didn't know how far up or down I was. Saw blood on the railing. Wasn't necessarily from Mo, or Innes. Dried in what looked like a partial handprint, mind.

And then it fucking hit us. Hard, like if a freight train and a Mack truck had a fucking baby.

That *was* Mo Tiernan's blood. And it *had* come from Callum Innes's hand.

Because I remembered the cunt's walking stick, remembered seeing something dark on the handle, smudges down at the other end. The fucker'd used it as a club on something. Not such a stretch to connect a club and the mincemeat that was Mo Tiernan's face.

Which could only mean one thing: Callum Innes killed Mo Tiernan.

TWENTY-EIGHT

Innes

I hear Donkey before I see him. There's the roar of an engine, a screech of tyres, and one of the lads comes barrelling through the doors, yelling about the five-oh like he's a dealer in the fucking projects. Paulo's head snaps up and he looks at the double doors. I'm already at the door to the office with a sick, sinking feeling in my gut.

This is it. What I've been afraid of. I've run out of time.

Donkey barges through the doors, red in the face with a full shine of a sweat going. And he's looking for someone.

No prizes for guessing who.

'You want me to do something?' says Paulo.

'No. It's okay.'

I've got a ton of excuses that I can hand Paulo, but there's not one of them that'll stick any longer than a second and a half. Which is about the length of time it takes Donkey to make it across the gym.

I throw up a hand, palm out. 'Hang on.'

He grabs my wrist, yanks it down and twists me round before I get a chance to breathe out. Then it's a short trip into the wall as I feel fingers grab at the back of my skull. I feel the pressure on my chest as Donkey holds me in place, feel my breathing become shallow.

'Whoa,' says Paulo. 'The fuck you think you're doing?'

I hear Donkey shout, 'You back the fuck off, Gray. I didn't know any better I could have you in an' all.'

'Have me in?' I say.

He leans close to my ear. 'What d'you think, I'm fuckin' *daft*, Innes?'

'I don't—'

'You must think I'm a right fuckin' idiot, eh? That I'm not going to ask questions? That I'm not going to know about what happened up in Newcastle?'

I'd shake my head, but my face is pressed hard against the wall. 'Wait.'

'I know all about you, you fuckin' bastard,' he says. 'You and Mo, and his fuckin' *sister*.'

I don't say anything.

'And I know that I'm well within my fuckin' rights to bring you in on it.'

He wrenches me from the wall and I stumble forward, my nose almost to the fucking floor. My right leg goes out from under me, and Donkey adjusts his grip, must put both hands on my collar, because I hear some tearing material and feel myself skimming the wood floor. He hauls me to the double doors, kicks them open and throws me into the small foyer. I throw up my hands again. Glance behind him, and I see my walking stick lying on the floor in the gym.

'*Wait*,' I say. 'Please.'

He kicks me in the face. Once and hard, but once and hard is all it takes. I hit the deck, stare at an upside-down sky for a few moments before he shouts something at me that I can't make out through the ringing in my ears, and then he starts planting his shoes in my ribs.

I black out for a second. I think it's a second, anyway. Could well be an hour. And suddenly the blows give out, only the pain remaining. I open my eyes, and the sky is a touch darker, looks like it's going to rain. As the whoosh in my ears gives out to shouting voices, I turn my head in that direction.

Paulo has Donkey cornered against his Granada. Donkey's pointing at me, Paulo's in his face. I blink and squint through my roiling vision, pull myself over onto my side and get a punch of agony when I try to breathe, praying that Donkey hasn't broken a rib with those cheap fucking shoes of his. I manage to get onto my hands and knees, blink away the tears, bring one scuffed hand across a bleeding nose.

Then I realise that I'm not the only one bleeding here. As I focus on Donkey, I realise he's holding a hand to his face, and there's that brown opaque stain running over his mouth and chin that means Paulo's planted a hard right on him. I struggle getting up to my feet, have to use the wall as a guide.

'Get the fuck off my property, Sergeant.' Paulo's pointing at Donkey, and I can see the blood on his knuckles. 'I see you around here again, I'll beat fuck out of you.'

'Can't do that,' says Donkey.

'I can do whatever the fuck I want to do.'

Then Paulo drops his finger, moves in closer to Donkey. For a second, I think Paulo's going to kiss him, the way he smiles. But then he says something quietly to Donkey, and Donkey's face goes even paler under the bloodstain. Paulo backs off a couple of steps, the remnants of the smile still pulling his lips tight. He raises both eyebrows at Donkey.

'You get me?' he says.

I lean against the wall, press a knuckle to one nostril that refuses to stop bleeding, wheeze through battered lungs. Then something rattles that I have to cough up. The sound brings Donkey's attention. We stare at each other.

'Go home,' Paulo says to Donkey.

Donkey snaps back a glare at Paulo, then gets into his car, slamming the driver's door as he gets behind the wheel. There's a brief swell of muffled music as Donkey turns the ignition. Sounds like Norah Jones, which would be weird if it wasn't Donkey at the wheel.

I watch him roar off, spit blood at the ground. The gob hits and splatters, and I'm reminded of Mo Tiernan again. Paulo turns away from the road, heads my way, shaking his head at the state I'm in.

'You hit him,' I say.

'It's okay.' Getting a closer look, he says, 'Jesus Christ. That fuckin'—'

'It's not okay.' Shake my head. 'He's a copper. He's a cunt. The two don't mix . . . with a punch.'

'Really, it's fine. Let's get you indoors.'

Paulo puts my arm around his shoulders and hunkers down, puts his arm around my waist. He squeezes my side too hard and I flinch away from him, grunting in pain.

'Sorry,' he says.

'He'll be back.'

'No, he won't.'

I cough and it hurts like fuck. What's the point in me doing everything I've done, if Paulo's just going to plant one on Donkey and ruin it all. 'He *will*. I know how—'

'He's not going to do anything, Callum.'

'He won't stay . . . scared.'

'He's not scared.' We reach the office. Paulo nudges open the door and eases me over to my chair. Then he goes to retrieve my walking stick.

'Then how?'

He appears in the doorway again, breathes out. 'I had my suspicions.'

'About what?'

'He's not on duty,' says Paulo.

'That doesn't matter—'

'I called the police station, thought it was odd that he backed down so quick when he was around, y'know. And I was going to put in a complaint, anyway.' He hands me my walking stick. 'Fucker's been suspended, hasn't he?'

I look at Paulo. Doesn't look like he's pulling my leg, and this would be a weird fucking joke if he was. But it can't be right, either. Donkey's never been suspended his entire career. Doesn't matter what heinous shite he's been accused of through the years, nobody's ever had the balls to call him on it, or do anything about it.

'What for?' I say.

'Don't know, they wouldn't tell me.'

No, they wouldn't, right enough. I shake my head, still can't believe it. There's me, willingly giving Donkey information when he's not in any position to do anything about it. Not officially, anyway. Which makes him fucking dangerous to my situation. Extremely dangerous.

'You going to be okay?' says Paulo. 'Look like you could use a once-over at the hospital.'

'Nah, I should be . . . alright.'

'He break anything?'

'Don't think so.'

'You sure?' Paulo's pulling that old familiar face again. The worried look, the one he reserves for whenever I get my arse kicked. I'll admit, it's been a while since I've seen it. Not since he saw me the first time in the hospital after the stroke. And I'll admit this, too: I've kind of missed it.

'Yeah,' I say. 'I'm fine. A brew . . . would be good.'

'Course, right,' says Paulo.

And off he goes. Soon as he's out the door, I pick out my mobile. Turn it on, and it seems like it still works, which is good. I stare at the display, scroll through my contacts and think about what damage Donkey's already done.

Time to put an end to it.

Used to be, you wanted to speak to Morris Tiernan, you had to call the Wheatsheaf and wait for Brian the landlord to get his arse in gear, pick up the phone. Then you had to put up with him swearing blind that Tiernan wasn't on the premises when it was patently fucking obvious that wasn't the case. Then, once you'd managed to threaten your way into a conversation with the man himself, Tiernan would be full of hell, because the last thing he liked doing was talk on the phone. His mood was a throwback to the party line days, when they were still trying to pin the scally Godfather tag onto him.

But I'm above all that now. Now, I have a direct line to the man. And as I punch the numbers, I don't know if that's a sign that it's already too late for me.

'Yeah,' he says after two rings.

'We need to talk.'

'Urgent?'

'Yeah.'

'Northside tonight. Seven sharp.'

And he hangs up.

TWENTY-NINE

Donkin

Fuck.

Fucking *stupid*. Fucking idiotic fucking thing to do.

Hindsight kicked in, my blood settled to a low simmer, and the only thing I could think of was how fucking daft I'd been. I needed to watch that. Christ, I'd been told enough times. It was like calling your mother a cunt – soon as you said it, you wished you could take it back.

Anyway. My point was, I never got any warning when I lost it. The counsellor, that jumped-up, pot-bellied little prick with a degree and that expensive-looking ballpoint he kept clicking when I talked, that little fuck said that I'd see something, I'd hear something, I'd *feel* something when I was about to lose control.

'When you hit your wife . . .' he'd start.

And that was usually the moment I got up and left the room.

Because if I'd just been able to talk to Annie after it happened, if she hadn't up and disappeared for a month after, took the kid with her, then we might've been able to sort stuff out. The problem was, she was jittery about shite like that, and I knew it. Bad history, worse boyfriends, and back in the day, I was a bloke like a knight in shining armour, took care of a couple of them ex-boyfriends for her. She didn't know when she met me that I was a copper on account of my nose was burning with some seriously nasty coke a wog dealer'd try to palm off on us. Winston never found out I was blue until much later on, never suspected a thing until I caught him on the back end of a steep coke slide, nudging into OD territory, and then I turned him into a prize grass. But when Annie found us with frosted nostrils and *then* clocked that I was a copper, well, that was her wet as a Manc summer.

According to her, she'd always had a thing for the bad boy.

But apparently the bad boy shite wore thin fast as you liked. People got older, and it became too much of an effort to keep up the drama when you spent most of your working day arse-deep in the filth of the city. She got bored and we had a kid, thought that would sort it. It didn't, just bolstered her side of the fucking argument, because it turned out to be a girl who grew to hate us just as much as Annie did. Shannon didn't get the whole copper thing, didn't realise that I wasn't oppressing her and her middle-class Goth mates.

No, wait, I remembered. They weren't Goths. They were something else: *emo*. Like Goths but without the commitment.

Anyway, my home life wasn't great. That should've been a sign. But when you're in it, you don't *see* it. I mean, it was only in fucking hindsight that I saw the cables fray, but it was all I could do to keep my work head on.

Then I hit her.

Once, but that was all it took, and as soon as I did it, I saw all those bad memories dredged up in a second. And she looked at us like she was shocked to see us turn into a mixture of every single bad-beat boyfriend she ever had.

She went round her sister's that night, took Shannon with her. I sat and decided to drink myself comatose with whatever we had left in the kitchen cupboard, which turned out to be half a bottle of Gordon's and some Pimm's.

And that was the fucking start of it all.

She only came back once, and she cleaned the place out – anything she could lift and carry was gone. Got off shift one night, come home to find the place gutted. Only the big items of furniture left, but they were still her taste, so it looked like someone'd burgled us, ripped the heart out of my home.

I got angry. Yeah, that was bound to happen. Called her sister's, called her mam's, didn't talk to her at either place. She'd moved out, gone on and got herself a new flat with Shannon. Hadn't took her that long, either.

So I got angrier, and then that subsided into 'good riddance to bad rubbish'. Because then I got to do all the shite that married men couldn't do. I could eat kebabs in the front room, drink as much as I fucking wanted without the eye-rolls and the tuts. I got to smoke big fat cigars in the house, instead of shivering my balls off in the back yard, and I got a whole big bed to myself at nights, instead of creeping upstairs to find out she'd gone all diagonal on us.

Then it turned into me sitting at home and staring at a dead telly. A habit of watching the screen even when the thing wasn't turned on. After a while, I heard noises in the house that I'd never heard before. At first, I thought it was just the telly next door: the bloke who lived next to us was old and deaf as. But I didn't do anything about it, thinking if I had the energy to turn on my telly I wouldn't hear *him*.

The truth was, I liked hearing the noise from next door. It was something I couldn't control. Made us feel like there was someone else in the house, almost. And it made the drinking I was doing seem less desperate. Otherwise it was us pissed in the front room with the big light on because the bulbs'd gone in the lamps and I couldn't be arsed remembering to replace them.

I was wrong to hit Annie. I knew that. I wasn't fucking daft. But the problem was, I didn't know I was doing it until it was over.

I knew what people called us down the nick, knew what they thought about us. It never really bothered us before, because I always knew that however I did the job, it got results. Brass didn't bother with us because of that, and fuck the rest of them – they never had any fucking imagination.

It was easy enough to figure out – if you had enough grasses working the streets for you, you didn't need to do much to keep your collars up. It was the same mentality behind those big-time dealers, the ones clever enough to keep their hands off the product. You had enough people out there doing your grunt work for you, then all you needed to do was tour once or twice a week. And right enough, all I had to do was bring 'em in and sweat 'em down, maybe put a slight beating on them to stop the lip, remind 'em who the gaffer was. It was dirty every now and then, didn't involve all the doorstepping that some of the others did, but it meant I could sit back and watch the top cops head straight for the cardiac ward.

But then – too many looks. Too many background sniggers, words pointed at us that I didn't always hear, but caught the fucking gist. It wasn't the usual shite anymore – 'Donkin, yeah, you wanna keep an eye on him, he spends too much time with his grasses, you know how dodgy that looks, eh?'

No, it was that my collars didn't mean anything. Because, according to the desk sergeants, I was bringing in the same people time and again. Didn't matter that they were criminals, fucking stone-cold recidivists who went on a crime spree the second they were left unsupervised. It was like I needed to, what, keep it fucking fresh for the sake of appearances?

Bollocks.

In the end, though, you hear something enough, you start to believe it. And it got so's that was all I could think about. That I wasn't a real copper. That I was just a chauffeur, ferrying in the usual suspects every week or so.

So I took some of the leave I'd built up, spent it drinking away the insecurities.

And now, maybe I got to thinking that I hadn't done the right thing. It was entirely possible I was wrong. I mean, I was wrong about Annie. Mind you, that hadn't exactly been a rational fucking thought.

I looked at the road. It was raining again. The sky looked like it was going to open at any moment. A rumble in the distance woke us up properly.

Annie wouldn't come back to us, not the way I was. She was best off out of my life at the moment. Because it was obvious I wasn't a bloke to be around, couldn't be trusted to hold my fucking temper. And if I wanted her back, it couldn't be like I just told her I was better. There had to be a real change, a hard change. It had to be visible, actions louder than words, all that. I'd have to clean the house out, bring in new furniture, show myself capable of being domestic if I was going to promise her a stable home life. And I'd have to go to that counsellor, share my fucking feelings, get well, get shot of whatever the fuck it was that had made us pull that punch in the first place.

Before I did any of that, though, I had to sort this case out. Because there was no way she'd take us back if I didn't have a job, especially if I lost that job because I beat someone up. I had to make it up to the fucking job before I ever made it up to her, which meant I couldn't go around half-cocked.

So even though I knew Innes had killed Mo Tiernan, I couldn't just go back there and beat a confession out of him. That was the old Donkey.

No, what I had to do was gather evidence. And when I had enough evidence, I'd find some way of arresting the bastard properly.

That was it, like. Thinking. Because I needed to be clever about this.

I pulled my baccy tin, rolled a nice fat one and licked the paper. Sparked it and eased my seat back a notch.

I couldn't afford to give up, not now. And certainly not over Callum fucking Innes. There was no way I would allow that little bastard to be involved in my final days on the force. I especially wouldn't let the fucker walk on murder, not when he'd dangled it in my face like –

That wasn't the way to play it. Getting angry again, getting emotional.

I breathed smoke.

Had to be calm about this, think it out rationally. It was all about being clever, all about thinking shit through. For once in my life, I reckoned I'd have to investigate without going to my usual sources.

There was something about that I didn't particularly like, but I reckoned I'd have to get over it. After all, justice had to be served, didn't it?

Another rumble, getting closer. Rain spotting the windscreen.

There was a fucking storm coming.

THIRTY

Innes

When I get to the Northside, I'm buzzing from a couple of painkiller beers and running late. Tiernan's nowhere to be seen which isn't unusual, considering the place is packed.

A couple of local lads dominate the bill and, from what I can make out, both are rising stars, so this exhibition's brought in pretty much everyone who's interested in the Manchester boxing scene. Won't find many fair-weather Hattonites in this place, but you might bump shoulders with some of his close mates. It's a watch-what-you-say crowd, so I keep my mouth shut and my head down. As I push through, I get growled at, pushed back, and a full compliment of dirty looks and idle threats. The guys in here are built like bears, but shaved to the skin on the top. The women are either made up and stinging people's eyes with their perfume, or else bat-faced bean bags chain-smoking their way to an aching left arm.

I see Tiernan through the wall of his lads. I have to push further and harder just to reach the first bodyguard, who takes one look at the bruises on my face and decides I shouldn't be anywhere near his gaffer. One large hand comes out and braces my chest. He's about to tell me to fuck off when I catch Tiernan's eye.

'The fuck have you been?' he says.

'Got caught up.'

'Drinking,' says the bodyguard.

Both Tiernan and I look at this bloke, wondering where the fuck he got the idea he was part of the conversation. He's young, looks aggro enough to be new blood.

'Watch the fight,' says Tiernan. 'We'll talk later in the van.'

The fight doesn't have long. Heading into the eighth with five to go, but I'll be surprised if we get all of them. One of the lads, a white kid with swollen eyes and a fierce cut on his temple that doesn't want to close, is already lurching about as if he's about to jack it in. His guard is up, but wavering, looks like a supreme effort just to keep his hands up at his chest. The Asian lad he's fighting doesn't look that much better off, but there's an urgency in his step that means he's set on winning this. That's if the ref doesn't call it first.

I try to get comfortable standing, but there's too much jostling, too much noise for me to watch the fight properly. I'm too hot, my brain already going from buzzed to swimming, and it suddenly strikes me as odd that Morris Tiernan would come out in public if he thought someone was gunning for him. And he might have blokes around him, but the one that put his hand on me looks to be the most experienced. Got to wonder what the fuck Tiernan thinks he's playing at.

The Asian lad throws a weak punch that still puts the white kid to one knee, and the ref starts counting it, the white lad trying to wave him off with one glove. Kid's got heart, I'll give him that, but all the heart in the world can't stop a ten-count.

And that's the bell.

Tiernan moves on the second ring, his boys moving with him as a unit. I see it, follow it, hobble in the slipstream of the entourage.

Then I'm out in the real world. Fresh, cold air slaps some of the alcohol out of my system and aggravates the bruises on my face. Behind me, people are filing out of the club, and their presence is making Tiernan tense. I follow him as he moves off to one side, turning his collar up and his back to the crowd.

'The fuck is it?' he says.

Something new in his expression. Could be something *like* fear, but I don't know for sure. It's not something I've ever seen before, especially when it comes to Tiernan.

'Darren,' he says, 'You called the lad, didn't you?'

One of the bodyguards, fattish, starts nodding slowly. 'Yeah, no problems on that score, Mr Tiernan.'

'The fuck does that mean?'

Darren's mouth hangs open for a moment. 'Uh, that it's all being sorted.'

'No, there *are* problems, Darren. If the lad was here, there wouldn't be any fuckin' problems, but he's *not* fuckin' here, is he? And neither's the fuckin' van.'

Darren, still nodding, says, 'Yeah.'

'You called him again?'

'Right.'

'Not *right*. Fuckin' do it. Now. We had this timed for a fuckin' reason, you daft cunt.'

Darren pulls a mobile from his puffer pocket. Tiernan turns away from him, looks as if he's about to grab my arm, then drops his hand. I watch Darren poking at his mobile while Tiernan stands next to me, breathing through his mouth and shifting his weight from one leg to the other. He reaches under his jacket, tugs at something I can't see, then zips up again.

He looks back at the entrance to the Northside. I follow his gaze: there are still people coming out of the building.

A car door slams loud up the street. Engines, talking, some loud laughter, a mess of noise that appears to tense Tiernan right up.

And Darren's still on the phone.

'Darren, get the cunt here right now.'

'It's ringing.'

'It's ringing, you want to go fuckin' *look* for him.'

Darren moves the phone from his ear. 'What, now?'

'Fuckin' keep ringing him, get your arse moving while you do it.'

A fat bloke in a T-shirt shuffles past Tiernan, jostles him. Doesn't realise who he's nudged and how fucking dead he's about to be until Tiernan's almost on him.

'Sorry. Jesus, *sorry*,' he says.

Tiernan backs up, watches the guy head on. His mouth hangs open. 'Fuck it. Can't get the fuckin' . . .' His eyes wide, he points at me. 'You wanted to talk.'

'Yes.'

'Let's do it now before I fuckin' kill someone.' He gestures to the aggro lad. 'Glen, you tell Darren to keep phoning, right? We're going to take a walk around the block and when we get back, that cunt better be sitting here with the fuckin' van, you understand me?'

'You want me to come with?' Glen eyes me up like I'm about to hold a knife to his boss's throat.

'No, fuck's sake.' Tiernan grabs me by the arm, hurries me along, away from the crowd that's developing in front of the Northside. Glen jogs over to where Darren is ambling up the road. Tiernan breathes out, shaking his head. He attempts a kind of rueful smile and says, 'No fuckin' point in me leaving early if I'm going to be stuck in all that, is there?'

I grunt in agreement. Have trouble keeping pace with him. We hit a corner and Tiernan slows down.

'That cunt out there, he's got one job to do and that's have the fuckin' van outside when I need it.'

'You had threats?' I say.

He glances at me, then stares down the street. 'More importantly, what happened to you?'

'Got a problem.'

'Thought you might.' He jerks his head for me to follow. I do as I'm told.

'Police,' I say.

'Right.' Tiernan fishes in his pocket, brings out his cigarettes. 'You told me that wasn't going to be an issue. Told me you had that sorted, Callum.'

'They're not a problem. As a *group*.'

'So,' Tiernan lights a Rothmans as he walks, 'it's an individual gave you that. What's his name?'

'Donkin.'

'Why's that name familiar?'

'Donkey. He's a sergeant. CID.'

'Right,' he says. 'Got you now. Heard about him. He's a right piece of work, isn't he?'

'Yeah.'

'Should be kicked out by now, eh? I mean, the stuff I heard he got up to.'

'Still does.' I shake my head. 'The only people he hurts . . . they're *grasses*. Nobody really cares.'

'And you.' Tiernan stops and looks at me. 'What does that make you? You got worked over—'

'I'm not a grass.'

'This copper your police contact?'

'Was.'

Tiernan sniffs loudly, and we've arrived round the back of the Northside. He pulls out his cigarettes, offers the pack to me. I decline – smoking *and* walking is tough on me. He blows smoke straight up at the sky, showing me his throat.

'So what do you want?' he says.

'Help.'

'With the copper?'

'Yes.'

'What kind of help?'

'You know.'

'I don't like dealing with police,' he says, working his mouth as if he's desperately trying to stifle a smile. 'There's rules in place.'

Obviously Tiernan's gone fucking soft on me. Should've seen it coming – the bloke's been popping at the seams the past couple of days.

I nod. 'It's okay.'

'No, leave it with us. Let me look into it. I'll let you know if it's doable.' He leans against the back wall of the club. 'In the meantime, you got anything?'

So that's what it comes down to. You scratch my back, I'll get the copper off yours. Fair play, he's been working on trust for a while now.

'Been working the hair,' I say.

He tenses up a little. 'Okay.'

'Kevin Ross . . . doesn't know. Baz, again, nothing.'

'Anything else?'

'Police know . . . it wasn't robbery.'

'They're sure?'

'Yeah.'

'So what now?'

'Check on Mo's . . . love life.'

We stare at each other for a short while. Tiernan's obviously trying to work out if that was a dig at his daughter. It wasn't, but it's not a bad thing to get Alison back in the man's head. To all intents and purposes, I'm off the Alison lead, but there's no harm in refreshing his memory every now and then.

Tiernan nods, drops his cigarette. He digs into his jacket, revealing what looks like a bodywarmer underneath. As he brings out a thick envelope, the light catches the fabric of the body armour he's wearing. When Tiernan notices me staring, he zips up and smiles.

'It's a lot of money,' he says, handing me the envelope. 'Plenty more where that came from an' all. C'mon.'

He heads off around the side of the club. I follow him at a distance. As we emerge from the alley on the other side, Darren spots us, twisting round with his mouth open. By the kerb is a large black SUV, its engine idling. The guy behind the wheel – bald, heavy eyebrows, face on him like a bulldog chewing a wasp – glances at Tiernan, then faces front, staring at some obviously uncomfortable point in the middle distance.

'Thought we'd lost you,' says Darren.

Tiernan strides towards the SUV. As he passes the driver's door, he slams his hand against it. The driver flinches. 'The fuck were you, you lazy cunt?'

The driver opens his mouth, flaps for a second before he says, 'Thought you said—'

'Don't make a difference what you *thought*.' The SUV door slides open noisily; Glen's already inside. 'You *be* here when you're supposed to be here. And you keep your fuckin' phone on, dickhead.'

The driver starts to say something else, but his mouth's long stopped working in tandem with his vocal cords. All that comes out of his gob is what sounds like a throaty cough. Darren steps ahead, holds the door to one side for Tiernan.

Before he gets into the van, Tiernan stops and looks at me. 'That thing we talked about. We'll sort it. You keep on doing what you're doing.'

'Thanks.'

He ducks into the SUV. 'And you lot get your fuckin' heads out your arse. Safer with him over there than I am with you bunch of twats.'

Darren shoots me a glare that makes me think he wants to chop me in the fucking throat. 'You can never be too careful.'

'Yeah, you never fuckin' know, son.' Tiernan laughs, stretches out in his seat. 'Wake the fuck up, Daz. Look at him.'

Darren does. Tiernan waves a hand for him to get in and close the door. He backs up, slides the door across and into place with a loud metallic bang.

But before Tiernan disappears from sight, I hear him say, 'How the fuck is he a threat to *me*?'

Too right.

After all, I'm just a mong, aren't I?

PART THREE

Nobody Walks

It was supposed to be a family meal, but we weren't much of a family, so it wasn't much of a meal.

My last night in Scotland, the night after the funeral. Promised my mum that I'd show up for a farewell dinner, just me, her and Uncle Kenny. Supposed to be a nice way of saying goodbye, but as me and her sat there – nine o'clock, Christmas tablecloth spattered with wax from the guttering candles, the throat-closing smell of a roast dinner that had gone from succulent to husk about an hour before – I realised I'd had enough of watching my mum try not to show the tears and pushed away from the table.

'Where are you going?' she said.

'Going to get . . . *Kenny*.'

'He's—'

'I know where.'

Out in the hall, and I knew she wouldn't follow me, but I turned around anyway. I saw her silhouette flicker in the candlelight, then I was gone.

Port Edgar was more boneyard than boatyard when the bad weather rolled in, foul icy winds sweeping in across the Firth of Forth that took the skin from your face, dug in and put a chill right through the marrow. I caught a cab out to the marina, left him outside the main gate with the engine running.

Place was supposed to be closed at this time of night, but it was a home away from home for my uncle, and he didn't need to tell me why.

Thing was with Kenny, when I was a kid, I barely remembered him. He was a wallpaper-suit kind of bloke. Whenever we'd have to trudge round to my Auntie Linda's for Christmas and she got out all the spare chairs, there'd always be one missing, and that would be Kenny's. So he'd stand by the wall, try to blend in. And when the conversation faltered between the adults, plunging into a thick silence, he'd be the one to break it with a nonsense sound – 'Uh-huh . . .' – as if that would get people talking again.

He faded into the cigarette smoke. He barely registered, even when he started fucking that nurse in Bo'ness and him and Linda called it a day with fourteen years and two kids under their belts. After that, we didn't go round for Christmas anymore. Can't say I shed any tears. Nor did I when I heard that Kenny and the nurse split up, and he was living the lonely bachelor life in Leith.

Anyway, with nothing else in his life, Kenny did what any man would do. He threw himself into his work. Which is how I knew exactly where to find him in a time of stress.

When I found him, he was out by one of the pontoons, the wind and rain lashing him. He didn't feel it much, though. Judging from the dregs in the whisky bottle he was holding, Kenny wasn't feeling much of anything.

I shouted his name. He responded as if he'd been kicked in the back.

'Callum,' he said. At least that was the way his lips moved. The wind whipped the sound away from him.

I fought the gale, hobbled out towards him. Nodded at the bottle he was holding. 'Least you didn't . . . miss dinner.'

Kenny dropped the whisky to the ground. It bounced and rolled towards the end of the pontoon. 'I'm sorry.'

'What was that?'

'There's something . . .' Shook his head. 'I didn't mean to.'

I looked at him. 'Kenny.'

'Didn't want to live. I mean, we *talked* about it.'

I didn't say anything. Tried to stay cold, which wasn't difficult considering it was freezing as fuck out here. Watched the wind whip the smoke from his cigarette, already sodden from the rain. Kept my hands down, even as I felt them tighten.

'I didn't kill him,' he said. 'He killed himself.'

'Because of . . . the baby.'

'No.'

He shook his head quickly. 'He would've done it anyway. That's the thing about our family, Callum. About the *men* in the family. My brother, your brother, *you*. Self-destructive. Weak in a *fundamental* way, do you understand me, Callum?'

I stared at him. Realised he'd been waiting for me to find him. Spent all his time draining the bottle that rocked at his feet. I felt drunk, myself. This was a guy who'd spent a majority of my life not saying a fucking word, especially not to me. Look at him now, the seal was broken, and a tsunami of shit sure to follow.

'We're all fucked, Callum. From . . . *birth*, a genetic flaw. I've been thinking about it for a long time, and it's all proven true. You know your dad, he couldn't take the idea of settling down, hated the idea of having *one* kid never mind the pair of you. You know the worst thing you ever could've done to him, you did. You knocked him down. That was it, he needed out. Same as your brother when you hit him. Only way you'd get him sent up here was to hit him first. We all run away, try to escape what hurts us, because we don't want to admit that we're killing ourselves, Callum.'

'Shut up,' I said, trying for dismissive and failing miserably. There was still time to play this as if Kenny was a daft old drunk, time to forget all about it. But we both knew that wasn't going to happen.

'You don't believe me,' he said. 'That's fine. But he killed himself. And I had to help him. Because it's what we all want.'

'Not me.'

'You're *exactly* the fucking same,' he said. 'You get a family, you'll fuck it up, try to kill yourself in the process.'

That was when I hit him.

My first punch was weak, but then so was he. Caught him sharply in the side of the head with my hand, still wrapped tight around the handle of my walking stick. Pushed him back, swung the stick in a short arc, connected with the top of his head.

Again, and a swipe that knocked the hand he'd brought up to his cheek. Kenny folded, stumbled back. I lurched forward, kicked the whisky bottle, sent it skittering into the water. Swung my stick again, caught Kenny behind the knee. He dropped to clutch where it hurt, and I pivoted on the good foot, brought the bad one into his face. His head snapped back. His legs shot out from under him, and he landed on his right arse cheek, swaying over the edge of the pontoon.

'Cunt,' I said.

'I know,' he said.

'You killed him.'

'No.' Kenny had his hands up. 'He did it to himself. I told you, you don't *listen*—'

'I'll fuckin'—'

But I couldn't move. I wanted to kill him, push on, beat fuck out of him, kick what was left into the Firth of Forth and let the cunt float to Norway. Even if they found him before that, he'd be another one of those bloated corpses they skimmed around the Forth Bridge, miserable twats who took a header to prove a point.

Let his theory ride out.

And he wanted me to do it. If I killed him, it would be the same situation as him buying smack for Declan, knowing full well what he was going to do with it. It was a mercy killing, pure and simple. And somewhere in the fog of alcohol that had swaddled his brain, he believed that he'd done my brother a favour. Hoped I'd do him the same.

I wasn't about to end it there. Because Kenny wasn't really to blame. All this shite started long before he scored for my brother.

Besides, I had a cab waiting. And he was still on the meter.

THIRTY-ONE

Donkin

A bolt of sunlight woke us up. That was what it felt like, anyway.

Except it wasn't that sunny; outside the skies were grey and it was coming down in fucking sheets.

Then the banging kicked in. I had a twelve-can, half-bottle hangover, so it took a moment for us to work out that the banging noise was coming from out in the hall, not the inside of my head. Sounded like someone was getting ready to kick the door in, so I pulled myself off the settee. Tried to get steady by grabbing the coffee table, but I just ended up knocking all the empty cans onto the floor. There was the sudden stink of ciggies and beer, and I realised I must've been using the cans as ashtrays the night before.

All the while, whoever it was outside wouldn't stop hammering on the fucking door. I managed to haul myself out into the hall where it was nice and dark. Colder than the lounge, and I reckoned that I must've gone to sleep with the gas fire on again. Meant that this bastard behind the eyes wasn't going anywhere soon, and my nose and throat were all dried to fuck.

A pause in the banging when I got to the door. Silhouettes behind, looked like two blokes.

When I pulled it open, it was more like two and a half, because one of them was big as a fucking house. Suited, looked like bailiffs, which meant they were in for a surprise, because everything in this house was paid off. And then I reckoned Annie sent some blokes round to pick up the rest of the stuff she thought was hers.

Either way, they weren't getting in.

'The fuck do you want?' I said.

The House hit us in the face. I lost my balance, stumbled back, my legs gone wide and I hit the wall with my back as I turned. The breath went out of us. I grabbed at my face, felt the blood running hard, just as those two bastards came storming in the house. I opened my gob to shout for help, but the smaller one kicked the door shut behind him and, for a second, they dropped into shadow. I braced my back to the wall, pushed off and made a run for it.

Something hit us hard in the back. I bent and something else knocked out my legs. Pain lashed across the backs of my knees. I grabbed out at the wall, missed it, hit the floor. Caught an up-close-and-personal whiff of the chicken korma I spilled on the carpet about a month ago and was too pissed to clean up properly, and my gut did a triple fucking somersault. I gritted my teeth, spat blood, tried to focus on the carpet. Reckoned if I just got my head right, I'd be able to put at least one smack on this pair of clowns.

Then the big bastard put the boot in. Made us do this scratchy belch and then the chicken burger I had last night came up for a fucking encore. When the boot came back at us, I made sure I rolled out of the way of the spew. Might've taken an extra couple of kicks because of it, but there was no way I was going to be covered in my own puke as well as my own blood.

Hands on us. It was the smaller one, because the big bastard's Chelseas didn't move. Pulling us up. I didn't put up a fight, not yet. If this twat wanted to drop his guard, I'd be in there, but seeing as there was two of them, I'd have to be clever about this.

'Y'alright?' The big one said. I got a decent look at his face through the haze. Big face, small features. Unibrow.

'I know you?'

'Nah.'

'I do.'

He looked at the bloke behind us. 'Let's get him in the lounge.'

'I do,' I said, staring at him. 'I know you. Fuckin' *lounge*, you fuckin' ponce.'

The pick-up merchant shoved us towards the front room and my legs buckled. I grabbed onto the doorway, but the big lad knocked my hand away. I dipped, was pushed, hit the settee and then bounced off onto the floor. I knocked the rest of the cans off the coffee table, heard laughter from somewhere. When I looked up at the big bastard, he hadn't cracked his face, so I guessed I'd amused the little fucker. I pulled myself back up onto the settee, mopped at the blood on my mouth, the hangover long fucking stifled with new pain.

'Now,' said the big lad. 'Y'alright?'

'Now what the fuck d'you keeping asking us that for?'

'I want to know.'

Giggles stood to one side, watching us with a twitching smile on his face. Like he was gearing up to twat us one, like this was the most exciting thing that'd ever happened to him. I reckoned that I'd have to keep an eye on him; looked too much to me like he was straining at whatever invisible leash the big lad had him on.

'Here,' said the big lad, snapping his fingers at us.

'What?'

'I asked you a question.'

'Eh?'

'Are you alright?'

I stared at him. 'No, I'm not fuckin' alright, am I? I'm fuckin' bleeding, and what the fuck do youse pair of cunts think you're doing in *my* house?'

'Mouth on him,' said the smaller bloke.

'Mouth on *you*. Thought you were a fuckin' mute.'

The big bloke snapped his fingers again.

'And you,' I said, 'I'm not your fuckin' waiter, so I don't know what you think you're snapping at, son.'

Mouthy smiled, moved under his suit. One fluid movement and his jacket was unbuttoned. 'I'm just trying to get your attention. You're easily distracted. I just want to make sure you're completely focused when I'm talking to you.'

'Then spit it out, for fuck's sake. Haven't got all fuckin' morning, have I?'

Mouthy took one step – barely saw it – and smacked us in the exact same place he'd smacked us before. I shook and kicked out at nothing with both feet, heard something crunch and my nose just give it up. When my head came back down, blood started scooshing again, splattering the settee. I put a fist under my nose, wedged it up to stop the blood and put my head back. Looked at the mouthy bastard with horse eyes.

'So,' he said. 'Y'alright?'

I didn't say anything.

'Asked you a question.'

I knew he'd asked us a question. And it was one I already saw coming, because it was about the only thing that came out of this bastard's gob. He was like a broken fucking record.

'So?' he said.

Moved the fist to a cup, felt my hand filling up with blood. I wanted to flick it at him, but I held my temper. 'Yeah, mate, I'm fuckin' super-duper.'

'No pain, nowt like that?'

'Actually, yeah, funny you should mention it.'

'Yeah?'

'My nose does smart a little.'

'That's a shame.'

'Nah, I think it'll be alright.'

'You look like you might need a hankie.'

'Oh, you think?'

'Yeah.'

I smiled, said: 'Fuck yourself.'

The giggler stepped in, smacked us right in the ear. Snapped my hearing out and sent a jolt through the side of my head. I jerked, lost my hand from my nose and sprayed blood across the carpet, which pissed us off more than the sting in my lug. I turned and looked sidelong at the fucker. Giggles held his fist, staring at us like it was my fault he misjudged his punch.

He'd be easy taken. Couldn't throw a punch for toffee, bring it the fuck on.

I spluttered out a laugh, dug my feet into the carpet, got braced, and made to barrel the bugger. I managed three steps before the big bastard put his fist on the other side of my face. When he clipped my nose, a flashbulb went off behind my eyes and I went down like a dropped dog. I blinked at the carpet, and as my vision cleared, the first thing I noticed was more of my blood. Place was beginning to look like a fucking abattoir.

'Sergeant,' said Mouthy.

'Detective Sergeant,' I said. 'And you both know I'm a copper, right?'

'Yeah.'

'So you know that I'll fuckin' *have* you.'

The big lad shook his head, grinned at us, and somewhere near the back of his smile, I caught the flash of a gold tooth. I hoped that someone had knocked out the original – the way this bloke took pride in his appearance, a missing tooth would've been cause for a three-week crying jag.

'Doesn't work like that, Detective.'

'Right, so how *does* it work?' I pulled myself to the edge of the settee. Kept one eye on Giggles, who was itching to plant a square blow on us. But just because he didn't get the first one right, didn't mean I was going to let him have a freebie.

'You're listening now,' said Mouthy.

'Yeah.'

'Good. We have a message to deliver.'

'Uh-huh, thought you might.'

'You need to back off from Innes.'

I stared at Mouthy, cocked my head. 'Come again?'

'You heard.'

'I heard *something*, but it was probably my ear playing us up, thanks to your mate. Sounded like you said I had to leave Innes alone.'

'That's right.'

I shook my head, playing gobsmacked. 'And who's this message from?'

'Doesn't matter.'

'Not from Innes. That lad doesn't have either the cash or the stones to hire you two.'

Mouthy tapped his ear. 'Listen to me.'

'I am.'

'Then you'll have heard. It doesn't matter.'

I nodded. Because I knew only too well where this was coming from. Took a bit of thinking, what with all the knocks to the head, but I was sure now.

'Tiernan,' I said.

Mouthy looked at Giggles. Giggles looked back. It was almost sweet, the way they dropped a fucking bollock.

'Aye, you're fuckin' *Tiernan.*'

Mouthy took a slow step forward, like he wasn't going to do anything except maybe whisper at us. I caught Giggles moving, too. Pair of them, closing in on us.

'Doesn't matter if we're working for Innes, if we're working for Mr Tiernan or someone else with a lot more pull.'

'Who? Come on, lads, who's got more pull than Tiernan, eh?'

'All that matters is that you understand the message I've just delivered to you.' He cleared his throat, tried a smile. 'Do you understand—'

'Yeah, mate, I understand your fuckin' message.' I shifted on the settee. 'And you're a couple of cunts think they're above the bastard law.'

Mouthy started shaking his head. 'That's not—'

'I know that's not *your* message, mate, but that's what I'm saying to you. You know what I am? I'm the fuckin' *police.* I'm the *law.* You can't do what you've done to a copper without expecting the whole fuckin' force to come after you. We protect our own.'

Mouthy looked at us, his head still. The smile had faded to a smirk that would've been invisible if it wasn't for the fact that I'd been staring him in the face for so long.

I lowered my voice. 'You know you're already in the shit, old son. And you know that if you keep fucking around the way you are, I'm going to make it my sole fuckin' life's work to track you down and make your life as uncomfortable as the five minutes you've been in my fuckin' house. But I'll make you a one-time deal right now. You tell us who sent you, and me and you, we'll forget this ever happened.'

He worked his mouth. Looked to me that he was thinking about my proposition. Course, I hadn't said anything about his rat of a mate. That bastard would get strung up as soon as I got the rope.

Finally, the big bloke sighed. 'One thing, though.'

'What's that?'

'I'm not in the shit.'

'You what?'

'You're not a copper,' he said. 'You're suspended. And there's not a lot you can do if you're just a civilian. Isn't that right, Donkey?'

That was it.

I pushed up off the balls of my feet, lunged at Mouthy. He switched out of the way, and I followed through, staggered a couple of steps and brought the coffee table halfway across the fucking room before I pitched to the floor. Then I saw a blur of movement, realised that Giggles was coming up on us. Mouthy must've dropped the word because I honestly didn't see this simple rat-fucker do anything without the big man's say-so. Giggles kicked us once, then twice in the gut and I retched and rolled. Mouthy brought his foot into my back. As I swung back, he brought his heel down in the middle of my chest, tore the breath out of us. I choked a scream, couldn't do anything except look up Mouthy's nose until Giggles snapped a short kick across my nose.

I threw up a hand as the flashbulbs went off again.

And then I was gone.

THIRTY-TWO

Innes

When Tiernan calls me on the mobile to let me know that Donkey's been taken care of, I don't bother to ask how. He sent lads round, or he managed to have a word with Donkey's superiors. Either way, Donkey's had his arse handed to him, and he shouldn't be a problem. Not for the time being, anyway.

So what d'you reckon, Cal?

Reckon you can go through with this?

Truth is, I don't know.

I've been stuck in the Micra all morning, watching varying strengths of rain stream down the windscreen. Now there's one of those low-slung stretch-bonnet hairdresser cars heading towards Alison's house, I'm ducked down in my seat, watching it. Pretty sure Alison's behind the wheel, but I don't know for sure until the car pulls into her driveway and she gets out.

What about now? Different when she's there, isn't it?

I look down at the wallet in my hands. Belonged to Mo, still got his blood on it, probably. Not much in it apart from the usual identification. A bus pass with a recent photo, Mo staring out at me like a challenge. It doesn't look like much, but it could be everything.

That's what I fucking thought.

Look up and Alison's face is creased at the drizzle. She pulls the front passenger seat forward and leans into the car for something. I watch her fuss about for a few seconds. Turns out the something was a someone, a toddler dressed in a coat so puffy he can't put his arms down by his sides.

This must be the same kid I saw being looked after by Morris Tiernan a year ago. And as Alison sets him down on the ground and reaches in for some shopping bags, I can't help but wonder where the time went. He's walking by himself, arms out like some miniature bodybuilder, waddling towards the front door. He looks up, gets his face wet, then rubs at the water with one mittened hand.

Meanwhile, Alison is trying get her key in the door. When she manages to twist and open, she calls the kid's name – Sammy – and ushers him into the house. I see her bring him back onto the doormat to wipe his feet, then she closes the door and all I can hear is the random spots of rain on the car windows.

It is different seeing her.

This is Alison Tiernan in real life, and a straight one at that, from what I can see. Far from the gangster's daughter who had me beaten almost to fucking death in a motorway lay-by, this girl looks to the world to be the usual young single mother, albeit one living beyond her means thanks to her father.

And what do you have to thank her father for?

Right. I might have some lingering doubts over what I'm about to do, but there's no question that she's still very much a part of the Tiernan family, and that's all that matters.

Besides, I'm not sure I have much of a choice now, my mobility limited to a single course of action. Mind you, if there's anything I know about these days, it's limited mobility, and while Donkey might be out of the game, he won't be out for long. So I should make the most of the opportunity I've been given.

Then do it.

I wait another fifteen minutes by the clock in the dashboard, just to make sure that Alison's managed to unpack her shopping and get settled. Then I get out of the Micra and hobble towards her front door.

The trick is to look like I've just arrived, and as harmless as possible into the bargain. I'm hoping the rain will do me good, add a certain pathetic quality to me when I ring the doorbell.

Just because the circumstances have changed, doesn't mean the person has. I just have to remember that. And even if Alison Tiernan *has* changed, that doesn't alter what her and her family did to me and a load of other people over the years.

I press the doorbell. A soft chime sounds behind the door.

I hear her before I see her. She's saying something to the kid, looking at him as she opens the door. When she turns my way, there's that flicker of disgust. And somewhere in her mind, she's calling herself all the names under the sun for opening the door without checking first.

'I think we . . . need to talk,' I say.

'I told you the other night—'

'This is important,' I say, nice and loud.

She glances behind me. Not as easy to keep me under wraps in broad daylight. And she's obviously worried about how she's perceived out here. Which is handy for me.

'Make it quick and wipe your feet.'

She backs off to one side as I step into the house. She hurries me through into the hall as I struggle to wipe my feet on a doormat that's too small to be practical.

When I look at her again, she looks like she'd quite happily murder me. That's the Alison Tiernan I knew back in Newcastle.

She heads up the hall, urging Sammy to stay in the living room. 'Mummy'll be in in a minute, okay?'

I unzip my jacket and follow her to the kitchen.

'You'll want a brew, will you?' she says.

'Yes, please.'

And as she goes to put the kettle on, I put a hand in my pocket, feel for Mo's wallet. I'll need to be quick and precise when the time comes.

THIRTY-THREE

Innes

'I don't know what you want us to tell you.'

'The truth?'

Alison raises both eyebrows at me, then goes back to stirring her coffee. She's noisy about it, clanging the spoon against the side of the mug as if she's about to make a speech. Then she tosses the spoon into the sink and stands with her back to the kitchen counter.

'I kept the baby,' she says. 'And I was scared about it. Don't think I wasn't. I mean, you know what they say about brothers and sisters . . . I didn't know if it stretched to *half* brothers and sisters, didn't know if he was going to be alright or have one eye and a hole in his heart. But what did I know? I was a fucking kid myself.'

She shakes her head, picks up the two mugs and brings them over to the table. Somewhere behind me in the living room with its cream carpet, IKEA furniture and fake flame gas fire, the kid's playing. That waddle I saw him do outside has more to do with his pudgy little frame than the coat he was wearing. He's active, and he's interested. Come a long way from the kid with a face like a bag of rocks.

'So you left,' I say.

She looks at me to see if I'm taking the piss. As it turns out, I'm not. I'm actually interested. Because whatever I've heard about Alison, or the way she was back then, there's still a disconnect between that and the way she is now, and I need to sort that out. The car, the semi-detached, the whole fucking lifestyle change, looks to me that it's paid for by her daddy, which she's already made clear to me isn't the case. But that's got to be a lie.

'Yeah, I left home. With a man I shouldn't have. And . . . all *that* happened.'

All that – nicking ten grand from her dad, absconding to Newcastle, me after her and about to get run over, beaten up and hung out to dry. Dismissed with two words, and it's all I can do not to laugh.

'You had it worked out,' I say, shaking my head. 'With Rob.'

'I didn't expect Mo,' she says.

'Neither of us did.'

'And I was a different person then.'

That's the chorus for the conversation, something she's keen to tell me whenever she gets the chance. It's as if she knows why I've come round, that she feels the need to tell her side of the story, make me see that she's not to blame for what happened to me. But it's really too late for that now. I'm just listening because I'm interested, not because I need persuading of anything. So I just nod and try to look like she's having an effect.

'I was angrier then. There were issues I had to deal with.'

'Right.'

'And you've got to understand what it was like for me. Growing up in that house. With my dad, with Mo, you've got to understand why I thought maybe being stuck with Mo's kid wasn't the cleverest life decision.'

'Life decision?'

Sounds like she's been up to her nose in self-help and paid therapy of the ineffective British kind. It would explain a lot.

'What about now?' I say.

She sips her coffee, stares beyond me at the kid in the other room. 'Now I won't be without him.'

'What about Mo?'

Her eyes snap back to me. She blinks. 'You know, then.'

I don't say anything. Better she assumes I know more than I do.
'He came round,' she says.
'When?'
'A month ago. Maybe longer, I don't know. Doorbell rang, and Mo's on the step, asking if he can see Sammy. I tell him no, he can't, I just put him down for the night. It was like ten at night. Even if I wanted Mo to see Sammy – which I didn't, not for one *second* – I wouldn't have woken him up. But he kept shouting that he wanted to see his kid, and . . .'

She trails off, takes a moment to blow some air and blink furiously. Looks as if she might start crying in a minute.

'The neighbours,' I say.

She nods. 'Nobody around here knows who I am.'

Right. She's off starting her new life and then has her half-brother screaming that he wants to see his kid? Not going to do much to endear her to the community, is it?

'So you let him in,' I say.

'Yeah. Had to. And I said he could see Sammy, but he wasn't allowed to touch him or wake him up anything like that. So we went upstairs and I let him look in on him, and then brought him back down. Then he started talking about the future.' She pulls a face as if the word stuck to her tongue like a gob of phlegm. 'Like he wanted to be part of Sammy's life. Not like an uncle or anything, but a *dad*. Y'know, I felt sorry for him and everything, but I couldn't . . .'

Tears in her eyes now. She puts both hands round the coffee mug. She frowns quickly and the tears seem to dry up.

'I couldn't let him in like that, I didn't know what Dad would say – I mean, it was *over*, he wasn't part of the family, I couldn't just let him into my life, could I? It was *different*. I was different, I wasn't the same stupid girl who let . . . ' She drinks from her mug, sighs after she swallows. 'So I told him no, he had to leave.'

I wait. She presses one hand to each of her eyes in turn and sniffs.

'He said was there anything he could do. Like, he was sorting himself out, he was going to get a job, he'd already talked to Rossie about it. He was going to get straight, stop dealing, and when he did that, could he be a part of Sammy's life? And he seemed so fucking *genuine* about it.'

I nod, playing at understanding. This is all news to me. Not like Mo to show vulnerability like that. But then, I never knew him the way his half-sister did.

Thank fuck.

Alison sits for a while. I don't say anything until it looks as if she's caught up in her memory.

'You let him?' I say.

She looks up at me, and for a moment I see the rage in her eyes. 'No, of course I didn't let him. I'm not stupid, am I? Mo's a fucking liar, probably just wanted a pity fuck, so I told him to get out, didn't I? And when he didn't go, when he tried it on, I fucking hit him.'

'You hit him.'

'In the face.'

'And then?'

'Then he went,' she says. 'I got rid of him. Told him not to come back.'

I nod slowly. 'And that's it.'

'Yes.'

'You haven't seen him.'

'Not since then, no.' She pauses, manages to collect herself. 'Is that why you came here?'

'No,' I lie. And then to add more inches on the nose, 'I wanted to . . . apologise.'

'For what?'

'For the other night. Turning up . . . *uninvited*. Must've been unwelcome. I'm sorry.' I whirl my hand around at the kitchen. 'You're trying to . . . do something. With your life.'

She regards me over the lip of her mug, then puts it down. Her gaze flickers to something behind me. 'Sammy. Sammy-love, put that down.'

'I should go,' I say, starting to get up.

'No, it's alright,' she says, still watching Sammy. 'Just . . . you're fine, really.'

She stands and I watch her quick-march into the living room. Sammy's busy looking guilty as hell with three fingers in his mouth. Alison tugs on his arm and he removes his wet fingers.

'Sammy, don't do that, sweetheart, alright?'

Sammy nods. Smiles. Then he looks around the place. I don't know much about kids, don't even really know how old Sammy is, but there's something about the lad telling me that Alison's original fears were probably on the money. He looks spaced, maybe a bit touched.

'D'you want to play with your cars? Is it your cars?'

Sammy stares at me. He's seen something in my face that he finds fascinating. Just like everyone else, except this kid doesn't have the social skills to know he's being rude. Alison follows his gaze, then puts a hand on his cheek.

'Sammy, no. You want your cars?'

'Brum-brum,' says Sammy.

'Right y'are, brum-brum.'

'Brum-*broooooooooooooom*.'

Sammy's noises get louder as he toddles off to a corner of the room. He yanks on a small plastic box, then there's the sound of die-cast hitting die-cast as he organises the kind of multiple pile-up that would mean a bloodbath in real life. Alison stays crouched in the middle of the lounge. Behind her, Sportacus zips about the place with his rubber muppet friends. It's a grotesque programme, seems oily to me, makes me a little sick watching it. I have to turn away from it.

'I'm sorry, too,' she says.

'What for?'

'For everything that happened to you because of me.'

She does blame herself, then. Maybe she saw me the other night and it spooked her into rudeness. But I come around again, she sees me in broad fucking daylight with no real excuses to keep me out and with neighbours who'd query the freakshow on the front step, so she lets me in. And now I've been sat here talking to her, it's difficult to ignore the damage caused, in the first instance, by the injuries sustained in a hit-and-snatch organised by her.

I get to my feet, take my cup to the sink. Pass the bin and find it half-empty. Yeah, that should do it. I check to see Alison playing with Sammy, then I drop Mo's wallet into the bin as I put the cup in the sink. There's a slight rustle, covered by the clink. Alison turns at the sound, and I'm already unwrapping a new pack of chewing gum.

'It's okay,' I tell her. 'No harm done, eh?'

And she sees me to the door. It's still raining outside, so I pull up my collar again and hobble through it towards my car. Alison holds onto Sammy's hand. I look back to see Sammy waving at me, his fingers closed around a toy car. I wave back before I get into the Micra and, behind the curtain of rain on the windscreen, allow myself a long, slow exhale.

Then I turn the key in the ignition and watch the wipers sluice the rain from the windscreen.

THIRTY-FOUR

Donkin

When I came back to the world, it was the colour of my carpet, and I had one thought in my head – Innes is a fucking dead man.

I took it slow getting up, ticking off each ache as I did, making a mental checklist of every fucking kick I'd taken, holding onto it so I could remember it when I finally got my hands on the bastard. Took a breather at the doorway to the front room, staring at the mess on the carpet. My blood, beer and cigarette butts strewn across the floor, the table turned over. I felt my jaw, waggled a loose tooth. Reckoned one of them twats had kicked us in the mouth, even though I didn't remember it. And as I stood there, looking around the place, something struck us harder than any of them kicks.

Thank fuck Annie and Shannon hadn't been here.

Because it was obvious that Tiernan didn't give a shit, would've hurt the pair of them if they'd been here. And even though it was small mercies and all that, that single what-if was enough to get my blood going and me moving. I grabbed my jacket from the settee, dug out my phone. Called Innes on his mobile, but he wasn't answering. Didn't exactly surprise us, that, and I was about to leave him a message, but I decided to hang up instead. Nothing I wanted to say to him that wouldn't be better spat into his bleeding, screaming face. So I went upstairs, got myself cleaned up, trying not to look too hard at my own face. Then I got changed and stormed out to the car, pulling a face against the sunlight that threatened to burn the backs of my eyes out.

I sat in the car for the first two songs off of *Come Away With Me*, just so I knew I wasn't going off half-cocked here. I needed to stow all that rage for the moment. Use the energy in a more productive way, just like that therapist told us I should do. I couldn't go grab the cripple and beat the shite out of him, even though I knew if he wasn't behind my wake-up call, he was certainly fucking involved. Because that would be the old Iain, the fucking *Donkey*, right? And if I was serious about change, I'd have to be serious about *now*.

Put both hands on the steering wheel, breathed through my nose, closed the one eye that hadn't already started to puff itself shut. And I calmed down.

Then I turned the key in the ignition, started the engine. Headed for the poof's club, went straight past because there was no sign of the Micra. For a second, I thought about going in, rattling the poof's cage, but reckoned it'd be best if I kept a low profile for as long as possible. No sense in letting the crippled cunt know I was coming until I was already there.

So: no Micra, no Innes. I turned at the top of the street, headed out to Regent Road and further up to the block of flats where I knew Innes lived. As I was about to get out of the car, I stopped.

Saw the white Micra coming my way.

I pulled the door shut, moved down in my seat. Hoped he didn't see us. I watched the Micra slow up a bit as it came to the gates that led to the car park, but then he moved on, like he wasn't sure. I waited until he was well past us before I turned my motor round and followed.

Yeah, the fucker'd seen us, but he'd hoped that I hadn't seen *him*. And I might've had one eye swollen shut, but I wasn't all the way blind yet. I followed him up the road, watched him turn towards Eccles.

Then I followed the bastard all around Greater Manchester, a slow game of lose-the-tail, going round in bastard circles. After a while, I didn't know where the fuck we were. I'd been dragged through that many concrete fucking estates, they all started to blend into one, and by the end of it I wasn't two cars behind him anymore.

There was no point. We both knew what was going on here.

I was about to lean on the horn, or hang out the window and shout at him to stop fucking about when the Micra slowed to a stop.

I pulled in right behind him. Kept the engine going, just like him. Just in case he reckoned he could make a break for it, which would've been just like him.

I waited. Saw him watching us in his rear-view. I watched him right the fuck back.

Saw Innes roll down his window. He put his hand out, waved it in an overtake gesture. I thought I saw half a smile on the bastard's face as he looked at us in the mirror.

Having a fucking giggle at my expense, right enough, like this was one big fucking game to him.

Well, fuck that. No more games. I had the bastard on his own, now was as good a time as any. I unclipped my seat belt, shoved open the driver's door. Ahead of us, Innes revved the engine till it roared.

I had one foot on the ground when he let go of the handbrake.

Then the Micra leapt backwards, connected hard with the front of my Granada. There was a quick shake under my arse, I heard my shoe scrape against the tarmac, and my car lurched out from under us.

I whipped my leg back into the car, clamped both hands round the steering wheel, knocked the volume on the CD and Norah was soon belting out 'Don't Know Why' so loud I thought my fucking head was going to burst. I wanted to knock her off, but Innes kept grinding his car against mine. I hammered at the brakes, shouted at him.

Then he chucked the Micra into gear and jumped it forward.

I saw my chance, made for the door. When I glanced ahead, I saw the Micra bearing down on us again, twisted a bit like he'd catch us if I got out the car. I managed to yank the door shut just as his car hit it bang on, throwing a nasty shock up my arm and punching the bodywork right in.

Tried the door handle. It didn't work. I saw Innes kick the accelerator again, kangaroo forward.

'The fuck d'you think you're doing, you daft—'

And he only slammed the car into us again. I got thrown back in my seat this time. Grabbed at the handle to get out. Couldn't see straight for the red mist, wanted to get out there and throttle this cunt.

Then I looked up and there he was, getting out the Micra. Limping across to us, this foul look on his face.

I didn't know what to do. First time in my life one of these bastards had the brass balls to fight back.

Innes reached the driver's door. Stepped back, lifted his stick like a club.

'The fuck—'

Flinched when the stick hit the window. Didn't break, but there was a crack in the glass that I'd take out of his arse if I ever managed to get out of this fucking car.

'Innes, you fuckin'—'

Second time he hit the window, the glass cracked thicker and longer. Another crack jutted out of the frame.

No, fuck this. It got too much for us, so I stamped on the accelerator. Heard the engine roar. The Granada was playing funny buggers.

A third swipe, connected hard. I realised the handbrake was on. Saw another crack. Knew the window wouldn't take –

– another hit, and the fucking window exploded all over us. I flung up my hand to protect my face, felt the tiny bits of glass dig in. I tightened my grip on the handbrake, slammed it down and the Granada leapt forward. Threw me against the steering wheel, but I kept my head up. I didn't think my nose could take another smack. I went back into my seat, my eyes closed. When I opened them again, I saw an arm whipping out of the car.

Innes.

I made a grab, but he was already out of the car and away. He'd nicked something, I just didn't know what. I looked around the inside of the car, my ears ringing. Looked up and saw him limping backwards, one hand held up.

Realised the engine wasn't running.

The bastard had taken my fucking car keys.

I pushed hard on the handle then, felt something grind against something else inside the door. Brushed the glass off my hand, watching Innes gimp it back to his car. The Micra was all smashed up in the back, and he'd have a shitload to pay on it. I turned back and smacked Norah off the CD, then hauled myself across the gear stick, got out the passenger side.

'You,' I shouted. 'You fuckin' better hold your bastard horses, son, I want a good hard fuckin' word with you.'

Reached the side of the Micra. He was waiting for us with the engine running. Still had the window wound down. I made a grab for him, but he kicked the gas again, jumped forward so the inside of the window frame smacked us in the elbow.

'Give us the fuckin' keys or you'll get your rights.'

'Really, Donkey?'

Innes hopped the car again. Kept us from reaching in there, grabbing the twat around the neck. He held my car keys in one hand, shook them till they jingled. He drove slowly up the street. I walked alongside the Micra, holding my aching elbow.

'Yeah, really.'

'What happened to your face?' he said.

'Like you don't fuckin' know. It was your wake-up call.'

'Alarm clock . . . beat you up?'

'I took care of it. And I'm not off you, so it was a waste of fuckin' time.'

'You took care of it?' One of Innes's eyebrows went up. Probably the only one that worked. 'I find that . . . *difficult* to believe.'

'Course you would, you fuckin' mong, your brain doesn't fuckin' work.'

'That's not nice.'

'You want nice?'

I made another grab. He made the car jump again. A fresh jolt to my fucking elbow. Hardest part of the body, my arse.

'I wouldn't,' he said. 'Wouldn't do that.'

I relaxed a bit, backed off. Tried to be ice about the whole situation, because the last thing I needed was for that twat to feel like he was in charge.

'You know this is doing nowt but piss me off, Innes.'

'I know.'

'And you know this doesn't end with you winning.'

Innes shook his head and half-smiled out of the windscreen. 'Depends.'

'Nah, this situation, this is just something I'm going to hold onto, you know that. I'm the bloke who holds a grudge.'

'You don't fuckin' say.'

'So you also know that when I get a chance, I'm going to break your fuckin' neck.' I kept my voice low so he'd know exactly how fucking serious I was about this. 'Make you a full mong, proper shoulderbiter. Put you in a wheelchair, put a fuckin' bag on your hip.'

'Uh-huh,' he said.

'So you're listening to us. You can hear us.'

He nodded, driving on. It was getting cold, and I didn't fancy being stuck out here for any length of time. I pulled my coat tighter.

'You know the minute you get back to your poof's club, or you get fuckin' home, I'm going to come in there with a couple of thickneck constables and we're going to work all your fuckin' pressure points, leave no bruises on the outside. Then I'm going to bring you down the fuckin' station and I'm going to make up some terror charges so I can keep you in a cell without food or water for a month. And we'll see who's the fuckin' smug-arse then, eh?'

Innes did this noise, like a dog laughing. He jingled the keys and glanced at us. 'So when's this . . . going to happen?'

'Soon.'

'Right y'are, Donkey.'

'That's not helping your case, son.'

'Arrest me, then.'

He looked at us. And I couldn't stand the twinkle in the bastard's eyes.

He knew.

'Course you fuckin' know,' I said, nodding.

Then I stopped walking. Innes carried on driving at the same speed. There was no point in following him. I couldn't arrest him. Didn't have the authority. And he bastard well knew it. I might as well have been a community support officer.

Halfway up the street, Innes slowed down and I saw his arm come out the side of the car. Heard the jingle fade as he pitched them as far he could. Saw something bounce into the grass, but I wasn't going to run for them. Didn't have the energy. Instead, I watched him drive off round the corner.

The Micra disappeared, and I breathed out. Tried to remain calm.

I started walking again, headed for the wasteland.

If Innes knew I was suspended, then it was probably all over the fucking city by now. I couldn't make out like I had any power, couldn't play that game, because I had to take it on faith that this particular nugget of information had already caught and travelled through my network. Grasses wouldn't talk to us, and neither would the average street scally. In fact – and, Christ, here was a new thought that made my arse chew on my skids – I'd have to watch my back, because if it got out that it was open season on us, then other people might get the same bastard idea, think they could take a free shot. And these lads – especially the ones who might reckon they owe us some pain – weren't too clever. They'd just ape, maybe go further. What they wouldn't realise was that Innes and Tiernan's lads already got us up to the limit of shite I was willing to take. And they wouldn't cotton on to the fact that even if their memory was long, mine was *way* fucking longer, and this suspension wouldn't last. Soon as I got officially badged again, they'd be in the shit.

So I wasn't all that scared. As long as I watched myself, kept out of my usual haunts, I reckoned I'd be okay.

I found my keys next to a big pile of dogshit. A stroke of luck that Innes hadn't thrown a couple inches to the left, else I'd have been picking my keys out of that mound with a twig. When I straightened up, I looked back at my car. The bonnet was fucked. You could see it even at this distance, which made us think it was only going to get worse the closer I got.

But I did go back, and when I was back, I switched on Norah Jones and I listened to the whole of 'Thinking About You' before I started the engine.

She calmed us down, did Norah. And I needed to maintain it. Even if it felt like I was about to lose my fucking mind.

THIRTY-FIVE

Innes

'Sad, really. The way things turn out.'

Frank's talking to Paulo in the back office as I come in. On my desk is a large white cake with a couple of pieces missing. Frank has cream in the corner of his mouth and Paulo's trying to look interested, but it's obvious that Frank's been nattering non-stop for quite some time.

I frown at the cake.

'Mrs Sadler,' says Paulo.

'A thank you.' Frank goes back for another piece. 'Payment, if you want.'

'She didn't have cash?'

Frank shoots me a look. 'No. And I wouldn't have taken it even if she did. You want some?'

I shake my head. 'Had a big lunch.'

'Turns out I didn't need your help, anyway,' he says.

Paulo heads for the door. I watch him. He looks at Frank, then raises one eyebrow. 'You should hear this.'

Frank smiles through a mouthful of cake at Paulo as he leaves. He gestures at the closing door with a fork, says: 'I've been boring Paulo with the details.'

I put a juice down on the desk. Wave at it. 'Peace offering.'

'What for?'

'Should've . . . helped you out. Sorry.'

He picks up the juice, nods at me. 'It's alright, Cal. You've got your own stuff to do, right?'

'Right.'

'And I don't think you'd be up to a long stakeout.'

I close my eyes. It's only right that I suffer, at least for a while. Frank's obviously proud of himself.

'So,' I say, 'you going to . . . fill me in?'

Frank swallows some juice, replaces the cap on the bottle. 'Well, you know I had surveillance set up at her house, right?'

Surveillance. Frank can't even spell the word, let alone do it. But I'll play along. I nod.

'Cameras,' I say. 'I brought one.'

'Yeah, so you did. Well, I didn't move, kept a watch on her place on account of she said it was a regular occurrence, these lads coming round and terrorising her. And I told her there was nothing I could do if they came round. To stop it, y'know?'

I nod. 'You can't get . . . *involved.*'

'Yeah, that's what I said. And she was okay with it.' He leans against the desk. 'I mean the point of the job was to find out who was causing her all this bother.'

'And you saw them.'

He doesn't hear me. Or if he does, he doesn't care. 'It was her car, you see, *mostly*. Sometimes the front window got put in, but she said that only happened a couple of times, both times Saturday nights, so I reckoned they were drunk and got some confidence from that. Anyway, most of the time they took their frustrations out on her car.'

'Off-street?'

'No,' he says, smiling. 'See, that's another reason why they took to the car. Mrs Sadler always parked on the street, right under a streetlight.'

I nod. Frank shovels a forkful of cake into his mouth, pulls a yummy face and I have to wait for him to finish chewing before he continues.

'My thinking was, they *knew* her.'

'Why?'

'They did the car. They knew it was hers, because when they got the courage, they put out her window, so Mrs Sadler was right about one thing – it was personal. And they needed the courage to get onto the property, because we both know that Mrs Sadler's the kind of lady who'd put up. At the very least, she'd recognise whoever it was if she saw them.' He takes another bite, talks through the cake. 'They had a point they wanted to make.'

'There was a point?' I glance out at the club floor. Jason Kelly comes out of the changing rooms, all ready for his workout. Paulo slaps the lad on the shoulder, points to the heavy bag, then heads for the cupboard. He brings out a pair of focus pads and watches as Kelly goes to work on the heavy bag. When I look back at Frank, he's polished off the cake, set the plate to one side.

'See, Mrs Sadler's a teacher, isn't she?' he says.

'I didn't know that.'

'She mentioned it, Cal.'

I glance back out the window and Jason Kelly's going hard into the bag. 'I've been . . . it's been a long week.'

'So she thought it was someone in her class. Someone who happened to know where she lived.'

'Right. And you saw 'em.'

He nods, grinning. 'Got 'em on camera. Two of them, both pupils in her class, they're both thirteen.'

'That's young for here.'

'They're not *from* here. Not ex-offenders. Paulo's never seen them before.'

'But you passed it on.'

'Better than that.' He smacks his lips, runs his tongue into one of his back teeth. 'Soon as Mrs Sadler put an ID on the pair of them, we went round to see the parents.'

'You didn't inform . . . the police?' I frown at him.

'Didn't need to.'

'Didn't Mrs Sadler—'

'No, she didn't want the police involved. She wanted it sorted amicably.'

I stare at Frank. He keeps using that big old vocabulary of his, he's going to lose the Daft Frank nickname quick enough. 'So what happened?'

'Showed the parents the photos I took, let them identify their own boys. And then we talked.'

'About what?'

'About compensation. About how much it would cost to repair the damage. We split the cost down the middle. I mean, we didn't want to make it official, get these lads in serious trouble. You know how that ends up, you can't shake it off.'

I nod. I want a cigarette, look out at the club again. 'Well done, Frank.'

'Sad, though.'

'Come again?'

'That she did what she did,' he says, nodding at the gym. 'I asked her about it. She said she was positive she'd seen one of the boys come here. When she found out it was an ex-young offenders' place, that was all she needed.'

'They weren't offenders.'

'Didn't matter to her. She wanted revenge, she lashed out. Didn't matter that it was wrong. Somebody had to get hurt.'

'She was angry, Frank.'

'Yeah, but *anyone* would do? Any young lad.'

I look at him. 'People get emotional.'

'But, y'know, it was the wrong person,' he says. 'I mean, where d'you get the revenge in that?'

I shake a cigarette out of the pack, move towards the door. 'Doesn't always matter.'

'You going out for a smoke?' he says.

'Yeah. Listen, well done, mate.' I nod at him. 'You did well. Reckon you could *run* . . . this place.'

'It's a partnership,' he says.

I make an agreeing noise so I don't have to lie. Then I leave the office and limp across the gym. Haven't needed a cigarette like this in ages.

I shouldn't be here. Smoked two already, leaning against the wall of the Lads' Club, staring at the street. There's a part of me that's willing Donkey to come roaring around the corner. At least that would put an end to it, and it'd be no more than I deserve. But after the second cigarette, I know he's not coming. Probably off somewhere licking his wounds, wondering how the fuck a mong like me managed to put one over on him.

Let him wonder.

I light another cigarette, promise myself the third's my last for the moment. After this I should head back home, see if he's turned up there. Or else I could get the ball rolling. I glance back at the Lads' Club, see Paulo heading for the double doors, and shift my arse so he doesn't hit me when he comes out.

'I was looking for you,' he says.

'Yeah?'

'Yeah, and I wasn't the only one.' He lowers his voice. 'Sorry about before.'

'No problem.'

'What did he want?'

'To mess. Same as usual. He's like that. It's okay.'

'You sure?'

I nod, blow smoke. There's a chill in the air that Paulo appears to have brought with him out of the club. He has his arms folded. Partly because it's a natural position for him, partly because he's trying to warm himself up.

'You're worried,' I say.

He doesn't answer for a few seconds. Then he says, 'You blame us, Cal?'

'I told you already.'

'I know.'

'Nothing to worry about.'

'You say that, but then what do I see?'

My turn. 'I know.'

'Police, come round looking for you. Not once, but twice in as many days.'

'They found Mo.'

'I know they did.'

'So Donkey wants to . . . *question* me. Wants to take me in. Except he can't.'

Paulo looks at me. 'Because he's suspended.'

'Sacked, more like.' I pluck the cigarette from my mouth. 'It'll be fine. You worry . . . you make *me* worried.'

'Okay.'

Best change the subject. 'How's Jason?'

'He's great. Now. Back on form.'

'Glad to hear it.'

Paulo looks at the pavement, breathes out. He might as well be smoking, the way his breath comes out in a long plume. He scrapes his bottom lip with his teeth, then straightens up.

'Listen, whatever you're doing—'

'You know . . . what I'm doing.'

'Make sure it's on the level. Make sure you're not going to take all this onto yourself.'

'I can't—'

'I don't want that on my conscience, Cal. Don't need any more shit weighing us down like that.'

I shake my head. 'Blame's got to fall . . . *somewhere*.'

'Not on you,' he says.

'No. I've got it covered.'

'Do I want to know?'

Shake my head once and ditch the cigarette. I've lost my taste for it. 'Probably not.'

He stares at me for a long time. 'What the fuck are you doing?'

'Not sure,' I say, half-smiling. 'But if Donkey . . . comes back. You know what to do. Right? Don't take a chance. Call the police. Let them handle him.'

'Okay.'

I pull my jacket as I walk round the side of the building. I parked the Micra round there so Paulo wouldn't see it and start asking stupid questions. These days it's hard enough to talk, never mind come up with reasonable explanations as to why the back of my motor's suddenly bashed in. And he would ask about it. The way he's been acting recently, I wouldn't have been surprised if he asked me for a cigarette himself. Constantly on edge, drinking way too much coffee in some misguided attempt to keep him away from the booze. Only need to spend five minutes in his company to know his mental health's all over the shop, but he can't admit it, especially not to me.

It shouldn't be long now, though. Then it'll be all over one way or another.

They destroyed us, the Tiernans. Mo Tiernan turned my brother into a smackhead, then a thief. I was along for the ride, so they turned me into a scapegoat and a jailbird, a walking fucking menagerie.

Nobody's business what happened to me in prison. Not something I want to dwell on now, either. And besides, when I came out, I had more important things to worry about. I entered the legit world after two-and-change to find that the Tiernans had strung Declan out. But they kept him in the bosom, just in case he got any ideas that he was better than his friends.

Judge a man by his mates, and watch him burn.

And because they strung him out, they were the ones to blame for his eventual suicide. Mo Tiernan killed my brother, and Morris Tiernan helped.

They put me in that place. Made me impotent. Destroyed what little life I had, put a stain on me I couldn't scrub off.

They killed my brother, tore up my family and stamped the remnants into the dirt without even fully fucking realising it.

Which is why I'm about to do what I'm doing. Because I already know who killed Mo Tiernan, and I can't let him take the fall for it.

After all, Paulo's the only real friend I have.

THIRTY-SIX

Innes

Of course it comes down to Jason Kelly in the end. One of the reasons I've been staying away from him, especially after when Paulo tells me how it all happened. The lad was trying to stay on the straight and narrow. Difficult enough on your own, made harder by the dealer that insisted on hanging around the club, looking for all the world like a stray dog nobody wanted to shoo away. Considering that dealer had the name Tiernan, ringing big bad bells for those who didn't know the back story.

The way Paulo told it, it was Jason Kelly he was looking out for. He saw that spark in the lad's eyes, wanted to focus it on the right thing. One bad spar, and a lad a couple years younger than Jason marked him up because Jason hadn't been watching his loose guard. He'd started wavering after that, looked to the dubious comforts of the past to see him through.

Now Paulo tried to pull him to one side – he'd already seen Mo nosing around the place again, didn't want to get into it if he didn't have to. Besides, Mo hadn't actually come onto the premises as yet, so Paulo didn't think he could get too demonstrative. Anyway, Jason was all understanding, the usual smiles and denials. Course he wasn't back on the wraps, Paulo. No way he'd do that anymore, is there? That was the shit got him in trouble in the first place.

The rehabilitation song, and Jason was in full voice.

But Paulo's never been an idiot, despite his palooka-looking face. So he kept an eye on Jason. And after a week or so, he saw Mo come out of the shadows. Paulo'd made a show of locking the place up and leaving, and it was only then that Mo showed his face.

'Should've seen him, Cal. The bloke was a walking corpse. Anything I did to him . . .'

'Okay,' I said. 'Carry on.'

Jason Kelly with his kitbag, moving into the darkness where Mo was skulking. Paulo watching from the club. Saw Jason emerge from the shadows a few minutes later with both hands in his pockets.

Paulo waited long enough for the suspicion to die down, waited for Jason to head up Coronation Street. He'd deal with Jason the next day, in the office, the kind of intense whispering that put the fear of God into the other lads, and which I remembered from my early days at the club.

Once Jason had gone, Paulo came out of the club, stopped by the front doors. 'Mo?'

Nothing.

'You're out there, son, I know it.'

A shuffling sound, but not much else.

'Think we need a word, don't you?'

'I'm not on your fuckin' property,' he said.

'I know.' Paulo tried to keep his voice friendly. Calm. 'But I think we should still have a talk, you and me.'

'Fuckin' joking, I'm not coming anywhere fuckin' near you.'

'Don't be daft, Mo.'

'Fuck off.'

'Don't make this difficult, son.'

'Here, I didn't do nowt wrong. Got nowt on us.'

Paulo didn't hang about. Off the steps and into the darkness, grabbed a handful of greasy Berghaus before Mo could react, wrenched him out of the shadows, the breeze throwing a stink into Paulo's face. He gritted through it, dragged Mo into the club and shoved him into the middle of the gym.

'Take a good look around, mate,' said Paulo. 'Want you to see exactly what you and your scally mates did. Reckon you haven't had much of a chance to admire your fuckin' handiwork, eh?'

The walls were still blackened then. They were still using the old rings, the old equipment, all of them with a layer of engrained soot.

Paulo brought Mo into the club to look at it all. The way he told me, he just wanted Mo to see what he'd done, show him that the place was still standing. He wanted to see the lad's reaction, and as he watched Mo look around, he already had a nice long speech for him, the usual warning and lecture rolled into one.

He'd just started when Mo said, 'Ah, fuck it.'

'You what?'

Mo danced back into the club a little more, his eyes almost hollowed out. And when Paulo told me how bad Mo looked, it was difficult not to think of a dancing skeleton, with a rictus grin and junkie tremble.

'Fuckin' *deserved* it. What, you want to fuckin' tell us that it didn't work? It worked.' Mo pointed at Paulo then, still grinning. 'Went right off the fuckin' rails, you did. Think I'm having problems? You was almost back on the fuckin' sauce, don't think I don't know about that. And so the fuck what anyway, man? What, you think you're better than me? You're not better than me. This – all this shite – it was a fuckin' *warning*. You got nobody to help you, nobody to protect you, we're gonna come at you any fuckin' time we *choose* to, know what I mean? You are not safe.'

'Don't be a dick, Morris.'

'You think I give a *fuck* anymore?' he screamed. Eyes bloodshot. 'You think I got owt to fuckin' take *away* from us now? What, you think I'm going to look around here and realise how fuckin' great you are? Fuckin' daft cunt.'

'You're out of your fuckin' mind,' said Paulo.

'The fuck?'

'Get out of my club.'

'You brought us *in* here, man.'

'And now you have to leave.'

Because as soon as Paulo brought Mo into the light, he saw the damage and knew how deep it went. Saw what he told me – a walking corpse, held together with a rare raging electricity, moving through sheer force of will. Mo's face twitched, a spasm of fear or hatred, as if he'd seen his reflection in a mirror, saw the mixture of faces in his own – the mother who left him, the father who hated him – and realised that they'd both been right to do so. Because somewhere amongst the misfiring synapses in his head, Mo knew his weaknesses.

But there was a difference between knowing your weaknesses and having them pitied by someone you hated.

'Aye,' said Mo. 'I know why you brought us in here, like. You want to have a pop at us. Because your fuckin' mate knows, I'm not going to stop if I don't want to, and there's nowt you can do to persuade us to back off. So you want to fuckin' end it.' He waved his hands – a come-and-have-a-go gesture – and stepped towards Paulo. 'Course you want to fuckin' end it. We all want to fuckin' end it.'

Paulo stood his ground, told Mo that he wanted him to leave. He didn't want to put hands on him, not like this. In the end, though, he didn't have a choice.

It was what Mo was waiting for. Soon as he felt Paulo's touch, Mo twisted, ducked and brought his forehead into Paulo's left cheek.

You could barely see the mark on Paulo's face by the time he told me what happened that night. And it wasn't so much the pain – Mo was weak as fuck, barely able to throw enough solid punches to get him out of the proverbial brown paper bag, so there was no chance he'd knock down Paul Gray – but the shock of the blow, the fact that this little prick had managed to plant one on him. And like a lot of ex-fighters, it wasn't even a conscious decision on Paulo's part to hit Mo back. It was as natural an instinct as breathing out when your lungs were full.

But he was pro enough to keep his punch loose. Told me that he didn't hit Mo hard at all, just enough to burst a lip and put him off-balance. A few steps, a one-two, three-four, then Mo dropped.

But not before he smacked his head off the end of the bench behind him.

The wet, heavy crack hung in the air long after Mo hit the floor. Paulo watched him roll onto his side. Looked at the bloody mark on the end of the bench, thought he saw something solid stuck, glistening, to the wood. Then he watched more blood begin to pool under Mo's head.

Paulo told me he was sorry.

'It's okay,' I said.

'I'm so fuckin' sorry. I didn't—'

'Don't . . . worry about it.'

The reason he told me was Tiernan. When he found out I was seeing Tiernan, he knew the game was up. If I hadn't been contacted, there would've been nothing said, I know it. The new club was open for a while, the bench gone along with the rest of the old gym equipment. All the walls of the place were painted, the trace evidence destroyed.

But guilt had a way of lingering. And as soon as Paulo knew I was on the case, he felt the need to spill his guts. Sitting forward in his chair, leaning on his knees, looking through me. His voice hoarse from all the talking, from trying to keep back tears. As he spoke, I watched his big hands clenching each other, the knuckles scuffed and scarred from a million punches that hadn't ended up in someone's death. But Paulo knew it only took one. Did the last time, the reason he went to prison, which was why he was stuck to his seat when he told me.

'I checked him out,' he said.

'And?'

'He was breathing.'

'Sure?'

'Yeah.'

But either way, it wouldn't look good. If Mo had been alive, he'd need a hospital. And there'd be an assault charge or worse pinned on Paulo. Plus more bad publicity for a club that had just made a couple of page fours by being firebombed.

And if Paulo was mistaken, that Mo was dead, then that would mean the end of everything. Without a doubt, all the hard work Paulo put in to get the club up and running would be totally worthless. Because all people would see was a man who'd previously done time for beating a man to death, up on trial for exactly the same thing. He'd be an ex-con who couldn't even rehabilitate himself, let alone the lads that came into the club.

'He couldn't stay there,' said Paulo.

I nodded. Of course he couldn't.

'Where?' I said.

'Miles Platting.' Paulo was shaking his head now. 'There was a thing in his pocket, something from the Job Centre. I reckoned that was where he was crashing these days, so I took him back there.'

'Right. In the car?'

'Yeah.' He looked up at me now. 'I didn't – I mean, I reckon he was still breathing, but I couldn't—'

'It's okay.'

We sat in silence for a bit. Outside, it started to rain, the water spackling against the window with a gust of wind. I breathed out, reached for my Embassys and wished I had a drink. Paulo probably did, too.

'He's dead,' he said.

I nodded. Trying to think.

Remembering – 'He's long gone, Callum. Trust us on this. Don't go looking for trouble when there's nowt to find, alright?' – and thinking that it wasn't so much advice, more a fucking warning.

Don't go snooping around and accidentally find out he killed Mo. Don't open that box, no matter what the fucking voices in your head tell you to do. It's not worth it.

When I looked at Paulo then, I understood the situation. He was trying to sort it himself, but couldn't reconcile what he'd done with the consequences. It was like when I saw my brother for the first time when I got out of prison. There was some shift in our relationship, like we'd somehow swapped places.

And I knew that Paulo and I were the same now. I wouldn't be intimidated by him for my own good, nor would I ever really seek his approval. There was nothing to look up to, now I knew the bloke was just as weak and stupid as the rest of us.

Didn't mean I didn't love the bloke to death. Just, things changed.

'He's dead, isn't he?'

'He'd be . . . at the club. If he wasn't. You know . . . what he's like.'

Paulo lowered his head again.

'What's the address?' I said.

Paulo told me. I struggled to my feet, told him to wait here. I'd call him when I got there. He said he'd come with me. I told him no, it was better if I went alone. The drive there would give me enough thinking time, because an idea had already sparked in my head.

It's still there now. And it's time to do what Mo wanted, and end it.

Once and for all.

THIRTY-SEVEN

Innes

I call Uncle Morris, sitting outside Sutpen Court right now. Thinking there's no easy way to break this to him, and there's no way I can do it over the phone, either.

Tiernan's mobile keeps ringing, as if daring me to hang up and forget about it. But I can't. Not now. Not now I've planted everything I'll need. And it's not even as if I've done an immaculate fucking job of it, either. It won't matter. If there's one thing I've learned from my constant fucking slog through this life of mine, it's that the truth doesn't matter – it's what *pretends* to be the truth, what someone *believes*. In that respect, every day is a leap of faith.

And in that respect, Tiernan better pick up this phone soon before I lose my fucking mind with worry.

He does. And it's only when he answers that I realise how late it feels. Already dark outside. More rain in the air. My side aches.

'Hello?' he says.

'It's Innes. We need to talk.'

'Now?'

'Yeah,' I say. 'Where?'

He grunts something, moves the phone away from his mouth for a moment. I can hear him talking in the background. Probably to one of his fucking apes. Telling them to either back off or saddle up, depending on how much he trusts me. I'm hoping it's the former, hoping the last few days and the marbles I've chucked under his feet haven't done too much damage. Because I need some swinging room here.

'What is it?' he says when he comes back on the line.

'I have a name,' I say.

He breathes out. Like he was hoping for it, but now he's having second thoughts. 'Okay,' he says.

'Where?'

'Tell me.'

'No.'

'What?'

'I can't. Not now.'

'Why not?'

My turn to breathe out. 'You trust me?'

He pauses. There's some more talk off-line. Somewhere deep beyond him, I think I can hear a door closing. Then another pause. His voice seems cracked when he speaks again. 'Who is it?'

'I told you. I can't tell you.'

'I'm paying you—'

'I know. But not on . . . the phone. Trust me.'

'The Wheatsheaf,' he says.

'Twenty minutes,' I tell him, then hang up.

Sit in the car some more, staring at the rain that's now battering the windscreen. Then I turn the key in the ignition, warm the engine up a little before I head out to the Wheatsheaf.

Brian the landlord looks like he's about to shit a cat as soon as he sees me push the doors. He stops a Guinness halfway down the pint and shouts at a small, busty blonde to finish it off once it's settled a bit. He scurries down to the end of the bar just as I'm approaching. To be fair, he needn't have bothered rushing. I'm taking my time. Old aches have surfaced again. Must be the cold. And I'm thirty next year. What a fucking waste.

I nod at Brian. His face is white, and already moon-shaped. Looks like he's this close to passing out, hating every second of this meeting and it hasn't even taken place yet.

'Where is he?' I say.

'He's upstairs in the function room. You're to go right up.'

I want to ask if he's alone, but I realise it doesn't matter if he's brought an entire fucking army with him. The man has to be told at some point, and if he doesn't trust me then so be it. We'll deal with whatever arises. Or I will.

Brian shows me to the stairs, which is good because I need a fucking pointer. He honestly looks like he's pointing the way to hell when he backs off from the staircase. I take it slowly, the way I take all stairs now.

Push into the function room, which is just a normal room with a laminate six-foot square in the middle that acts as a dance floor. The place is harshly lit right now, not the usual lights, I'm guessing, considering there's a DJ booth set up in one corner of the room. Looks like it should have Fisher-Price written on it. In the opposite corner, facing the door and the booth, is Morris Tiernan.

And he's alone.

He doesn't move as I approach. But I notice there's a chair already pulled out opposite him.

How very fucking thoughtful.

I don't take the chair. Look around the place.

'Well?' he says. 'You got a name for me or not?'

'Yeah.'

'Who?'

I take a moment, wonder how I'm going to phrase this, but then that's all I've been doing since I made the decision. There's no easy way, like I said.

'Alison,' I say.

'You what?'

'Alison.'

He blinks once. I can see his hands tighten a little as the idea flits across his mind. I let it churn around in there for a bit, make sure he's seriously considered the idea before I open my mouth again.

'I have proof.'

He nods. 'Right.'

She has motive. That jaunt up to Newcastle was spoiled by Mo's appearance. She lost a boyfriend to him, and she had a kid by him too. Could be argued that Mo Tiernan ruined his little half-sister's life. And it was obvious to her that her dad couldn't handle the situation, so she decided to take matters into her own hands. Hell, maybe Mo brought it on himself. Tiernan knows as well as everyone else that his son was hardly the kind of bloke to leave well enough alone. His trek up to Newcastle in hot pursuit of her was testament to that.

But then Morris knows all of this, doesn't he? He's thinking about it right now.

'You going to tell me what proof?' he says.

'Police found a hair,' I say.

'A hair.'

'In Mo's hand.'

'Uh-huh.'

'Under his . . . fingernail.'

'Right.' He looks at the table. 'And that's it?'

'No. There's more.'

'You know what I said would happen,' he says.

'I know.'

'Someone's responsible, they've got to be made an example of, right?'

I don't say anything. He looks up at me. And for the first time since I've known him, I really get what people are so fucking scared of. His blue eyes flash almost white and there's this granite-set look on his face that means he made a decision about his life a long time ago, and he's had to stick to it, come hell or high water, ever since. And it's been eating him the fuck up from the inside out.

It's the kind of look people see before they're killed.

'You're sure about this?' he says.

'I'm sure enough. To come to you. With the name.'

'Her name.'

'Yes. Don't think . . . it was *easy.*'

He puts one hand on his face, pinches the bridge of his nose like he's suddenly got the worst headache in the world. He's one word away from throwing the table over. There's a part of me that wants to ask him if he's okay. But I know that won't do any good. Morris is way into himself now. He'll come out when he's ready. Too much to take on right now. He moves his hand and sets it on the table. His fingers are crooked in a way that means his heart is hammering the inside of his chest.

I stand there. Watching. Waiting.

Tiernan sucks his teeth, breathes out through his nose. 'I think you should go downstairs.'

I nod. Turn towards the door.

'Have a pint or something. Not too much. But wait down there for me.'

Another nod. I make it to the door without falling down. Then I close it quietly behind me before I take the stairs.

It's a shitty thing to do, dropping Alison in it. Especially considering I've seen her since Newcastle. Especially considering it looks like she's trying to do something with her life, be a decent mother to a kid that she mustn't be able to look at without picturing Mo on top of her. That alone should be enough punishment.

Should be, but it isn't. Not really. These people fucked my life. They deserve everything they get.

Besides, who's going to believe that Paulo killed Mo? And who's going to believe that I took my fucking stick to him?

Then again, who's going to believe that a single mother did the deed, either?

Only one person has to. And that person is tearing himself apart up there.

Good.

I get to the bottom of the stairs, haul myself round to the bar. Brian makes his presence known almost immediately. Same expression on his face as before, and seeing me doesn't help it.

'Well?' he says.

I lift my chin at him. 'What?'

'How's it going?'

'How's what going?'

Brian wags his head. I lean closer.

He lowers his voice: 'How is Mr Tiernan?'

I lean in close. 'None of yours.'

'Come on, I need to—'

'You don't.' I point at the pumps. 'Kronenbourg.'

Brian locks stares with me for a moment, then he backs off towards the pumps. I lean against the bar, wish I could light up in here. I was told to sit down here like a good boy, which means I don't get to leave the place for a sly cigarette. Which is a bastard, but I'm sure I'll be able to ride it, knowing full well that any discomfort I might go through is like a fucking pin prick compared to the agony he's dealing with upstairs. My only real problem is keeping the fucking smile from my face.

I look down and there's a pint of Kronenbourg. I reach into my pocket, but Brian's already waved me off. There's no paying, not while I'm supposedly a guest of Mr Tiernan's. I pick up the pint and hobble over to an empty table. Set the pint down and breathe out.

When I'm about halfway down the pint, I wonder if I'm going to make it out of this pub alive. It's not so much a sudden thought, more one that creeps out from my subconscious. There's a chance Morris is keeping me down here so that I won't do a runner. Making me stay in one place so he knows where to find me when he plucks up enough energy or courage or whatever it is a man like him needs to come down here and finish me off. But then I look around the place and realise that even Morris Tiernan wouldn't kill someone in front of a pub full of people.

Two thirds down the pint, there's a noise from outside. I turn in my seat, squint through the frosted pane at the road. There's Tiernan's usual ride, the SUV, gleaming in the streetlight. A thump from upstairs and I turn back to see Tiernan emerge from the hall. You can feel the temperature of the entire room drop, the oxygen going with it as everyone turns and breathes in at the same time.

Tiernan stops by me, holds out his hand. 'Lead the way.'

I put my pint down. Get to my feet. 'Sorry?'

'You know where we're going.'

I look at the unfinished pint, then nod to Tiernan. I haul myself towards the door, step out onto the street.

Here goes nothing.

THIRTY-EIGHT

Donkin

I knew it would take balls, but I also knew that nobody reckoned us dogged enough to do it by the book. In fact, it was abundantly fucking clear to us now what everyone expected – they expected us to go right after the cunt, all guns blazing, not give a fuck about the consequences of my actions, all emotion and no fucking brains. And if they were basing it on past experience, then they were probably right.

But here was the thing. They'd never managed to kick us off the force before, because I always got the bastard responsible. Now I was suspended, it'd be the same deal, except I had to be really fucking careful. Which meant there was no way I could do it on my own. Innes already knew I was suspended, wouldn't take being cuffed without a good kicking, and that wouldn't help us in the long run.

I didn't need to put the cuffs on him myself, though. And not everyone knew I was suspended. Which was why when I showed my ID to the first streak of piss constable I saw back at the nick, he said, 'What's up?'

'Need your help on something,' I said. 'Urgent, like.'

He nodded, followed us out to the car. I kept my head down.

'What's your name?' I asked.

'John,' he said, smiling.

Excellent, a fucking probationary.

'Alright, Constable John, you better drive us. I think I've had a few too many sherberts and I don't want us pulled over.'

PC John looked at us funny then, so I gave him my best I'm-just-kidding grin and got in the driver's side. He was a conscientious bastard, this one, which meant he'd be a good one to have on my side when the shit eventually hit the fan.

'Where are we going?' he said.

'We're going round to see someone that I want a word with.'

'And you need me—'

'As back-up.' I put my seatbelt on, started the engine. 'The lad we're going to see, he's got form – did two and change in the 'Ways not so fuckin' long ago, and it looks like he's itching to get back inside. Thing is, though, me and him, we got something of a past.'

The constable looked at us cock-eyed.

'Which is one of the reasons you're here. This history me and him have, it might make him think he can prod us into something that would be detrimental to the case. So you're adding a bit of balance to the proceedings. You get me? I mean, I got the right bloke, didn't I? You're good at your job, you're impartial.'

He nodded, then looked confused.

'You know the name Callum Innes?'

'No.'

'You will by the end of tonight, I'll tell you that.' I put my hand in my pocket, pulled out my baccy tin and rested it against the steering wheel as I rolled one-handed. 'That stretch he did, it was for the Tiernans, so he's connected. You'll know the Tiernans.'

'Morris,' he said.

'You're that familiar, huh?'

The constable swallowed. 'No, I didn't mean that.'

'Thought I might have to second-think my back-up there, son.'

Shook his head. 'Sorry, no.'

'But you know *of* him, which is a good start. Means you know we're not dealing with small fry here, right? You know what the cunt's capable of.'

Constable John got noticeably paler. So I decided to put the bloke's mind at ease a bit.

'Innes is connected,' I said, 'but he's not *that* connected. What I could make out, Morris might be keeping him on a salary, but Innes is spinning him a yarn. The lad's up to his balls in shite.'

'Right,' said PC John, his voice low, like he was trying to be all manly. 'So you want to bring in Innes to roll on Tiernan?'

'No. We don't go for the big fish. No fuckin' point. You grab Tiernan on something to do with Innes, he'll just chuck cash at it, pull a few strings and that case you had vanishes into thin fuckin' air. The man's got briefs so good, Tiernan could skin you – you personally, a fuckin' copper – and it'd come out self-defence. Flay you alive. With witnesses. Broad fuckin' daylight, middle of Piccadilly Gardens, and he'd get off. That's my point.'

I put one hand up to the back of my neck, pushed at the flesh. Getting a nasty stress crick up there, better I knead it out before we get to our destination. Didn't want it to affect what I had to do.

'No, we just go for Innes. Innes is our target here.' I pulled onto Regent Road. 'Usually, I wouldn't need any back-up on this, but the situation's different.'

'Your history.'

'Aye. Nice to see you've been paying attention. Now if he kicks off, you just leave it to me. No sense in getting your nice new uniform all messed up. And if he does kick off, I want you to back me up when it comes to the paperwork, alright?'

He kept it shut.

'It's all legit here, Constable, I promise you. I wouldn't have it any other way.' My mobile started ringing. I looked across at PC John. 'Okay?'

He was staring out the windscreen at the road. Chewing his lip. Knew he'd agreed to something that would end up biting him in the arse. His own fucking fault, of course. I knew the look in the bastard's eyes the moment I saw him – he was a career copper, but one that didn't want to do things the usual way. So he saw us, figured us for an easy promotion if he helped us out.

'Okay,' he said.

Soon as he answered me, I answered my mobile. 'Detective Sergeant Donkin.'

'Donkey, what the fuck d'you think you're doing?'

Kennedy. I scratched my cheek, watched the road but didn't really see it.

'You hear me?' he said.

'Yeah, I heard you.'

'So?'

'I'm wondering how the fuck you got this number.'

'How d'you think?'

'Derek.'

'If you want.'

'Anything that cunt *hasn't* told you, Colin?'

He laughed, but there wasn't any fucking humour in it. 'Yeah, one thing – whatever the fuck it is you think you're doing right now.'

'Right now? I'm driving.'

'You know what I mean.'

'It's a long story. Better you just tell us what you heard.'

'I heard you came into the nick and commandeered a fucking uniform. Basically kidnapped him.'

'See, that's how rumours start. He's here of his own volition.'

'And what about you going after Innes?'

I didn't answer that for a few seconds. Had to think about my reply. Because this twat had heard something, and it couldn't have been from Adams. Which meant the poof had grassed us up. Which was fair enough, considering.

'I'm not after Innes,' I said. 'I'm after Mo's killer.'

PC John looked at us then. I shook my head at him.

'Well, you need *someone* to straighten this out for you, Donkey, because if this gets anywhere near the DCI's ears—'

'Let him find out, Colin. Honestly, like I give a fuck. What, you were going to keep it a secret for me? Very kind of you, you slimy little wanker, but I think I can take this on my own. Ta, anyway.'

'I'm not offering help, I'm asking you what the fuck you think you're playing at. Obviously you've got a suspect, obviously you want to bring him in. So you're kidnapping constables for the arrest?'

I waved my hand, squinted. Wanted to hang up on the cunt, especially now we were getting close to the poof's club. 'Maybe we can talk about this some other time, eh?'

'Or is it that you know as soon as this disciplinary's over with, you're dead in the fucking water? And you reckon, what the fuck, you might as well deal with some personal grudges on the way out?'

I *did* hang up then. Turned off the mobile and put it in my pocket. I could feel the constable looking at us, but I didn't turn. Concentrated on the road instead.

Kennedy would have had a point if I was the old Donkey. Like, if I was a bloke that harboured grudges. I mean, I could see how that might look from the outside – like I was hounding Innes, trying to get him banged up again because of, what, some long-standing fucking enmity?

It was fucking ridiculous, but then that was obviously the way everyone saw it.

Including Constable John over there.

Well, fuck him, and fuck Kennedy. This had to be official. I couldn't have my case blown out of the water because of a technicality, like I wasn't *officially* a copper, and couldn't *officially* make an arrest. What I said to PC John before about Innes kicking off, well, that could happen and I'd be ready for it if it did, but I also knew that the old days of me being able to clout a cunt and get away with it were over. And I knew the constable sitting next to us was a bastard jobsworth, just like the rest of them. Which was good, because I was playing it straight, meant that I'd end up collaring the right lad – a lad who'd been walking away from shite for far too long, you asked me – *and* I'd be doing it right. I'd also be slipping a case out from under Kennedy, which explained why he was so quick to call.

Fuck it, if I was lucky, I'd be able to get Kennedy up on some kind of investigation himself. After all, it wasn't like he was breaking his back trying to find out who did it, was it now?

But I was getting ahead of myself. First I had to deal with the poof again. I couldn't go in there steaming again, not after the last time. To be honest, I'd forgotten that the bloke used to be a handy fighter in his day.

And as I pulled the Granada into Coronation Street, I took a deep breath. I'd have to be fucking clever about this, right enough.

Parked outside the poof's club. Turned in my seat.

'Wait here,' I said. 'If I start screaming for help, you come running, alright?'

He didn't nod. Didn't shake his head, either.

Fair enough.

THIRTY-NINE

Innes

'Need to talk to you, love.'

Alison Tiernan looks over her dad's shoulder at me. I look at the ground. Next to me is the big lad Tiernan called Darren. He's holding his hands in front of him. I feel movement in front of me, hear a kissing sound, and look up to see Tiernan walking into Alison's house, his head bowed. Squint across at Darren and he nods towards the open door.

I head into the hall. See Alison leading her dad into the living room. Feel Darren behind me, hear him close the door and feel the swift breeze turn to the cloying heat of the radiators. You can almost hear the fresh air get sucked out of the room. There's also the sound of something live and obnoxious on the television, quickly muted as I enter. Talent show of some sort, can't tell which one because my eyes are hurting too much. I rub them as Sammy comes into the room, staring up at us all with large blue eyes.

Alison goes to her kid, hoists him up to her hip. Looks at us, standing there in the middle of her living room like a bunch of fucking bailiffs. And, for a second, I'm scared and guilty about what's going to happen.

Then I get control of myself, hoping it didn't show.

All this is necessary. I need to remember that.

'What's up?' says Alison.

Tiernan holds his hand out to Alison, jerks his head towards the kitchen. 'Need a word with you in private, love.'

'What's he doing here?'

'You want to give the kid to Darren, he'll—'

'Nah, what's *he* doing here?' she says, nodding at me.

'I'll tell you in a second.'

Darren moves to take the kid from Alison and her eyes flicker wide.

'No,' she says. 'What's up, Dad? Tell us now.'

Tiernan looks at me, breathing through his nose, his eyes slits. Like he's already blaming me for coming here, for the questions he has to ask. I look back at him, hopefully with the right face for the situation.

'Darren,' he says, 'look after Sam for us, will you?'

Alison gets it then. Something bad's happened. What she doesn't know is that something worse is *about* to happen. She looks at her son, then puts him on the floor. 'Show Darren your Legos, Sam.'

Sam looks at Darren, then back at his mum.

'It's okay. Show him your Legos.'

'You want to show us your Legos, eh?' says Darren, trying to be as non-threatening as possible.

Sam heads for the door to the hall. Darren pauses before he follows him.

Alison waits until she hears them climbing the stairs before she says, 'It's about Mo, isn't it?'

Tiernan looks like he wants to burst into tears right then. But he doesn't. 'Makes you say that?'

She points at me. 'Because *he's* here. And the last time he was round here, he was asking about Mo an' all.'

'He's dead,' says Tiernan.

Alison shakes her head and moves towards the kitchen. 'You'll want a brew, then.'

She sticks the kettle on, pulls out some mugs.

'Just the two. Callum's not staying.'

Alison does as she's told. Then she leans against the counter and says, 'Where'd they find him?'

Tiernan sits at the small kitchen table. Pulls a chair out. The legs scrape loudly against the tiles. 'Miles Platting, wasn't it, Callum?'

I nod. 'Squat.'

Alison nods to herself. 'Right.'

'You know he was squatting?' says Tiernan.

'No.'

'See him much?'

Alison looks at her father. 'No, Dad. Why would I?'

'Just wondering,' he says, lacing his fingers together on the table. 'Just trying to . . . I heard something about him recently, I'm trying to get my head round it.'

'What's that?'

Tiernan frowns. 'That he was killed.'

She doesn't stop with the coffee, moves to the fridge and grabs some milk. You can tell she's a mother – she doesn't have to sniff the milk to see if it's alright.

'Alison,' says Tiernan.

'Was he?'

'Police seem to think so.'

'Okay.' She turns back to her father, glances at me. 'And what's he got to do with it?'

I don't answer. Tiernan says, 'I asked him to look into it for me.'

'Why?'

'Because he's trustworthy.'

'Seriously, Dad, why?'

'I told you—'

'Right,' she says, and her tone hardens. 'You got him to investigate. And the first place he comes is round here.'

Tiernan doesn't say anything for a while. He rubs his nose with one hand, then shifts around in his seat and stares at me. Looks me up and down as if it's the first time he's ever seen me. After a moment, the kettle boils. Alison moves to it and pours the coffees.

'I think you better wait outside,' says Tiernan. 'You look like you need a smoke or something.'

I nod. Make a move for the door. As I do, Tiernan turns back to his daughter and sighs.

I don't know what I expected, but it wasn't this. Standing outside a semi-detached Barratt Home on the edge of town, watching the sky light up with the first fireworks of the night.

I breathe smoke and drop the cigarette under my heel.

Inside the house, I can hear people moving around. I take a step back, look up at the first floor – see the lights on in what looks like the kid's room. Hoping to fuck he's not going to be around to see what's going to happen to his mother. From inside, more movement. And a loud voice, distressed, sounds like Alison. I can't make out what she's saying, but I catch the intent. She's defending herself, shouting back at her dad. In the middle of it, her voice cuts out.

Tiernan hit her. I move back to the hallway, can make out the sound of sobbing coming from the kitchen. It's quiet, as if she's used to keeping her voice down. A far cry from the last time I saw her – with a black eye, a black eye she got in self-defence from the guy she was beating the shit out of on a regular basis.

She was tough back then. Not so much now.

I reach the kitchen door. Push it open.

Alison Tiernan is leaning in the corner of the counter, one hand up over her face. No blood, but both her cheeks are flushed. On the floor, one of the mugs that I presume was hers is smashed and a thick brown river spreads into a pool on the floor. Tiernan is still sitting down, his hands over his mug. He's staring into the liquid.

'Something . . .'

His voice catches. He pushes the mug away from him.

'. . . something I don't understand,' he says, slowly, carefully, with his four-pack-a-day voice. He raises one finger to his temple, taps. 'I've been thinking about it, but I still . . . can't get my head right on it.'

I don't say anything. He doesn't move.

'You want to know what it is?' he says.

I still don't say anything. Wait it out. Maybe he's talking to Alison.

Tiernan turns in his seat. And, for the first time, I can see he's been crying. His eyes are red-rimmed and his cheeks shining to dry. He rubs one hand against his face in a rough movement. 'I'm talking to you.'

I clear my throat. 'Okay.'

'And I was wondering something.'

'What?'

'When you started thinking I was fuckin' stupid.'

I blink. My gut sinks. 'Sorry?'

'I was wondering when it was . . . *exactly* . . . when you started to play funny buggers with us. When you thought I was so fuckin' washed up you could have a bit of fun with us.'

'I don't know what—'

'I don't give a *fuck*, Callum.'

'Wait a second. You talked to her,' I say.

'Alison's got nowt to do with Mo's death, Callum.'

'That's not true.'

'She says she didn't—'

'She's lying.'

'You have proof, you tell us.'

'The police know.'

Alison looks at me. 'How?'

'Donkey told me. He told me what they found at the scene.'

Alison shakes her head and squints at me.

'They have ID . . . from his wallet,' I say, looking straight at her. 'She dropped it . . . when she took his wallet. They must have . . . taken *prints* from it. And they have a hair. A long hair, can't be his. Won't take them long . . . to find out it's *Alison's*. Even if she hasn't . . . seen him. Recently. The police reckon . . . I'm sorry. The body was there. For a while. Before it was found.'

Tiernan doesn't say anything now. He breathes out through his mouth.

'She has a motive,' I say, moving round in front of the table. 'I know it's difficult . . . to accept. But it's true. That *kid*.'

Tiernan looks up at me, then beyond me at Alison.

'You know whose it is,' I say. 'You know what Mo did. To her boyfriend. In Newcastle. She didn't forget that.'

'You're a fuckin' *liar*,' she says. Keeping her voice down.

But I move out of the way, turn so I can watch her. Just in case. She's standing next to the cutlery drawer and a knife block – I don't want my back to her.

I shift and point at her. 'I'm not saying . . . she killed him. Could've been an OD. But she was there. When he died. The hair under his fingernail. Ask the police. The wallet. And whoever was there . . . they did damage to him. Lot of hatred there. I don't know . . . anyone else in this room . . . with that kind of hatred? For Mo.'

Tiernan looks at the table.

'I know you . . . don't want to hear this. But it's true. Got to deal with it. I can help.'

'You lying bastard,' says Alison.

'Alison.' A quiet warning from Tiernan. She shuts up.

'It's okay,' I say. 'I can talk . . . to the police.'

Tiernan raises his head and looks at me. His eyes are half-closed. He looks tired as fuck, like all this noise has taken it out of him.

'I can make it better,' I say. 'Just leave it to me.'

A small smile appears in the corner of his mouth, spreading across until it becomes a full-on toothy grin. Then he closes his eyes for a few seconds, exhales.

'I can't let you do that,' he says. 'There's no point talking to the police for us, Callum. Appreciate the offer and everything.'

I hear thumping from upstairs and my heart joins in. Sounds like they're moving to the stairs.

'The police don't get involved with this. This is me taking care of my own. We're not fuckin' idiots here, Callum. You know as well as I do what's going to happen to the man who killed my boy.'

'I can sort—'

'You can sort nowt,' says Tiernan. 'Because I've got an idea who killed Mo, and it wasn't Alison.'

I watch Tiernan, don't say anything. Pray that we don't have to go round the Lads' Club.

Behind me, I can hear Darren come down the stairs.

And I stop breathing.

FORTY

Donkin

Getting late now, but Gray still had a light burning in the window. As I headed for the doors, I hoped that Constable John would keep his fucking head down. I wanted to keep this quiet for the moment and, while everyone in here knew us, they'd think bad thoughts if I came back with a uniform.

Besides, I had a fucking rep to think about. If I was going to walk in there, I'd walk in alone. The constable was back-up, not part of the team.

And I was the gunslinger, hefting open the double doors and catching the glare of the bright strips right in the eyes. When I got my vision back, I reckoned the place was pretty much empty apart from the black flies that danced in front of my eyes.

'For fuck's sake.'

I squinted in the direction of the voice. It was Gray, standing there with a mug in his hand.

'Yeah. I want a word with you.'

'Thought we'd been through what we had to say.'

'No, we haven't.'

'In fact, what I should do is call the police. Y'know, the *active* police.'

'Can if you want. I'm not here to cause any trouble.'

'Says you.'

'Won't take long.'

Gray watches us for a few seconds, then he takes a drink out of his mug and turns away. 'If you're really on your best behaviour, you might as well step into the office.'

There was me thinking I'd have a problem. But, no, he was calm as. I followed him out to the back of the place. Into the office, and there was that Frank bloke propped up in a chair, reading a wodge of papers, a bit of Neil Diamond chuntering away in the background, an old one. The bloke was singing the words in a half-whisper: "I got the feeling, I'm hearing goodbye . . ."

When he saw us, he moved his feet from the desk and glanced at Gray.

'Everything alright?' he said.

'Yeah,' said Gray. 'Might want to give us a minute, mind.'

'Sure, no problem.' Frank moved from the desk, pulled his jacket off the back of his chair. 'I should be off anyway.'

We watched the big lad go. Gray shut the office door and I said, 'What'd he do?'

'Sorry?'

'It's been bugging us. He did time, didn't he?'

'Yes.'

'So what was it?'

'Armed robbery.'

'Huh,' I said. 'He doesn't seem the type.'

'He's not. Which is why he got caught.'

'So where's his partner?'

Gray didn't say anything. Leaned against a desk and folded his arms. 'We've been through this. And I thought you agreed that you wouldn't come round here bothering him.'

'You went through it. This is different.'

'Yeah, it's important, right?'

'That's right.'

'And you're doing it nicely, because you can't throw your weight around. Because I don't have to answer a single fucking question you throw my way.'

I smiled. 'I know that. And there's no need to look so fuckin' smug about it, is there? Specially when your boy's in the shit.'

'I've heard that before an' all.'

'He been missing before?'

'He's not missing.'

'He's not at home.'

'So?'

'And he's not here, unless you've got him hid in a fuckin' cupboard somewhere. Which means, to *me*, that he's missing. So. Here I am. Looking for him.'

'Why?'

'None of your fuckin' business.'

'It is when I'm the one forced to listen to your bollocks,' he said, straightening up. 'You want to play that game—'

'There's a police constable outside in my car,' I said.

Gray stopped flapping his gums for a second. Another second passed and it sank in. 'How bad is it?'

'We need to make an arrest tonight.'

'Who?'

I didn't bother to answer that. Made a face like it was fucking obvious, wasn't it? Gray stared at us, waiting for us to say someone else, anyone but Innes. But I didn't.

'What for?'

'He's going to help us with our enquiries.'

'What's the charge?'

'At the moment?' I scratched my ear. 'Lad's looking at murder, but a good brief'll get it knocked down to manslaughter, I reckon.'

See, now that did something to the poof – made his skin crawl, got him all antsy. You mention murder to an average pleb, they don't take you seriously. Murder's the remit of the telly and movies, not something that worms its way into an average life unless you're either unhinged or unlucky. But you mention it to someone who's done time, you watch the skin crawl right off his fucking body.

He breathed out through his nose. 'Who?'

'Who the fuck d'you think?'

'Mo?'

'No prizes.'

'He didn't do it.'

'Oh, well, that's a fuckin' relief. There was me thinking he had something to do with it, on account of he physically assaulted Mo about six months ago, threatened to kill him if he ever saw him again, in front of a pub full of witnesses. And then there's the history the two of them had. And the fact that he was on the fuckin' crime scene the night the body was called in, with blood on that walking stick of his like he'd just used it to beat the shit out of a corpse. So, you've got to understand, even if he *didn't* do it, it's pretty easy for me to *surmise* that he's got *something* the fuck to do with it.' I rolled my shoulders, gave the poof a good hard stare. 'But if you reckon he didn't have nowt to do with it, then that's good enough for me, isn't it? I might as well fuck off home.'

Gray watched me, caught every syllable of my sarcasm and swallowed the anger, even though it was a tough fucking gulp. Because he knew I was right; he'd been around the bastard long enough to know he'd had something to do with Mo's death. And, for a second, I reckoned it might be worth bringing *him* in.

Then I figured, nah. I had to focus on my target here. Couldn't waste PC John on this nonce.

'You can't pin this on him,' he said.

'I'm not pinning nowt on anybody. Just enquiries at the moment.'

'You want to bring him in and sweat him.'

'And you need to call him,' I said. 'Right now. Before this gets fuckin' daft and we both do stuff we'll regret.'

'No.'

'Then I can't vouch for his safety.'

'You're the fuckin' *threat* to his safety,' said Gray.

'You can't honestly believe that,' I said, 'because if you do, then you're more of an ignorant bastard than I thought. You honestly expect us to believe you don't know he's working for Tiernan again?'

Gray didn't say anything. He pushed off the desk. Made for the door, but I got in his way.

'What?' All aggressive now. 'You want to start something, Detective?'

'No,' I said, trying to be as open as fucking possible. 'You know he's working for Tiernan, and you've been around here long enough to know what kind of bloke Tiernan is. And what he fuckin' *isn't* is the forgive-and-forget type. So, you know, the slightest fuckin' *breath* of your boy being involved in Mo's death – and there's going to be more than a fuckin' breath, you give it a couple days – and he's dead.'

'Fuck off.'

'He's dead. Because Tiernan doesn't take any prisoners. You know that. He can't afford to, especially not when it's his son that's been killed. He has to tie up all loose ends, and fuck's sake, your boy's out there flapping in the breeze, isn't he? I don't know what the fuck he's trying to pull, but he won't make it.'

'Because of you,' said Gray. And there was a genuine accusation in his voice. 'Because you'll bring him in. Doesn't matter that he didn't do it, you're going to pin it on him. So he's dead anyway, right?'

'Not if we do this right,' I said, raising both hands. 'I want to do this the right way. That's why I brought the constable along. He's the one who'll make the official arrest, and we'll do this by the book, and I'll do everything I can for him.'

'He didn't do it.'

'Makes no difference.'

Gray moves away from us, heads back to the desk. He looks down into his mug, looks like he's going to have another drink, then passes by. If I didn't know better, I'd swear the bloke was about to start fucking crying. I knew he wasn't, right enough – he *couldn't* have been – but he was emotional enough to listen.

'There's only one way out of this,' I said, 'and that's with me.'

Gray put one hand on the desk. A part of us reckoned he was feeling around for a weapon. Then he said, 'What do I have to do?'

'Call him,' I said. 'Get him to come here. We'll do it nice and quiet, won't be any trouble for you.'

He looked at the phone. Put one hand on the receiver.

'Then it'll be over,' I said. 'Promise you, on my daughter's life, I won't bother you again.'

Then Paulo Gray looked up at us. His eyes were dry, his jaw set.

He picked up the phone, started dialling a number.

'I'll take you up on that,' he said.

And, looking at him, I didn't doubt it for a fucking second.

FORTY-ONE

Innes

It's ringing.

Somewhere through this red fog that means I can't see, can't hear, can't move without pain, I can hear my mobile ringing. Bringing me out of unconsciousness and into a fresh, stinging reality where every breath feels like it's made of smoke, and the smell of shit and piss and blood and sweat hang heavy. I can't move. Can't even think about moving because the thought alone puts me on a bad route.

'Shit.'

Cutting through the haze. Tiernan's voice. A low growl, thick in his throat. Then there are hands on me, and they feel like they're made of fucking metal, gouging into my flesh. He's rifling through my pockets, but he might as well be wrenching out my fucking organs and throwing them to the floor.

'Dad. Don't.'

'You still here?'

'Yeah. So's Sam.'

'I told you to go to the bonfire, love.'

'I can't take him to the bonfire.'

'Why? Kids love fireworks.'

'Not Sam. He doesn't like them. They're too noisy.'

'Then he has to get used to them, doesn't he?'

'No, Dad, he doesn't.'

'It's going to happen every year. You don't want to have to tranquillise him, do you?'

'He's not a *dog*, Dad.'

'But he needs to go out for a walk, right? Busy here.'

'We've *been* for a walk, Dad. Remember?'

'Eh?'

And there's a moment where I picture Morris Tiernan standing there, his vest wet with my blood and spit, looking at me like he's wondering where all the time went. Then one hand clamps on my hip, I jerk like I've been shocked, and a weight moves from my pocket. I try to breathe out slowly, but it feels like boiling hot liquid spilling out of my throat.

'Fuckin' things.'

'Dad,' says Alison, 'I mean it. If Sam hears you swearing, he's going to copy it, alright?'

The ringing stops. Tiernan breathes out. 'Alright. Okay. Sorry, love.'

'And I'm not bringing him in here. The mess you've made.'

'Yeah.' Tiernan sniffs. 'Might want to put him to bed?'

'I will, but get it cleaned up. Properly, okay?'

'Right.'

'Seriously, Dad. I want it spotless.'

'I heard you. I'll get Darren in. You won't know we've been here.'

The kid screams from outside the door. The sound is enough to make me flinch on the floor. Alison tells the boy she's coming, but there's a pause before she leaves. I'm guessing she's shooting her father a glare.

Then there's nothing but silence apart from the sound of my own wet, sick breathing.

Tiernan shuffles his feet against the lino. 'You better be awake, Innes.'

I cough.

'Good.'

Another shuffle. Then he plants one in my head that knocks me out.

*   *   *

The smell of pine in here. The slow, steady thrum of a car engine. The SUV. I'm laid along the seats in the back, and when I move there's a plastic sound, which means they've taken the precaution of lining the fucking place.

Just in case they have to wrap and dump my body somewhere. And it's not far off. I should know. I've been there before. And there's that same smell in the air around me that I can't shake off. It's cloying, a musty mixture of sweat and urine that's overpowering enough to make me want to pass out. But I can't do that. Because if I do that, I know I won't wake up again. Something jarred loose in my head. I can almost hear it rattling around in there. Unconsciousness would mean it slides right into the fleshy part of my brain and then that'll be it.

Can't happen. Not the way Tiernan's talking now. Staring right at where he thinks I am in the rear-view. Darren – or someone who smells just like him – is driving. He hasn't said anything the entire time I've been awake.

'. . . you hear me?'

I hear you, Morris.

'Think I'm daft, Callum? You ought to know me better than that by now. Thought we had an understanding. I don't know. Since the Newcastle thing – I told you I appreciated that, right? Well, since the Newcastle thing, I thought I could count on you as part of the . . . extended family. I thought if I had a problem, I could come to you and you'd help me out. That was the way you seemed to approach the situation. But to have you mess us around like *this* . . .'

I hear a sigh from the front seat. Tiernan turns to Darren.

'You know what it's like, Darren? You trust someone and they play silly buggers with you.'

Darren grunts.

'Because that's all it is, Callum,' he said, back staring at me now. 'I don't know what you thought you were playing at, trying to make us believe my own daughter was involved, when I know for a fact she wasn't and wouldn't have owt to do with Mo. I mean, you were all adamant about this hair or whatever, but you honestly think you're the only bloke I asked to look into this?'

I shift a little on the floor of the van. Try not to let the fear show on the working half of my face. Although it's unlikely, considering I'm swollen to fuck. Tiernan doesn't see me, anyway. He might call me by my name, but he's talking to a bloke he didn't just pound into shit.

Tiernan looks out of the windscreen for a second. 'You want to know what I heard?'

I don't say anything. Can't say anything.

'I heard that you were at the scene of the crime before the coppers found the body. Which means you know where my boy was. I also heard that he was beaten to fuck, but he was beaten to fuck *there*. Not wherever he was killed. Which means you put a beating on my boy after he was dead. And I'm wondering why.'

He looks at me again in the mirror.

'You want to tell us? Nah, don't suppose you can, can you? Even if you could, I get the feeling you'd come up with some fuckin' excuse.' He rubs his face. 'You're a tough cunt, Innes, I'll give you that. But you're trying to protect someone and it's not going to fuckin' work, I'll tell you that an' all.'

Tiernan turns round in his seat, makes sure I'm looking at him. When he grabs my face, the pain is unbearable. 'I'll find out who killed my son, Innes. I'll find out who did it, because I'll pay the fuckin' police to give me a name. Your fuckin' bent bastard mate Donkin should do the trick – he'll give it up. Whoever you're protecting with this shite won't be protected anymore. You're not in a position to warn anyone, and I'll make sure that even if the cunt's arrested, he won't last a week. You understand, mate? You got off easy.'

He lets me go. I drop back to the floor, concentrate on my breathing.

'Because for all of this,' he says, 'I still like you. I just don't fuckin' trust you anymore.'

Streetlights flash through the van. I look at the roof, breathe slow and jagged out through my mouth.

And that's when I realise I'm going to die.

FORTY-TWO

Donkin

Gray put the phone back down.

'Well?'

'No answer.'

I knew he wouldn't. Somewhere out there, Innes knew I was coming for him, and he was laying low, wouldn't even take a call from his boyfriend.

'Try him again,' I said.

'This is ridiculous.'

'Don't fuckin' start.' I pointed at him. 'You try him again, and you keep trying him. He'll answer. And when he does, you tell him to come in. To me. Don't matter how long it takes, because I'm not going anywhere until I get some fuckin' face time with your boy.'

I went for my baccy, pulled out the tin and the poof's face started to blotch red.

'No,' he said.

'You what?'

Nodded at the tin. 'No smoking in here.'

'You're the boss, Mr Gray.' I backed out the office, grinning. 'But you make sure you keep trying that fuckin' phone. I want him here.'

I turned, pushed out of the club. PC John was up out of the car and watching the door. Up the road I could see headlights, too far away to see if they were coming anywhere near us. I leaned against the wall, pinched some baccy, dropped it into a Rizla.

'What's happening?' said PC John.

'He's calling our man,' I said, and licked the ciggie shut. 'You might as well stay out of sight. I don't want him doing a runner because he's seen a uniform.'

The lights swung round at the top of the street. Closer now. Something big, shiny, like a van or something, slowing to a stop. As I lit the ciggie, I tried to see beyond the glare.

'Detective,' said the constable.

'Thought I told you to get back in the fuckin' car.' I moved off the wall, headed back towards the Granada. Then I heard a door slide open, caught a glimpse of people.

Then I saw the bundle. About the length of a roll of carpet, but wider and wrapped in what looked like tarpaulin.

'Oh shit,' said PC John. He broke away from the Granada just as the car door slammed closed and the vehicle pulled away. 'You might want to call an ambulance.'

I walked towards the constable, took it slow. Couldn't run and smoke at the same time. He was bent over the bundle, his face white in the darkness. He turned to me as I approached – didn't take much detective work to realise this was a bloke wrapped in plastic. I stopped and stared at the disappearing brake lights. Couldn't see the plate.

'You get the registration?' I said.

'No.'

'Why not?'

'Didn't have time. It's *dark*.'

'The fuck kind of copper are you, Constable?'

It didn't matter, because when PC John pulled the plastic from the bloke's face, I forgot all about the vehicle, concentrated instead on phoning for an ambulance toot fuckin' sweet. Then I ditched the ciggie and got down on my knees.

'You hear us?' I said, nice and loud. 'You conscious, son?'

Innes opened his eyes, shifted in the plastic.

'Aye, best you don't do that, eh? Got help coming for you now.'

But he kept moving, the one eye that wasn't blood-red staring wide at us. I heard the plastic crinkle and buckle as he tried to pull himself out of it.

'Wait a second,' said PC John.

It wasn't that he wanted out of the plastic, Innes was trying to get away from us.

Fuck's sake, you had to admire the persistence of the bloke.

'Better move back. He's going to kill himself if he keeps that up. He's panicking.'

The constable got to his feet. I rubbed my face, looked down at the mess in front of us, then back at the poof's club. Wondered how long it would take an ambulance to get here, then realised unless it turned up sharpish, there wouldn't be much point.

'Stay here,' I said. 'If you see the poof, make sure you keep him away from Innes.'

'*This* is him?' said PC John, a bit too loud for my fucking taste. 'This is your suspect?'

'Yeah, aye, and keep it fuckin' down, will you?'

'You can't—'

'Listen to us, alright? The poof in there sees his boy like this, he's liable to think I had something to do with it.'

'But he's covered in plastic—'

'Going to be difficult to explain that to the poof when he's gone mental on us. So, better you shield the lad from the bloke's sight until we get the ambulance here, in case he loses it.' I started to walk away, then stopped. 'You know any first aid, now's your fuckin' chance, by the way. Don't be shy.'

Then onwards to the Lads' Club. I pinched the top of my nose, which sent my brand new headache into the middle of my brain for a second. When I let go, the pain rushed back to the bridge. I really needed another ciggie, but I didn't bother.

As I got to the doors, he was already coming across the gym. 'What's going on?'

'You managed to get a hold of Innes yet?'

He shook his head.

I waved him back to the office. 'Then what're you doing off the phone? Keep trying.'

More headlights, this time sweeping across the gym floor as a car pulled up outside. I didn't turn around, reckoned it was probably the ambulance and they'd take care of Innes just as long as I kept the poof indoors. I got close to him, put a hand on his arm and said, in my best soft and calming copper voice, 'I need you to keep trying that number, Paul.'

Then there was the sound of closing car doors and someone shouted my name. I heard the club doors open.

'Can I see you outside for a moment?'

Turned to see Kennedy in the doorway to the club. I rubbed my nose, looked over his shoulder and saw Adams questioning the constable.

'Everything's fine.'

'Are you alright, Mr Gray?' said Kennedy.

'Fine.'

'What're you lot doing here?' I said.

Kennedy and Gray swapped glances. Then, I realised that as soon as I was out of the fucking building, the poof had dropped a twenty on us.

'Hang on a second,' I said. 'He was supposed to be calling his boy in.'

'You do that outside?' said Kennedy.

I shook my head.

'What?' said Gray.

'Nowt.' I moved towards Kennedy, took his arm. 'You wanted to see us, let's get it over with.'

Kennedy pulled his arm out of my grip. 'At least tell me you called for an ambulance, Iain.'

'Ambulance?' said Gray. 'The fuck d'you need an ambulance for?'

'Nothing,' I said. 'It's nothing, honest.'

But it was too late. Gray was already storming for the door, and he looked like he was ready to deck anyone that got in his way. I didn't try to stop him. It was these arseholes' problem now. As soon as he clattered out through the doors, I heard Adams and PC John trying to calm him down, keep him back.

'I did call for an ambulance,' I said.

'When?' said Kennedy.

'Just now.'

'Did you say it was police?'

'No.'

'Why not?'

'Because I'm not strictly fuckin' police, am I?'

'Could've got your constable to do it.'

'Doesn't matter.' I pointed at Innes. 'He's my collar.'

'What fuckin' collar?'

I moved out of the club, Kennedy following. 'That bundle of shite over there, he's the boy killed Mo Tiernan.'

'No, he isn't,' said Kennedy.

Adams and PC John were still trying to bar the way to Innes. Gray was having none of it; he looked like he wanted to put both the coppers to the ground.

'Mr Gray,' I shouted, 'you want to calm it down there?'

He turned to us, his face red and twisted. 'Fuck yourself, Donkey.'

'That's it,' I said. 'Constable, you want to restrain Mr Gray, be my guest. Let's get this over with.'

Then there was a shout that stopped everyone in their tracks. Came from Innes, this animal roar. Adams shook back from his crouched position by the bloke. Gray made a move towards Innes, and PC John got in his way, just like I told him. I saw the flash of the cuffs in his hand.

'Iain, you want to get over here,' said Adams, and there was a sickness in his voice that got me interested. He turned and said to Kennedy, 'He wants to talk to Donkin.'

Kennedy followed us as I approached Innes. I glanced at Gray, and the fight was seeping out of him. Looked like he was crying. I wasn't surprised – Innes had taken a serious turn for the worse. He was gasping for air, spluttering wet sounds out at us. When he saw us, his one good eye showed recognition. There was that fucked half-smile of his under the mess of a swollen, broken cheek, more like a fucking *quarter*-smile now. He said something I didn't catch.

I leaned in. Kennedy was right next to us. Didn't want to miss a thing, did he?

Innes said, 'It was me.'

'What was?' I said.

'Mo . . . Tiernan.'

He coughed, and I thought that was it. But Innes had more balls than I reckoned him for. He swallowed and closed his eye, repeated until he'd built up enough energy for what he had to say.

'I killed Mo Tiernan.'

Then he fell quiet. Still breathing, but only just.

I looked around at the coppers struck dumb, and the poof with the heel of one hand pressed against his eye, silently sobbing. Behind us, I could hear the ambulance pulling up to the Lads' Club.

'I told you,' I said, walking away. 'I told you he fuckin' did it.'

FORTY-THREE

Donkin

I watched them load Innes into the back of the ambulance on one of them folding trolleys. Gray insisted that he rode in the back; Adams went along to make sure everything was by the book.

I wasn't going anywhere. Didn't need to. Innes had already admitted everything to everyone here; I didn't need to track him all the way to the hospital for a follow-up. In fact, I didn't see the need for any follow-ups. The cunt did it. Pat on the back for Detective Sergeant Me, and I'll have my job back, thanks very much.

'Iain.'

I looked up and saw Kennedy coming towards us. For someone who was all set to beat the shite out of us not so long ago, he looked all kinds of knackered now. And the way I saw it, he *was* all kinds of knackered. The constable followed him at a short distance, looking at the ground as he walked, like he was scared of stepping in dogshit.

I blew smoke at the pair of them and smiled. 'Y'alright?'

'You proud of yourself, are you?' Kennedy said.

'Nah.' I sniffed. 'Well, yeah. A bit.'

'That was your collar, was it? That's the one you were fighting for all this time?'

'I was right.' I pointed at Kennedy with my ciggie. 'And you were all set to let the case go.'

He nodded to himself, watching the ambulance go. Then he rubbed at the edge of his mouth with a finger and said, 'That's what you were doing here, then. You were still running the case, despite what we'd told you, what Adams told you about. That, you know, being suspended and all, you weren't actually *legally* allowed to do any of this.'

'Can't keep a good man down,' I said. 'And I might not be allowed to arrest anyone, but I'm allowed to be curious. And I was just waiting on Innes—'

'Yeah, I understand that. But I've got to know, Iain, why did you bother?'

'Don't get you.'

Kennedy folded his arms and looked at us. 'You knew what the likely verdict was going to be, and you know how difficult it's going to be to prosecute this, now your chief fucking suspect is at death's door. So where's the perk for you?'

I took a hefty drag on my ciggie, blew the smoke out through my teeth as I smiled. My chest got tight; part of us reckoned I was about to have one of those heart attacks you don't shake off, but then the feeling passed.

'The perk is seeing you know you're fuckin' wrong,' I said.

He nodded. 'Right.'

'I'm not fuckin' finished. Because you're one of those coppers, you think it's all a matter of reading textbooks and greasing the right fuckin' palms, you'll be set for life in this job. But you couldn't catch a criminal if your life fuckin' well depended on it. Because you haven't got the first clue as to how their minds operate, you've never been out in it. When two plus two doesn't equal four, you're fuckin' flummoxed. Y'know? Whenever the answer isn't right there on a fuckin' *plate* for you, you can't deal with it. And the last thing you're ever going to do is get your hands dirty, because that's what you've been taught to avoid. And that's what you're all about – you're a fuckin' collection of stuff you've been told, you're not a person. You're just going through the fuckin' motions. You lot, you know the insides of your brand new cars, you know your HD tellies and your new-build fuckin' houses, and your *X Factor* as quality time spent with the kids on a Saturday night. You know what you're having for your tea and when your missus fancies a bit or when she wants you to leave her the fuck alone. But the one thing you do *not* know, the one thing you *should* fuckin' know but don't, is this fuckin' job.'

Kennedy didn't say anything. Standing there watching us with a thin smile on his lips. But his eyes didn't seem amused. His eyes told us he wanted to punt us into the middle of next week.

'You've known for a while, I'm not like you people. This is just another example. I go out there – I went out there – and I fuckin' investigated this the best I could, and what did I come up with? A solid suspect who just confessed to me with witnesses. And you've been at this just as long, with the kind of resources you have, what've you got?'

I opened my arms.

'You've got *me*,' I said, 'standing here in front of an empty club.'

'And a suspect who looks like he's been worked over to within an inch of his life.'

'I didn't do that.'

'Wouldn't be the first time you did do it.'

'Ask the constable.'

'I will. Once we have you in custody.' He nodded at PC John, who came towards us with the cuffs.

'Constable, you think you're putting them cuffs on us, you can also think about me knocking your fuckin' teeth out.'

'Come on, Donkey, that's hardly the sensible option, assaulting a police officer?'

'You *don't* arrest *me*.' I moved out of the way of PC John, dropped my ciggie, and pointed at him. 'Hang on to yourself there, mate. What's the fuckin' charge?'

'Obstruction of justice do you?' said Kennedy.

'No. It's a bullshit charge.'

'Assault on Innes?'

'Can't prove it.'

'Or how's about,' said Kennedy, 'we just pop down the nick and work through your story, see if we can't find something to pin on you. That's the way you work, isn't it?'

'Go fuck yourself.'

'You sober, Iain? I'm guessing you might've had a couple pints, maybe a short or two, a touch of the Dutch courage. So I'm thinking—'

'You're thinking drunk and disorderly, disturbing the peace, you can fuck right off—'

PC John came at us then. I thought about smacking him in the face, but once I'd let the idea roll around my head for a few seconds, I realised I couldn't do it. Couldn't give Kennedy the satisfaction of bringing us in on something proper. Because this entire thing was fucking wank, and it was all more evidence for Kennedy being bent as a nine-bob note. Because the only person that could've plausibly worked over Innes like that was Morris Tiernan, and this fucker wanted to make sure I wasn't going to blab about it.

Well, I'd make sure to convince him of that.

Then I'd have his fucking job.

So I held out my hands, let the constable cuff us. He was a good lad; he didn't do it too tight or anything. Then he steered us towards the back of Kennedy's Rover.

'You understand my position, Iain,' said Kennedy. 'If I let you roam free on this, you'll fuck it all up. Because that's what you are – a fuck-up. It's in your nature. You've never succeeded in a single thing your entire life. Only way you managed to hold on to your job was because of your grasses. Imagine that, eh? Only reason you had a job was because of shit like Paddy Reece. Next time you see him, you should thank him.'

'Rather hang with shit like Reece than the turd you work for,' I said.

Kennedy opened the back door to his car, the constable putting a hand on the back of my head; guided us into the back of the car and was about to shut the door on us when Kennedy held him back, told him to get settled in the driver's seat. Then he leaned in to the back of the car.

This was it. This was him telling us that he was going to kill us, something to drop him in it, admit he was working for Tiernan.

Christ, I wished I had a tape recorder on us to capture it, ready for when I put my appeal in, assuming I managed to get that far.

I would. I knew I would. I was strong. Not like Innes.

'Callum Innes didn't kill Mo Tiernan,' said Kennedy.

'That right?'

'Yeah. You know who did?'

'Who?'

Kennedy smiled. 'Mo Tiernan.'

'Fuck off.' I couldn't help myself laughing. 'You're out of your fuckin' mind.'

'Oh, we know Innes beat the *corpse* up, but he didn't *kill* him.'

I sniffed, cleared my throat, but I was still smiling as Kennedy put his hand on the roof of the car, leaned in further.

'You see, if you'd been doing your job like us *wankers*, Iain, you'd have been allowed on the actual crime scene. And if you'd been allowed on the actual crime scene you would've seen the blood and everything, right enough, but you *also* would've seen the empty wraps lying around the place, and the pin cushion your boy Mo made out of his arm.'

'Mo wasn't a smackhead,' I said. 'He dealt uppers. Didn't bother with smack.'

'Official cause of death was overdose.'

I shook my head. 'He didn't.'

'Just started. Must've had a reason. Maybe he was in pain, wanted to end it.'

I stared at him, my mouth open. 'Mo fuckin' Tiernan?'

'People change.'

Kennedy slammed the door shut. I watched him go round the car, get into the passenger side. He grabbed his seatbelt, nodded at PC John to start the engine.

I stared out the window for a long time as we drove back to the nick.

It was all shite, what Kennedy said. As much as it started to make sense in the back of my mind, I refused to believe it. Innes confessed to Mo Tiernan's murder, loud and clear. Let Kennedy explain that. A fucking confession, right from the horse's mouth. Then I realised that Kennedy didn't need to explain nowt. He'd already made his arrest, and he had Adams and PC John as back-up. Whatever Innes said, it was long forgotten.

But I knew better.

Innes killed Mo Tiernan.

Kennedy was bent as fuck.

And people didn't fucking change.

FORTY-FOUR

Innes

There's a copper in the back of the ambulance. He's watching Paulo and trying to ignore me.

I'm used to that.

Paulo's on my right side. I think he's holding my hand.

Poof.

Tiernan needed a name. He has one now.

'Callum.'

Paulo will be okay. That's all that matters.

'Callum.'

I move my head slightly. Look at him.

I hear him say, 'Thanks.'

His lips don't move.

So maybe he doesn't say that after all.

FORTY-FIVE

Donkin

The sun was out for the funeral. Even God was chuffed that this one wasn't trampling over His Nice Green Earth anymore.

Still, I never expected him to die. Didn't think the blokes that beat the shit out of him did, either. He was dumped outside the poof's gym for a reason. A warning not to mess. Whether it had anything to do with Mo Tiernan, I didn't know for sure. Probably. Wasn't going to bother my arse to find out, though.

Not now they'd fucking canned us.

It was Kennedy, of course. Couldn't handle being told off, couldn't handle that I knew more about what happened than him, and that Innes wanted to confess to me and only me. The fucking disciplinary about Paddy Reece was nothing more than a formality with Kennedy's oar in there.

Fuck it, they'd wanted us out for ages. Brass just saw their chance and took it.

No job meant no Annie. And no Shannon. It'd be official soon enough.

There weren't many people turned up for the funeral. The poof, obviously. The big lad, Frank Collier. A young lad I heard the poof call Liam, and a couple of other lads from the gym who looked like they'd been dragged there. I didn't spot any family. To be honest, I didn't know if Innes had any apart from his brother.

Nobody cried.

Mind you, from the turnout it would've been weird if they did.

I hung back at the edges, in the shade. Meant I didn't get too warm. Dressed in my one decent suit, and I didn't want to get too sweaty else I'd have to dry clean the fucker. When they finished putting Innes in the ground, I rolled a cigarette and started walking.

Didn't get far before I heard the poof's voice.

'You couldn't stay away, could you?'

I turned, pulled the cigarette out of my mouth, blowing smoke at the same time. Didn't know what to say to him. Didn't want to say anything.

But he was standing there, waiting for an answer.

'I'm sorry for your loss?' I said.

'You still on the force?' said the poof.

'No.'

'Kicked you out?'

'That's right.'

'So I won't be seeing you round the club anymore.'

'No.' I spat tobacco onto the ground, immediately wished I hadn't from the look I got. 'I didn't mean—'

The poof flexed his shoulders like he was ready to take a swing at us. And he could've done, no worries. Not like I was going to arrest him. He could've had a free shot, and with the lads coming up from the grave now, they could've watched his back.

But he never took the chance. Something stopped him, made him settle. Still that sour look on his face, like he couldn't believe what he was seeing. The lads passed by. Frank Collier didn't even glance at us, looked like a kid in a cream puff.

'You got a hole in your sleeve,' said the poof.

Then he walked off before I got a chance to reply. Good job, too. Because I was all set to tell him I wasn't sorry for his loss, I was sorry for *my* fucking loss. Wasn't like I wanted Innes dead; I just wanted the cunt behind bars where he belonged.

Just because he was dead, didn't make him a fucking angel.

But that's what you got for being polite. I watched him get into a taxi outside the cemetery, watched it pull away.

Then I went down to the grave. Took it slow because it was uphill and the shoes I was wearing didn't have grips anymore. The graveside was empty. The priest had done a runner back to the church. Something about that service was awkward for the bloke, like he wasn't sure if he was burying a poof or not.

I looked at the dirt, then I checked my sleeve.

Right enough, there was a massive hole in the elbow.

I wondered how long it had been there. How many times I'd worn my one good suit not knowing it was ruined.

Felt like a right cunt. I'd gone to job interviews like this.

Then I realised why the poof hadn't clocked us. He'd taken one look at that hole, didn't think I was worth the hassle. Like whatever had happened since that night made us a fucking derelict, one step from a ranting drunk on a street corner, like I'd lost my fucking mind or something, couldn't be trusted to take care of myself.

I blew smoke, realised my eyes hurt. Wasn't long after that, my throat started to hurt too.

I was still worth the hassle. Fuck him.

I smoked the rest of my roll-up, swallowed the pain at the back of my throat. I wiped the water from my eyes, then ditched the butt into the dirt. It sat there smoking by itself for a while, and I sniffed. I watched it till the smoke faded away, until I managed to get myself sorted.

Somewhere I heard a bird that sounded like it was laughing.

I looked at the dirt.

'Fuck you an' all.'